# THE
# GOOD LIE

## ALSO BY TOM ROSENSTIEL

*Shining City*

# THE GOOD LIE

A NOVEL

## TOM ROSENSTIEL

ecco

*An Imprint of* HarperCollins*Publishers*

HarperCollins books may be purchased for educational, business, or sales promotional use. For information, please email the Special Markets Department at SPsales@harpercollins.com.

FIRST EDITION

*Designed by Michelle Crowe*

Library of Congress Cataloging-in-Publication Data

Names: Rosenstiel, Tom, author.
Title: The good lie : a novel / Tom Rosenstiel.
Description: First edition. | New York, NY : HarperCollins Publishers, [2019]
Identifiers: LCCN 2018016636 | ISBN 9780062475398 | ISBN 9780062475428
Subjects: LCSH: Political fiction. | BISAC: FICTION—Thrillers—Crime.
  | FICTION—Thrillers—Politcal. | GSAFD: Suspense fiction. | LCGFT:
  Thrillers (Fiction)
Classification: LCC PS3618.O8388 G66 2018 | DDC 813/.6—dc23
LC record available at https://lccn.loc.gov/2018016636

19 20 21 22 23   LSC   10 9 8 7 6 5 4 3 2 1

For John and Katherine,
and R, L & K, always

I . . . solemnly swear that I will support and defend the Constitution of the United States against all enemies, foreign and domestic, that I will bear true faith and allegiance to the same, that I take this obligation freely, without any mental reservation or purpose of evasion . . . so help me God.

**—oath of office for all federal employees,
other than president of the United States**

You can't be less ruthless than the opposition simply because your government's policy is benevolent, can you now?

**—"Control" in *The Spy Who Came in from the Cold***

Only the dead have seen the end of war.

**—Plato**

# PART ONE

# *FIASCO*

## DECEMBER 7 TO DECEMBER 9

## ONE

## SATURDAY, DECEMBER 7, 5:35 P.M.
## EASTERN STANDARD TIME
## WASHINGTON HILTON, WASHINGTON, D.C.

Peter Rena watches the man who might be president pace back and forth in front of him.

"I'm not saying I'm running," David Traynor says. "But I've been approached."

The man looks different in person than on television, Rena thinks. On camera the billionaire's epic self-confidence could seem cartoonish. In front of Rena now, he comes across as more serious, even charismatic. He also seems older.

Most Americans had an image of David Traynor frozen in time—from the famous photo of a college student operating his first business out of a dorm room, or as pro basketball team owner, adorned in his signature midnight-blue T-shirt, in the famous meltdown video screaming at a ref, or a couple of years later hugging his star player as they lifted the NBA trophy. There was also the now-legendary clip of Traynor at Davos telling fellow masters of the universe, "Man, we need to get over ourselves." The middle-aged man in front of Rena now is thicker and fleshier than in those images. But Traynor, a man who knows how to turn most things into success, wears this new layer of flesh proudly, like armor. And he conveys in his smile, the twinkle of his eye, the way he moves, just how sublimely he has enjoyed every meal, every popping bottle of Dom, every trip on his private Gulfstream, also midnight blue. Part of Traynor's appeal is the hint—with all his frat-boy antics and blunt charm—that he is the everyman tech billionaire, not a geek or financial wizard or ruthless bastard; he's just a guy with good instincts, common sense, and a little more chutzpah than most. You could be, too.

"And the people we're talking about, the people who've approached me about running, are serious people," Traynor says.

Peter Rena sits on a cream-white sofa in the living room of the hotel's penthouse suite. Two more men, the political consultant Sterling Moss and the money bundler Anton Sylvester, sit in armchairs flanking Rena, the three men forming a semicircle around Traynor, who is standing. All four are dressed in black tie for the evening ahead.

"If I did run," Traynor says, beginning to pace again, "I need to know what I'd encounter."

Thirteen months ago Traynor added U.S. senator to his myriad titles. He also seemed to offer a wholly new political blend—a businessman who argued for environmental radicalism, a Democrat who denounced his party's cowardice for not fixing entitlements, a billionaire who criticized Wall Street money managers for "building more summer houses than jobs," and a self-made billionaire who advocated redistributing wealth as a way to save the economy. "I'm rich enough to know trickle-down is a scam. The only way you build anything is up." Audiences relish what they see as scolding, refreshing candor, especially in his purple home state of Colorado. The press keeps debating whether Traynor is farcical or authentic.

He stops pacing. A sharp look at Rena. Steel-gray eyes under sharp black brows. A stubby index finger pointing.

"I'm told you can find out what they'd throw at me, Mr. Rena. That you'll discover what others miss. Into the deleted history. The wiped hard drives. Things even I won't remember."

Rena doesn't respond.

"Am I wrong? Was I misled about you?" Traynor says and turns to the political consultant, Moss. "Stir," he says, using Moss's nickname, "am I wasting my time?" Then back to Rena. "Aren't you the best, Mr. Rena? Best in the city? The guy who can learn anything?"

Traynor is famous for this kind of rhetorical grilling—part flattery, part bullying, part negotiating.

"I mean your resume, man. Special Forces, military investigator, unearths a scandal in the army that costs you your career. Now you have your own firm. Last year, the whole Supreme Court nomination thing. I mean come on. Aren't you the freaking best?"

Traynor's stroll through Rena's background is another calculated message: *I've done my homework. I have my own investigators.*

Some of what Traynor has referred to is common knowledge. Rena left the military a decade ago to become a Senate aide and later was encouraged by his boss, Senator Llewellyn Burke of Michigan, to open a consulting firm. Rena, Brooks & Toppin did investigations and problem solving for business and political clients. Eighteen months ago they helped vet and confirm the newest Supreme Court justice, Roland Madison. The confirmation process became notorious when someone threatened the nominee's life. Rena ended up killing the man in the waters of the Potomac.

Some of what Traynor has alluded to, however, is not public knowledge: the history of sexual harassment Rena uncovered about a three-star general, which cost Rena his military career.

"Senator, are you asking to hire me to do opposition research on you?" Rena says at last, stating the proposition Traynor has not yet spoken out loud.

"Is that what they call it? Opposition research?" Traynor says, pretending not to know.

"Oppo for short," Rena says dryly.

"I love it," Traynor says. "'Oppo'!" He claps his hands together. "I'd have a former top military investigator doing oppo on me! Dude!"

Rena looks at Moss, whose raised eyebrows convey a mixture of disbelief and enchantment.

"How does oppo work?" Traynor asks.

He knows the answer, Rena assumes. But Traynor wants to hear the consultant describe it, to learn more about it—and about Rena. Traynor's blustering frat-dude clownishness is a provocation and an act, Rena recognizes. He is smarter than he pretends, and a better listener.

"My team would dig into every aspect of your background as if we were your opposition," Rena says. "We would try to find everything we could about your life, your family, your finances, the people you had done business with, your personal behavior, any lawsuits ever filed against you, everything we could find to make you look bad. Anything you said or anyone else ever said about you in public, and every piece of paper that had your name or the name of any of your companies on it, including shell companies. We would unearth the papers you wrote in college, everything you ever posted in social media, and anything about any companies you have any ownership in, any board association with or hold stock in. We would put that information in the worst possible light. We would imagine how people who want to destroy you would see it. Then we would provide it to you, so you'd know how your enemies will come at you."

"Geeezus!" Traynor looks more intrigued than alarmed. "Isn't there some risk, I mean if you start digging, that you just loosen up stuff that's deep buried? You know, get people who have forgotten and forgiven to just start thinking about it all over again?"

Sylvester smiles at Moss.

"Yes," says Rena. "But the bigger risk is assuming anything will remain buried. Think of John Kerry and the enemies he had made in Vietnam who came at him with the Swift Boat campaign. If he'd been prepared, he would have had a rapid answer."

"He might have been president," Moss says.

Rena says nothing, but his expression makes it clear to everyone he doubts it.

"I'm not a cautious guy, Mr. Rena. I'm a disrupter. I break shit. First-generation digital: I didn't grow up with computers; I helped invent them. So I'm not John Kerry. I'm a rapid-response team all by myself."

"Perhaps then you don't need opposition research."

"Fuuuck that!" Traynor declares. "I need it more than anyone. People will come at me from everywhere. And I don't even know what it'll be. In my generation, you market yourself. *You* are the product. And you piss off a lot of people along the way. So, good goddamn right I need oppo!"

Traynor stares at Rena and laughs, a salty, infectious ain't-life-wild laugh. When it fades, his tone has become serious. "Tell me how you do it."

Rena describes his firm, the mix of lawyers, former military and police, digital sleuths. Traynor listens.

A striking blond woman in a sleeveless black evening gown enters from an adjoining room.

"Davey," she says. "It's six."

"Yeah, babe," Traynor answers. "Peter Rena, my wife, Mariette."

Rena, military polite, is already standing.

Mariette Traynor, fifteen years younger than her fifty-six-year-old husband, had been an executive in his third company, after a career as a top-level marathoner while getting degrees from Stanford and Wharton. Traynor himself had gone to a land-grant college and gotten his MBA at "whatever top-ten school had the cheapest tuition."

"I better powder my goddamn giant nose," Traynor says. "Think about it, Peter." Traynor gives him a hard look that morphs into a mischievous smile. Then he follows his wife into the next room.

Sterling Moss walks Rena to the door of the suite.

"What do you think?"

The smile on Moss's weathered face is half amusement, half excitement. Rena can see Traynor thrills him.

"I'll ask Randi," he says.

Randi Brooks is Rena's partner and, like Traynor, a Democrat. She's already been approached about their working for Traynor but wanted Rena, a Republican, to meet him first, before they saw him together.

"But I'm gonna tell her I wouldn't touch this guy for a million dollars."

A flash of worry tightens Moss's smile, but only for an instant.

"Oh," Moss says, "I think he might pay more than that."

## SATURDAY, DECEMBER 7, 11:29 P.M.
## CENTRAL AFRICA TIME
## OOSAY CITY, REPUBLIC OF MORAT,
## NORTH AFRICA

When he gets to the roof, Assam Baah lifts his ancient field glasses to his eyes and looks two streets away into the American compound.

He sees four armed men standing outside the gates next to a pair of aging pickups. Poor bastards, he thinks. You have no idea what is about to happen to you.

Baah glances at his watch. *Seven minutes.*

The poor bastards are members of the Liberty Brigade, the local militia paid to guard the American compound. Local governments are required to provide protection to all foreign properties on their soil.

There is little local government, however, in Oosay City in the fledgling Republic of Morat. Four years since the rebellion sent dictator Ali Nori fleeing with his billions to Saudi Arabia, the people of Baah's country practice freedom on whatever terms they can grab. One armed militia has seized the water system, another electricity, a third ambulance service, each of them little more than street gangs—including Baah's own group.

Another glance at his watch. *Six minutes.*

He thinks of Sulla, his wife, and the boys, and the long trench where their bodies now lay with their fellow villagers, like so many broken objects thrown into a dump. In six minutes he will jump over that trench and enter a new world, alone, and live a life of secrets and lies and vengeance. And everything up to now will be erased.

He sweeps the glasses inside the compound until he finds the large yellow house with a brown roof where they will make the attack. The Manor House had been a merchant's residence a century and a half ago, built by a mining executive from Burgundy, back when the French ruled Morat. The Americans bought it a few months after the rebellion so they could have an outpost in Oosay, a place to meet privately with the sort of Moratians whom Westerners considered "reasonable"—so-called moderate militia leaders, lawyers, intellectuals, and politicians.

Baah knows the layout of the Manor House, though he's never been inside. A large front parlor, a dining room, and a library on the main floor where rumor has it Americans hold their visits. A large veranda in back overlooking what remains of the gardens. Upstairs, offices, and security rooms where Americans monitor the cameras and bugs rumor has it they've placed around the city. On the third floor there are bedrooms where American dignitaries spent the night—until recently.

Through the field glasses he finds the new building called the Barracks. Two stories high, nearly windowless, hidden behind a tall dark gray wall. A compound within a compound. No Moratians allowed.

Standing on the roof of a building two blocks away, Baah tries to stay calm. He is a thin man in his late thirties, stronger than he looks, with a down-set face and a beard that will never fill out. He wishes he were more physically imposing. He wishes he were as large as he feels inside. He lowers the field glasses and glances at his watch.

*Three minutes.*

He leans against a railing and thinks about the Americans. They keep making the same mistake, though this is something he cannot say aloud to anyone—especially his new righteous friends. He thinks of it as a parable. Imagine a teenager who has committed no crime being rounded up, put in prison, and tortured for many years, as Ali Nori did to so many. When the boy is still young enough to be angry and remember everything that has happened, he is set free. The Americans tell themselves the young man will feel no longing for vengeance. They think he will forgive his jailor and forget the judge who sentenced him because he will want to live a better life. They think he will not seethe inside to kill the politicians who gave the orders. And they think, if you fired all the policemen and judges and politicians who falsely imprisoned all the thousands who were just like that young man, you can find new police, new judges, and new politicians who have no memories, no history, and no family.

But we are not Americans, Baah knows. We have history and memory and family.

He hears the sound of trucks now pulling in front of the compound. He raises the field glasses.

It has begun.

The six Toyota pickups arrive, one after another, until they surround the Liberty Brigade guards.

Each flies the black flag of the Islamic State Army. Each has a mounted machine gun in back. The Liberty Brigade guards are now outnumbered twenty-four to four.

Baah's heart races.

His friend Amin gets out of the passenger seat of the lead Toyota and walks up to the leader of the men guarding the Americans.

People from the neighborhood have begun to gather. They fill the sidewalks and spill into the street. Shouts rise. Men wave Moratian flags. Some wave the black flag of the Islamist cause.

Amin takes his bullhorn and begins to lead the crowd in anti-American chants. "Al mout li Amreeka." Death to America. A few bottles and rocks sail over the compound wall.

Lights burst on inside the American outpost. They flood the

street, and the small protest that has gathered there looks unreal, as if someone is shooting a movie. It is beautiful.

The crowd swells. The chanting grows. The men in the pickups remain calm, their guns still.

Now, Amin, Baah thinks. Now.

His friend begins to exhort the crowd to disperse. "Adhhab lil-manzil!" Go home! Be safe. Go now.

When the crowd thins the six Toyotas pull back to make a lane and the men of the Liberty Brigade, the poor bastards there to protect the compound, drive away. It is just after 1 A.M.

Then, with the sound of thunder, the front gates of the American compound burst into flames.

The mangled concrete and steel opening looks like a screaming mouth spitting fire. The six trucks of the Islamic State Army storm through the jagged opening like angels entering hell.

Baah hears the machine guns from the pickups begin to fire inside the compound.

The Americans will be better trained, but there are supposed to be only a few of them. One of them will be a brigadier general.

An alarm blares, bellowing over and over inside the compound. Then everything goes dark.

The Americans have shut off the lights to give their night-vision equipment the advantage.

He sees flashes of tracer bullets puncturing the dark. He listens to the gunfire and watches the flashes and has to imagine the rest.

Baah waits for his trucks to reappear.

Quarter to two in the morning.

Any minute.

Then the air begins to look like water, the world blurry and moving in waves. Baah is knocked from his feet.

The sound comes a moment later, louder than any he has ever heard.

Everything is black and all the sound is muffled, as if he is lying under blankets.

He staggers to his knees. His ears ring. The field glasses have broken free from his neck. He spots them across the rooftop, crawls to them, picks them up, and manages to stand. One of the lenses is cracked.

He orients himself and finds the view into the compound.

Half of the Manor House is gone. What remains is ablaze.

Something has gone terribly wrong.

## THREE

## SATURDAY, DECEMBER 7, 6:30 P.M.
## WASHINGTON, D.C.

Peter Rena exits the elevators of the Washington Hilton and looks down at the rented red carpet. A cordon of photographers in tuxedos glance his way, but they don't train their motor-driven cameras on him. After his moment of fame from the Supreme Court nomination last year, Rena has evidently returned to his place among the vaguely familiar but not-quite-recognized of Washington.

Maybe he didn't need to be here tonight after all, he thinks. His friend, the TV correspondent Matt Alabama, had persuaded him he would be inundated with invitations after the nomination fight. If he didn't accept Alabama's invitation, he would have to say yes to someone else. *The unreliable SOB.*

The blue backdrop behind the photographers reads *White House Correspondents' Association* in white letters over and over. Tonight is the organization's ghastly annual dinner.

Rena finds a safe observation point on the side of the hotel's large foyer to wait for Alabama.

Rena stands slim and tall in his tuxedo—if nothing else, a West Point education teaches cadets how to wear formal dress. Italian by birth, he is copper-skinned, black-haired, and at forty-one still lean and strong. Most people, however, are struck by his eyes, which are so dark they seem liquid. He has a stillness about him that, depending on circumstance, can seem menacing or sympathetic.

Rena recognizes Secretary of Defense Daniel Xavier Shane entering the hotel lobby with a four-person security detail in rented tuxedos. Shane is a former Republican senator who bolted from his party, then from the Senate, and finally joined the administration of Democrat James Nash to make a statement about the need for foreign policy bipartisanship: "We cannot win the war on terror abroad if we use that war as a partisan issue at home." Now he is a potential dark horse presidential candidate.

Shane steps around the red carpet and pulls a BlackBerry from his jacket, the device still used in government. He reads a message, and a shadow of concern sweeps across his face.

Rena watches Shane maneuver to a quiet spot in the lobby and compose a response. At least two more messages seem to pass back and forth between Shane and whomever he is communicating with. Then Shane looks up—jaw tight—nods to his detail, and together they head down the hotel escalators.

It is a reflex to have watched Shane like this: young officers learn early to keep an eye on superior rank, to anticipate moods and spot trouble. Something in Shane's exchange strikes Rena as beyond the ordinary stressful messaging that goes with power. Watch tonight, he thinks, half-consciously.

Then, while waiting for his friend, Rena loses himself in the oddness of the correspondents' dinner.

The cable anchorman Jack Anthem is posing on the red carpet with the actress from the superhero film series the Spectacular Seven.

She turns on a lithium ion smile and angles her body forty-five degrees, right hand on hip, and the photographers bathe her and Anthem in strobe. Her sparkling maroon dress fits like skin. Something in the middle-aged anchor's smile makes Rena uneasy.

In his decade in Washington, first as a soldier, later a Senate aide, then a consultant, Rena has seen the correspondents' dinner metastasize from an evening banquet into a weekend of Washington grasping excess. Media companies invite Hollywood celebrities, who come to witness a different kind of power. And corporations throw lavish parties for lawmakers, who come hoping to meet celebrities. It is a weird celebration of yearning: everyone seems out of place.

Last year, Senator Mullen of Ohio was caught on video asking for an autograph from the reality star of *Dumpster Divers*. This year's event has been postponed from spring to winter because of a terrorist attack in Philadelphia the day before the event's original date.

Anthem and the actress step to their right and begin interviews with E! Entertainment Network and Vice Media. Rena can't quite remember the actress's name. The interviewer calls her Ursula. *Yes, Ursula Carver.*

"Jack, are you expecting fireworks from Kenny Winn?" Winn is the comedian performing tonight.

"It should be quite a night!" Anthem says vaguely.

For many people Jack Anthem had become the symbol of American journalism by sheer ubiquity. He appeared as himself in movies, TV dramas, and for three hours each weekday on the BNS program *Focal Point,* in addition to anchoring the network's election and special events. He did all of it at a half shout, as if he were trying to be heard in a crowded restaurant.

Rena takes in more of the strange scene. TV actors being interviewed by newscasters from their own networks. Ordinary people either avoiding the red carpet altogether or hurrying across, smiling sheepishly as the photographers ignore them.

At last he sees the salt-and-pepper mane of Matt Alabama crossing the crowded foyer. Twenty years older than Rena, the senior Washington correspondent of the ABN broadcast network is his friend and guide in the unexpected world of Washington politics. The correspondent has a craggy handsomeness that projects on camera as witty gravitas. The image is accurate.

"You look ill," Alabama says with a grin.

"Not my kind of evening," Rena says.

"You've survived war."

"I trained for war."

Alabama's grin widens and they make their way down escalators to the hotel's cavernous underground. The Washington Hilton is best known to longtime residents of the city as the Reagan Hilton. For it was here in 1981 that John Hinckley fired six shots, wounding Reagan with a ricochet off the presidential limousine, paralyzing his press secretary, and wounding two officers.

At the bottom of the second escalator, they find Randi Brooks, Rena's partner.

"Been gawking starlets on the red carpet, boys?"

Rena gives her a scowl. Brooks looks elegant in her evening dress, though she would never believe it. At forty-two, she is tall and, though she would never discuss it out loud, sad about the way she thinks she looks. Her round, intelligent face is intimidating until she smiles. Then it becomes a sun enveloping everyone in its warmth.

"We have time for one reception," says Alabama.

"Then once more," Brooks says, "into the breach."

They choose the reception of the *Washington Tribune,* the city's main newspaper. Whatever its challenges, the *Tribune* was still the most important publication in the capital of the free world.

The place is full of elected officials. "It looks like the green room to a primary debate in here," says Brooks.

The midterm elections ended a month ago. A month from *now,* in January, the first presidential candidates are expected to announce, twenty-two months before election day. A half dozen people in the room are already lining up donors and consultants—the so-called "invisible" primary.

David Traynor is here talking to Vice President Phil Moreland, the former governor of Tennessee, a hot-blooded southern progressive, a rarity in itself, even more so in the cool moderation of the Nash administration.

A few feet away Rena sees Republican senator Wendy Upton of Arizona, a member of the Judiciary Committee whom he and Brooks came to respect during the Madison nomination. Some think Upton, an independent-minded Republican, could sweep into the White House if she could survive her party's primaries, but it is hardly clear she has the desire for the fight.

Rena is surprised to see her laughing with Kentucky Republican Dick Bakke, the Senate's most ambitious conservative. Bakke has surpassed his mentor, Senator Aggie Tucker of Texas, as champion of the hard right, in part because, unlike Tucker, he wants to run for president. Bakke is a lightning rod who delights in angering liberals and likes to tell cheering crowds about the four things that make official Washington hate him: "I'm against open borders, open trade, and open marriages, and the only endangered species I care about is jobs."

For all his bluster, however, the Kentuckian is smart. He was chosen as a Supreme Court clerk despite graduating from a no-name law school in Kentucky. And he has the backing of the Grantland family of Las Vegas, owners of the country's largest private natural resources company.

Behind them, Will Gordon, executive editor of the *Washington Tribune*, notices Alabama and starts to head their way. He is accompanied by a tall woman with a severe expression and a thin runner's body.

"Who is that with Will Gordon?" Rena asks.

"Jill Bishop," says Brooks. Bishop is the *Tribune*'s national security correspondent and a feared figure in town for the scandals she has unearthed—secret prisons, illegal wiretapping, fake intelligence scams. She has nearly gone to jail more than once to protect her sources. Rena knows her by reputation but not by sight.

She is carrying what appears to be a scotch the size of a movie soda.

"She looks unhappy," Rena says.

"She abhors the correspondents' dinner even more than you do," Brooks says. "But they're giving her a prize tonight." Rena's partner seems to know all things about everyone.

Even in a tuxedo Will Gordon looks a little unkempt. He must be six five and has the sloped posture of a very tall man who has spent too many years at a desk. His curly graying hair looks like a patch of steel wool and he peers over half glasses in a way that makes him appear to be squinting. The tuxedo, however, is expensive, and below the pant legs, Rena notices red socks. The editor's shabbiness, he thinks, is from inability, not lack of effort.

Gordon and Alabama exchange a greeting that hints of old friendship and then handle the introductions.

"Hello, Peter," Gordon says, turning to Rena.

"You know each other?" Alabama asks.

"Iraq, 2003. I was an embedded correspondent," Gordon says, pronouncing the word *embedded* as if he meant it ironically. "Peter was," he pauses, "an officer in Special Forces." Rena nods. "You look the same," Gordon says, recalling Rena's quiet, almost unsettling watchfulness and his budding reputation as a skilled interrogator. "I wish I could say that about myself. How's life as a fixer?"

Rena doesn't like that term. The consulting firm he and Brooks run, which provides research, backgrounding, and strategic advice, is thriving, but it is also controversial. The reason: they take clients from both parties.

"It's fine," Rena answers.

"Are you fully recovered?" the reporter Bishop asks, speaking for the first time.

Rena looks at her uncertainly.

"We put in our paper you were shot," she adds.

The man Rena killed in the Potomac, who had already murdered three people, also shot Rena during their struggle.

"All good now," says Rena. He tries never to say anything memorable to journalists.

Sensing two strong personalities about to clash, Alabama decides to rescue the conversation. "Who's your guest tonight, Will?"

"Apparently these parties are evaluated by how many celebrities you attract. I would have liked Julia Roberts. But most of the Hollywood types turned us down for Y'all Post."

Y'all Post is a giant social media company that relies entirely on its customers to generate its content.

"So I went with Dan Shane instead." Shane is the secretary of defense Rena had seen checking his BlackBerry in the hotel foyer. "And, Jill, we've probably left our guests alone too long." Gordon offers apologies, and he and Bishop drift back toward the bar.

"You known Gordon long?" Brooks asks Alabama.

"We were babies together at the *New York Times*," he explains. Gordon moved from reporting to editing, then from the *Times* to papers in Minneapolis and Dallas. He'd come to the troubled *Tribune* two years earlier and had shifted the narrative about the place from free fall to the unlikely notion of a newspaper improving He had the benefit of the *Tribune*'s being bought by two brothers who had figured out the dominant system for bill paying on the Web and then created the largest data integration company in the world.

"What's he like?" Brooks asks.

"Gruff, passionate, brutally honest."

"How'd he ever get to the top?"

Alabama laughs. "It's apparent pretty quickly if he's not the smartest person in the room, it's probably a tie."

Rena watches Gordon across the room talking to Shane. The secretary of defense seems to be making apologies. Then he signals his detail and leaves the room.

Something, Rena thinks, *is* going on.

They negotiate the metal detectors into the ballroom, and Brooks heads for her table while Rena and Alabama look for the one assigned to Alabama's ABN News network.

Anchorman Alan Tessier is standing with Diane Howell, the president's national security advisor. They are talking with Cary Allison, the actor who plays a villainous senator in the television series *Master of Deceit*. A baritone voice speaking through the public address system announces, "Ladies and gentlemen, would everyone please take their seats."

Rena recognizes the cue. Secret Service can more easily scan a crowded room when everyone is seated.

A moment later, most of the room down, the voice returns: "Ladies and gentlemen, the president of the United States."

With that, everyone in the room rises. President James Nash appears from behind a blue curtain and navigates his way to the center of the head table, shaking hands as he goes.

The room fills with the uneven, complex applause of political Washington, some polite, some enthused, some forced.

The president waves, smiles, nods, raises his hands to quell the crowd, and repeats the sequence until the applause finally fades, and he takes his seat. Then fifty waiters emerge through side doors balancing salads on trays on their shoulders.

Twenty-five months earlier James Barlow Nash defied nearly all prognosticators and won a second term to his enigmatic presidency. Tall, ruggedly handsome, and gracefully athletic, the fifty-seven-year-old Nash had built his career being underestimated. The heir to a pioneer Nebraska dynasty, he'd been dismissed for thirty years as too good looking, too ideologically suspect, too shallow, and too privileged to go very far. "He has the roguish charm of Harrison Ford and the rectitude of Gregory Peck," an early profile gushed, "but what does he believe in?" As he moved to national prominence in an era of political alienation, the condescending distrust of both party establishments turned out to be one of Nash's strongest political virtues. He had never lost an election.

As they turn to their salads, Rena notices one of the guests at his table, National Security Advisor Diane Howell, glance inside her purse. She is reading her BlackBerry. She looks up, face filled with worry. When the next message arrives, she says to her host, anchorman Tessier, "I'm so sorry. I am afraid I've got to respond to this." She navigates her way to the side of the ballroom and tries unobtrusively to leave.

Rena scans nearby tables and locates the chairman of the Joint Chiefs, head down, reading a message of his own. Two tables away, Secretary of State Arthur Manion is conferring with an aide, Aaron Rubin, who is kneeling at his feet. The elderly Manion rises stiffly, and he and Rubin leave the room in opposite directions.

That's three.

At the head table, the president is still sitting undisturbed, no aide whispering in his ear.

Rena looks back for the chairman of the Joint Chiefs, but the admiral's chair is now empty. Then he sees the director of the CIA, Owen Webster, trying to stroll out discreetly as well.

**WILL GORDON OF THE *WASHINGTON TRIBUNE*** has noticed the same departures as Rena.

His own guest, Secretary of Defense Shane, never made it to the ballroom. He excuses himself and at the next table whispers in the ear of reporter Jill Bishop to wait thirty seconds and then meet him in the back of the room.

"Something's up," he says when she arrives. "Dan Shane never came in. Now Diane Howell has left. Along with Arthur Manion, Owen Webster, and Admiral Hollenbeck. That's DOD, NSC, State, CIA, and Joint Chiefs."

"News breaking out at the correspondents' dinner? How ironic," she says.

"Run traps," Gordon says, his parlance that she should check with her sources. She glances around the room for signs of other reporters moving and, seeing none, slips out. Gordon follows a moment later. He finds an alcove to hide in and touches the name of a contact on his cell, the home number of Steve Packer, his Pentagon correspondent.

"Stevie, Will Gordon. What ya doin'?"

"Watching football."

"Not anymore."

\* \* \*

When National Security Advisor Diane Howell reaches the limousine pickup area, Defense Secretary Daniel Shane and CIA Director Owen Webster are already waiting for their cars.

"What do you know?" she asks.

"The U.S. mission in Oosay, Morat, is under attack," says Shane.

Howell has only received notice to come back to the White House; no details. She has told her staff to avoid saying anything of substance electronically.

"I thought it was some kind of protest outside the compound," she says, having seen that much in an early news report.

"Apparently it's escalated," says Webster. Shane's expression tells her it's more than that.

"You have something going on in Oosay, Dan?" she asks Shane.

"Brian Roderick is there."

Howell feels a rising, liquid anger mixed with suspicion.

General Brian Roderick is a brash, articulate, and ambitious military reformer famous for putting himself in danger. Howell considered some of Roderick's theories about the war on terror unorthodox, possibly brilliant and perhaps a little mad. The last thing the administration needs is a general in danger.

Shane's government phone rings. He answers and keeps repeating the word *yes* into it, his eyes fixed on Howell. His car pulls up and he tells the other two, "I'll be at the Pentagon. I'll talk to you when I know more."

Webster's car arrives a moment later. "I'll be in touch, Diane."

Neither will call, she thinks, though they don't mean to lie.

She checks her watch. A little before 8:30 P.M. Saturday, just after 3:30 A.M. in North Africa, on December 7, the anniversary of the attack on Pearl Harbor.

## SUNDAY, DECEMBER 8, 3:16 A.M.
## OOSAY, MORAT

Every war creates its own vocabulary.

The word that pops into General Brian Roderick's mind now, as he glances out the window of the Manor House into the fire zone, is *kinetic.*

It was coined by soldiers in Iraq to mean a whole lot of ordnance being fired at once.

It is getting pretty damn *kinetic* out there.

He must have seen a half dozen pickups as he came across, all of them cherried up with mounted machine guns welded to the beds. ISA tanks. Welcome to the Toyota War.

Breathe, General, he tells himself. Stay low.

Even if the men in the pickups aren't experienced, Roderick thinks, this old Manor House is a fixed target. And the hajji in those pickups have brought a lot of rounds.

It's a regular OK Corral out there.

The analogy has been in his head all night. He'd read a book about Wyatt Earp not long ago. The real shoot-out at the OK Corral lasted just thirty seconds, yet in that half minute, Earps, Clantons, and Doc Holliday still fired off thirty rounds. With just revolvers and shotguns. In 1881, *that* was pretty goddamn kinetic.

The mounted machine guns on those pickups outside are probably NSVs, Roderick figures, a weapon that can by itself shoot nearly six hundred rounds in thirty seconds. Each Toyota its own fucking OK Corral. There look to be six of them. And this thing has gone on a lot longer than half a minute.

Breathe, he tells himself. He looks for the stairs.

It is the sounds that get his attention. The rounds that miss the building sound like firecrackers—but with a little more *boom* than *crack,* the telltale sound of high-caliber rounds fired from automatic weapons.

The ones that worry him make a different sound. They're more a *pew* than a *boom.* Those are the ones hitting the building, coming inside and ricocheting around like popcorn. Tearing holes in the air and looking for your heart.

When is the last time a freaking brigadier had heard *that* sound in combat, he wonders? Not lately. None of his brethren is that stupid.

He finds the stairwell and pauses. The first few steps, he thinks, will expose him. He has at least a dozen to go till he is out of view.

Dash, boy.

He smells something burning downstairs. The kitchen. Something on fire? How much time does he have?

Down the hall, racing, head low, under the windows. To the bedroom at the end. He enters the room. There it is.

*Goddamn it.* Untouched. The mother FUBAR of all fucking FUBARs.

He wonders if he is thinking out loud.

Breathe. Keep your heart rate down. And do what you need to. He says a prayer.

The blast throws him against the opposite wall. His head hits the ceiling and his legs the wall. I just bounced off the ceiling, he thinks. I was flying.

He doesn't notice the sound of bullets now. They may have stopped. He hears something else instead. A goddamn song.

*When I fall in love, it will be forever*

Nat King Cole. Sappy fucking song. But he likes it.

Where is it coming from?

He is on the first floor. Has he fallen down the stairs? Then he thinks, no. There are no more stairs.

He sees lights. Truck headlights. In the distance. He hears the music. "In a restless world." Nat Cole. Man has a voice that warms you up and takes you in its arms.

I have no legs, he thinks. Or they don't go all the way down anymore.

There is no more gunfire. No trucks. No light. No sound. Just the song. Nat, here, with him.

He thinks of Clara.

Then of nothing at all.

## SEVEN

## SUNDAY, DECEMBER 8, 7:01 A.M.
## WASHINGTON, D.C.

The Situation Room, located in the basement of the West Wing, is actually many rooms, a five-thousand-square-foot intelligence-gathering nerve center. John Kennedy ordered the facility built in 1961 after deciding he lacked real-time information during the Bay of Pigs. The soul of the place is a network of five rotating watch teams, thirty people each, that monitor events worldwide twenty-four hours a day.

What people see in Hollywood movies, and the occasional White House staff photo, is usually "the Woodshed," the main conference room with a dark mahogany oval table and the banks of video screens on one wall.

This morning the Principals Committee of the National Security Council is gathered in one of the small rooms down the hall. Away from prying eyes. No aides and no notes. Notes are discoverable. And if anything *more* goes wrong today, someone will come looking for them.

At the small round table Secretary of Defense Daniel Shane is so bone tired he is struggling to remain in touch with his better self. He's been up all night at the Pentagon, changed out of his tuxedo an hour ago, showered, donned a sweater and slacks, gone to his daily mass, and come to the White House.

Next to him, Secretary of State Arthur Manion looks dapper and fresh in a three-piece gray herringbone, custom made from the same Jermyn Street tailor favored by the British prime minister; the courtly old man, a veteran of perhaps too many crises, has clearly had a good night's sleep.

Next to Manion, National Security Advisor Diane Howell is dressed in the same formal gown she wore to last night's correspondents' dinner, and, in an instant of uncharitable rivalry, Shane wonders if the outfit might be calculated, a signal intended to convey to the president that she has not left the Situation Room all night. Then Shane, who takes seriously the Bible's teaching about how people should treat each other, admonishes himself for the thought.

CIA Director Owen Webster is harder to read. The old spy and veteran bureaucrat, now nearly three hundred pounds, is a sphinx.

Shane knows about the other two in the room. He has been in regular contact much of the night with the chairman of the Joint Chiefs, John Hollenbeck, and the recently appointed director of national intelligence, Stan Tollenson, a former congressman and CIA agent, just three weeks into the job.

The door opens and President Nash enters, followed by Chief of Staff Spencer Carr. Everyone stands. The president instructs them to sit down and joins them at the table.

"I know most of you have been up all night," Nash begins. "And may not sleep again until this evening."

Even at this early hour, just after 7 A.M., the president looks impeccable in a blue suit and crisp white shirt.

"This is what I know," Nash says. "Approximately ten hours ago, in the city of Oosay in Morat, North Africa, Brigadier General Brian Roderick was killed in an explosion at a U.S. facility there, along with three other Americans in his security detail, his aide-de-camp, and two U.S. contractors. The U.S. facility in Oosay, I'm told, is now safe, under protection of both U.S. and local guards, and the attackers have fled.

"Now, tell me what I don't know."

James Nash is famous for his dislike of being "briefed" in the conventional sense. He thinks formal presentations waste too much time and invite aides to gloss over difficult details. Nash likes to ask questions and get answers.

Diane Howell starts. "Oosay, sir, is the third-largest city in Morat. It's one hundred fifty miles northeast of the capital city of Yul, and is the country's most unstable region. The revolution that overthrew Moratian dictator Ali Nori four years ago began in Oosay. Since then, various Islamist radical groups have gained stronger footholds there—ISIS, Borku Hora, and the Islamic State Army, or ISA. The city has gained the nickname the 'African Mortar-itaville.'"

Nash's expression is grim. As the United States and its allies have defeated ISIS in Iraq, the war on Islamist radicalism has become a kind of grotesque, blood-filled balloon, bulging in new places whenever the U.S. and its allies shift their pressure, changing shape but never shrinking.

Oosay is one of those new places on the map where the United States is secretly operating, another possible war zone most citizens have scarcely heard of.

"Tell me about General Roderick," Nash says.

Howell looks at Shane to answer. What should he say? How much would the president recall about Brian Roderick? Assume nothing.

"General Brian Roderick, you may remember, Mr. President, is something of a legendary figure," Shane says and then recognizes he has used the wrong tense. Roderick, he explains, was a prominent character in two different books on the war on terror, and a controversial iconoclast at the Pentagon. "Rod often challenged those of us making policy, including the Joint Chiefs"—a glance at Admiral Hollenbeck.

But for all that he ruffled feathers, Shane explains, Roderick was recognized as one of the bravest officers in the army—a front-line leader who had done seven tours in forward areas—more than any U.S. uniformed officer of his rank. He was beloved by both his troops and scores of local native people, often everyday people, whom he befriended.

"What were these controversial theories?" Nash asks.

Shane scans the room. Then, delicately, he tries to explain Rod's maverick "four principles" for waging a new kind of war. Rebuild war-torn nations by working intensely to reestablish civil infrastructure, working one city at a time. Make it a civilian-led program—ending what now seems a military occupation. Commit to remaining more than a decade at least; the Islamist radicals are winning because they are waiting us out.

And lastly, develop more aggressive covert special operations plans to systematically destroy the terrorist networks at the top—and to accomplish it, cultivate a much larger network of agents and informants on the ground.

"Roderick came from that world, special operations," Shane adds. "But he spent more time on the ground with civilians than almost any other American, military or diplomatic. He believed in both, winning hearts and minds and cutting off the heads of the enemy with black ops."

The president's eyes widen.

"I assume black ops also means advance action?"

"Yes, Mr. President, Rod was an advocate of advance action."

*Black ops* means highly classified special operations, but *advance action* is a newer term, one that implies higher risk. It refers to a policy that dramatically restricts how many people know about an operation, allowing commanders in the field more discretion. Developed in response to the growing number of damaging leaks of CIA and NSA data, advance actions are kept removed from even the most secure digital communications. Sometimes knowledge doesn't go all the way to the West Wing.

Nash nods, and Shane glances at the other faces around the room.

No part of Nash's cabinet is more internally competitive than national security. There are seventeen different intelligence agencies in all—too many to coordinate or reform. The whole redundant jealous mess, Shane thinks, needs reorganizing. Or starting over.

"What was Roderick doing in Oosay?" Nash asks.

A deep breath. "Meeting with moderates, trying to strengthen our network there," Shane says.

"Mr. President, I might add that in the State Department's view, General Roderick, while no doubt an innovative leader, would have been wiser to work in closer coordination with the embassy in Yul," says Secretary of State Arthur Manion.

People in town tended to mock Manion. The oldest member of Nash's cabinet, the seventy-three-year-old attorney didn't use email and didn't carry a cell phone. But Manion was a true public servant, and President Nash liked experienced advisors who harbored no further ambition beyond this administration.

"Tell me what happened yesterday," Nash says.

The CIA director now takes over. "The details are still confused," Owen Webster answers.

"So tell me what you know so far, Director," the president says tartly.

The CIA director and the president are not close. Webster rose through the ranks of the spy agency, and, though Nash made him director, Webster has a poor feel for his sponsor. He was accustomed to politicians who surrounded themselves with clonelike loyalists. Nash, however, has filled his senior ranks with subject experts he doesn't know well, in some cases adversaries. There had been a good deal of publicity about a Lincoln-esque team of rivals and robust Kennedy-esque debates. To Webster, everything in the Nash administration gets chewed over till it becomes a mushy, unhappy compromise.

He begins to tell the story of last night.

Four days ago, a cartoon had surfaced in Amsterdam that depicted the prophet Muhammad as unhappy about Islamic extremism. The cartoon had sparked protests outside Western embassies in Tunis, Tripoli, Algiers, Sana'a, and Nairobi. These protests were often accompanied by more violent planned attacks—but the Americans, French, Dutch, British, and Belgians had all thwarted incidents through listening to traffic online and interceding in advance, making last week one of intelligence triumphs.

"What happened in Oosay last night was part of this pattern of protests and attacks," Webster says. "It began just before midnight their time. The crowds grew for about an hour outside a U.S. compound there and at some point the gates were breached."

"What was this compound?"

There were two main buildings, Webster explains, moving to a whiteboard and offering a crude sketch.

"One was an old colonial mansion, well known locally, called the Manor House. The other building, about one hundred yards away, is new, only finished a few weeks ago, called the Barracks. It's a sophisticated listening post," Webster adds.

Technically, the compound is maintained by the State Department. But the Barracks is a classified intelligence facility, Webster explains. Both buildings are surrounded by a perimeter fence. The Barracks has its own bigger, higher perimeter around it, which made it impenetrable.

"How'd Roderick and the other three die?" the president asks.

"From what we have now," Webster says, "the vehicles that entered the compound had weapons mounted on the back. There was a firefight. General Roderick and his security detail were highly outnumbered."

"How many people did we have in the compound?" Chief of Staff Carr asks.

"Eleven total. Roderick's detail counted six, including the general. A base staff of five in the facility. Apparently Roderick's detail was trapped in the Manor House. Around two thirty A.M., the old house appeared to be hit. We assume mortars. It went up like a matchbox."

Webster is trying to read Nash but failing.

"Roderick may have been in a separate room from his security detail, which ironically was closer to the impact. The other three survived the explosion, but they were killed trying to make it back to the Barracks. A fourth man was also wounded."

The president's concerned expression confirms what everyone in the room knows: a brigadier general killed in an attack in a country where we are not supposed to be engaged in military activity is a shit show, a fiasco. It could end the careers of several of the people in this room. Not to mention cripple whatever foreign policy hopes the Nash administration had in its remaining months in office. An incident like this, late in a presidency, echoes Carter and the failed Iran hostage rescue or the Iran-Contra scandal, which paralyzed Reagan's final two years.

"What about the local guard?" Nash asks.

"In Oosay, it can be difficult to side with Americans over your own countrymen," Webster says.

"The status now?"

"The facility is secure," Manion says. "The soldiers and contractors who were in the bunker have been flown to Germany. New men are stationed in the Barracks.

"By law, Mr. President, the FBI has authority to formally investigate what happened," Manion says. "That will take some time. We will begin that formal process tomorrow."

"I think there is precedent for an interagency investigation here," CIA Director Webster adds. *Interagency* is code meaning Roderick was involved in some kind of special operation, something classified, something State did not know about. "That's how we approached investigating the attack on the embassy in Yemen in 2008. The FBI can be rather slow. There were issues with that in Benghazi in 2012."

Nash doesn't hide his irritation. His team cannot even agree how to investigate this.

"And Mr. President, the Sunday shows are asking for an administration voice," Chief of Staff Carr says. "They go on the air in two and a half hours, before our next meeting."

"We need to get in front of this," Howell says.

Shane nods.

Nash looks at Manion. "I concur, sir," the secretary says. "It does not serve you to allow a vacuum to exist."

"Diane and Dan, you do the Sunday shows," Nash says, referring to his national security advisor and his secretary of defense. "Roderick was a general, so Dan, you have to represent. But I want it made clear he was not involved in a military action when he died."

Manion coughs, but the president cuts him off: "Arthur, you're off the hook." The old diplomat is not strong on television.

"We need to work up talking points," Carr says.

"Let's do it now, here," Webster says.

"Keep it vague," the president announces. "Stick to what we know. Don't get out over your skis."

Whatever people think of James Nash, he often surpasses expectations, particularly during crises. After his surprise reelection he succeeded in getting an iconoclast on the Supreme Court, forced broad infrastructure rebuilding plans through a reluctant Congress, and guided the country masterfully during a domestic terrorist attack last spring—the one that had postponed the White House Correspondents' Association dinner to last night.

The president also has an uncanny ability to remain graceful and authentically eloquent at moments when the people around him are tense. This grace under fire is Nash's special élan, his runner's extra tendon, something even skeptics admire. The public sees his calm as distinctly American, the quiet reluctant hero from books or movies.

But this morning, to the people in this room, the élan seems absent. Nash is tense and irritated. Diane Howell thinks of the word *brittle*. And she has a suspicion why. Last night, she, the national security advisor, felt caught unawares about Roderick being in Oosay. No doubt James Nash feels that way, too.

The president is standing.

"Spencer, please brief the press secretary," he says. Press Secretary Doug Paterno had asked to be present at this meeting. Carr had declined the request.

"Yes, sir," Carr says, adding, "And everyone, we have a full meeting of the National Security Council at ten."

Almost before Carr has finished his sentence the president is gone.

When he reaches the Oval Office upstairs, the sun has risen, but Nash is struck instead by the gloom he's learned seems to attach itself to every president in the final two years of power. Just when you finally know how to govern, all attention turns to who will succeed you, and it becomes almost impossible to accomplish much more, after accomplishing too little already.

Nash stares into the Rose Garden. The manicured bushes, pruned for winter, look like skeletons in the predawn gray, and a sense of alarm sweeps over him, an undefined premonition of looming disaster, a feeling as desolate as a road visible in front of you for a hundred miles, empty and unchanging.

"Peter, it's George Rawls," a smoky voice on the other end of the phone says. "I hope I didn't catch you at a bad time." It is early afternoon the same day.

George Rawls is the White House counsel.

Rena is sitting in the den of his West End row house. Sonny Rollins is playing "A Night in Tunisia" on the stereo. It must have been quite a night. Rena is making no discernible progress in a new biography of Ulysses S. Grant. Instead he keeps picking up the legal papers that came the day before in the familiar gray of Halsted & Cummings, the law firm that represents his ex-wife, Katie Cochran. The envelopes arrive every few months, asking Rena to sign here and here and initial there, erasing point by legal point any residue of his marriage to Katie, which ended three years ago. Rena considers the papers a tangible reminder of the doubts harbored by the Cochrans of the Rappahannock about the marriage of their daughter to the Italian immigrant boy who had befriended their son at West Point.

"No, George, it's not a bad time," Rena says.

"Do you think you and Randi might manage to get free and come to my house this afternoon?" The voice is southern, courtly, and sounds like bourbon and cigars. "Now if possible," he adds, a little less courtly. "I could have a car pick you up in thirty minutes."

"I'll call Randi."

The black Cadillac CTS is idling in front of Rena's row house in twenty. Darkened windows. Silent driver. Rena, out of his sweater and blue jeans and into a charcoal suit and blue tie, slides in and they head wordlessly to Brooks's apartment in Kalorama.

"Summoned," his partner says with a crooked grin as she bends into the backseat. Brooks is trying to hide her excitement. She loves the game, the idea of being called by the president's personal lawyer behind the scenes into a crisis. And she is extraordinarily good at such moments.

They had met working as Senate investigators, Brooks for liberal Democrat Fred Blaylish of Vermont, Rena for a moderate Republican, Llewellyn Burke of Michigan. From the start, people considered them an odd pairing: Brooks, the loud New York lawyer, staunchly liberal and feminist, the product of private schools who talked like a sailor; Rena, the quiet, bookish soldier, military polite, who tended to believe in history and human nature and distrusted ideology.

But they bonded over something more hardwired than their political beliefs. A shared conviction in the importance—or was it sanctity—of getting to the bottom of things, all the way down to where the mulch of truth could be found. And they shared a belief that when the government used its frightening power to investigate, the inquiries should be real, not political or cynical. Facts were not something to be manufactured in TV ad production studios. They were real, and if you followed them, people would have something in common and the country could find its way.

They both had their own reasons for being suspicious of secrets, reasons from when they were young, reasons they had shared with each other once and then never talked about again.

In time, Rena came to feel even their ideological differences were less a gulf than others saw them. Randi, like most liberals he knew,

THE GOOD LIE 43

tended to see the problems with America and wanted to fix them. Peter, like most conservatives, tended to see what was right in America and wanted to protect it. But they both, he decided, wanted to make the country better. They just came at it from different directions.

"Rawls say anything about what this is about?"

"He did not."

"It's Oosay," Brooks guesses, and Rena says nothing. The big black car glides up Connecticut Avenue five miles to Chevy Chase, the Maryland suburb closest to Washington—"the Village," as it is known to residents—home almost exclusively to Democrats, a disproportionate number of them with law degrees, and a somewhat smaller concentration of journalists. Republicans tend to nest across the Potomac in Virginia.

George Rawls lives on Cedar Parkway, a tree-lined lane facing the back nine of the Chevy Chase Country Club, in a center-hall colonial built one hundred years ago to look one hundred years older than it was. They drive past the house to an unlocked gate leading to a small hut at the edge of the golf course. There, Rawls, in a cardigan sweater over a dress shirt and knotted tie, greets them from behind the steering wheel of a golf cart. "Just a little detour to avoid the press pool," he says. They drive a hidden trail about one hundred yards and stop at a gate behind Rawls's house; then they enter the backyard and walk up some steps and through French doors.

The cherrywood library is large enough for an ornate hand-carved desk, a couch, and four armchairs. Standing at one of the bookshelves is White House chief of staff Spencer Carr. In a red leather armchair sits the president of the United States. James Nash rises, gracefully, hugs Brooks, and extends a hand to Rena.

"I'm afraid I need to ask another favor," he says.

On a Sunday evening eighteen months earlier in the White House private residence, Nash had asked Rena if he and Brooks would vet and then shepherd the nomination of Nash's first Supreme Court pick. The full truth of what had happened was known by only a few people in the world, the majority of them in this room.

"Please, take a seat," the president says, settling back in the red chair. Then he looks at George Rawls to begin.

Rawls is a big man with a face that looks carved from granite, the square edges smoothed only a little by time. He is in his late sixties, but he is still imposing, a careful, calculating North Carolinian who had come north to wrestle at Dartmouth and then attend Harvard Law School. He had been helping people navigate power for more than three decades, and, as far as anyone knew, had never betrayed a secret. Rena and Brooks had worked closely with Rawls on the Madison nomination.

"I assume you know," Rawls begins, "what happened last night"—a pause and stare—"in Oosay, Morat?"

Rawls speaks painstakingly, the words doled out two or three at a time, as if he were adjudicating each one before releasing it to the world. When they finally come, they explode into life like they were banged out on an old manual typewriter.

"And you've been following, I take it, the statements on the Sunday shows and social media this morning from our friends on the Hill?"

The majority of the people on the Hill are not Jim Nash's friends.

"Some," Brooks says with a wry smile. Rena rarely watched the Sunday interview shows—the city's unofficial intercom, where officials delivered messages to one another and about 2 percent of the country listened in. He rarely heard much there he considered new or honest. But Brooks watched them faithfully. In the car, she'd described to Rena what she'd heard. Dick Bakke, the wolfishly ambitious chairman of the Senate Homeland Security and Government Reform Committee, had declared that the death of a U.S. general was "de facto proof of incompetence by the Nash administration." He'd carefully used the same phrase on four different shows to make sure no one missed it.

Curtis Gains, the young chairman of the House Foreign Relations Committee, said he was calling for an immediate congressional investigation.

The Nash administration, meanwhile, seemed to be singing out of tune rather than in harmony. National Security Advisor Diane Howell said the early evidence suggested Oosay was a protest outside the gates that had run amok—not an organized act of terror. Defense Secretary Dan Shane was more circumspect, saying it might have been planned. The dissonance between them was already being exploited by administration critics. It was uncharacteristically poor White House messaging.

"We expect . . . there will be congressional inquiries," Rawls says.

That was Rawlsian understatement. The last terrorist incident on a U.S. facility abroad, an attack on the embassy in Tunisia, had prompted seven investigations—three House, two Senate, plus those required of the FBI and State.

Rena considers this investigation mania a damaging national disgrace—a far cry from his military days. The attack on the Marine barracks in Lebanon during Reagan's presidency, which killed 241 Marines, triggered a lone congressional inquiry in 1983. So had an assault on the Nairobi embassy a decade later during Clinton's presidency. Attacks abroad once unified the country. Now they triggered congressional Star Chamber inquiries and were a standard part of the city's paralyzing culture of attack and guilt by suspicion. Rena found it offensive. He considered blaming specific acts of terror on the people fighting the terrorists as idiotic, like blaming police for crime.

"And of course there will be media inquiries," Rawls says. He adds a fatherly stare for emphasis. Then he delivers what he'd summoned them to hear.

"Randi and Peter, we need you to conduct an inquiry on this incident. We need to know what others might unearth before they unearth it. We need to stay two steps ahead."

"Isn't this an FBI investigation, George?" Brooks says.

"The formal inquiry will probably be interagency," he says.

Rena and Brooks share a glance. *Interagency* means the intelligence community needs to be involved. Meaning Roderick was involved in something covert. The general was not merely meeting with moderates in Oosay in an innocent diplomatic role.

"We need something," Rawls says, "more nimble than the formal interagency inquiry. And, to be blunt, more secure."

Rawls, who's been standing in the middle of the library, now folds himself into one of the leather chairs. "You would be working under the auspices of the White House Counsel's Office," he says with a sigh.

The White House Counsel's Office is one of the most ambiguous in Washington.

Before Watergate, the job barely existed. The president already had a personal lawyer, the attorney general, with almost ten thousand more lawyers below him. But after Nixon's attorney general went to jail for helping engineer the Watergate cover-up, the Senate began to insist the attorney general pledge first allegiance to the rule of law and the public—not to the president.

Thus rose, largely invisibly, the power of the office of White House counsel. Presidents still needed personal lawyers and legal protectors. Once that was no longer the attorney general, the counsel's office had swollen from four people before Watergate to more than a hundred. And the White House counsel had become one of the most powerful posts in Washington.

One reason for this power was secrecy. The counsel wasn't Senate confirmed, meaning the president could choose whomever he or she wanted. And the counsel's advice was covered by "executive privilege," meaning Congress couldn't haul the counsel up to the Hill to testify about anything.

What exactly the counsel did, or didn't do, depended on who had the job, but history showed one task more important than all others: keep the president from breaking the law and keep the president's staff from embroiling him in scandals. In other words, keep the boss's ass out of trouble—legal or political—and keep his minions out of jail.

That is one of about four hundred reasons that Rawls tells his staff to *write down as little as possible*. Don't rely on remembering to drop your notes in the "burn bag" at the end of the day.

Rawls gives Rena and Brooks a Cheshire cat smile. *Got you two caught in my trap.*

"If the counsel is covered by executive privilege, then would our inquiry be as well?" Brooks asks.

"That is my position," Rawls says.

"And what we learn is covered by lawyer-client confidentiality?" Brooks asks.

"By . . . executive privilege. But I think they are largely interchangeable in this context."

"Will we have the power to subpoena?"

"No. But you have the influence of the counsel to the president."

All of this will be a challenge, but it's what Rawls hasn't said that worries Rena most. Why is Nash turning to a pair of outsiders to conduct an investigation into Oosay? He has a whole government to investigate this.

Spencer Carr, the president's chief of staff, is leaning against bookshelves, watching Rena.

If James Nash is charismatic and often underestimated, his chief of staff derives much of his power from something different—fear. He is tall and good looking in a dry, villainous sort of way, and Carr's presence here means he would help Rena and Brooks, but only so far as it served Nash's interests. If their inquiries turned up anything that would hurt the president, Carr could turn on them.

"Can you do this?" Rawls asks.

Brooks looks at Rena, who has been quiet up to now. "I have a couple of questions," Rena says.

A droll smile forms and just as quickly disappears on the face of the president of the United States.

On his best days, Rena thinks, Nash is now a 50-30 president—meaning about 50 percent of the country is inclined to believe him, 20 percent isn't sure, and 30 percent think he lies about everything. It is, Rena knows, about as good as a president gets these days.

"Mr. President, most Americans will think you already know the truth about what happened in Oosay," Rena begins. "And if you discover any of your people misspoke about it, they'll expect you to correct the record as soon as you do."

Nash's endless blue eyes hold Rena's dark brown ones.

"And your critics," Rena continues, "they'll think if you *didn't* know what happened in Oosay, you're incompetent. And if you *did* and don't share it immediately, you're part of a cover-up."

Nash's smile broadens slowly—until it becomes that famous, magnetic, hard-to-resist smile known around the world. "This, Peter, is why you're here," he says.

"And if we find a mess in Oosay, will you tell the American people?"

Rena can feel Carr's displeasure from the other side of the room radiating at him.

"Yes, Peter. If we are going to win the war against terrorist Islamic extremism, we need to know what happened last night," he says. "So your interests here and mine are aligned."

From the bookshelves Carr asks: "Satisfied?"

"I have one more question," says Rena.

Nash glances toward Carr with an amused look and nods to Rena.

"Do you know what happened in Oosay, Mr. President?"

"Jesus Christ," says Carr.

Rena and Brooks have learned the hard way to always ask: get every client on record telling you the truth, or at least find out if they won't give it to you. They aren't the president's lawyers who have to defend him. They are investigators trying to find out what really happened. If you are being lied to from the start, you may need to run.

Nash finishes whatever amber liquor is in his glass and says, "At seven A.M. this morning I was briefed by my national security staff about what they knew. That is what I know. That is what you will know."

Peter Rena's political mentor, Senator Llewellyn Burke, had a theory about Washington and lying. The city had two faces to the world, Burke said. One was public. The other was private and personal.

Politicians knew that when they spoke in public, they often had to talk in broad hyperbole and bright colors, usually in vagaries and sometimes in evasion.

Because Washington people operated with these "acceptable public lies," as Burke called them, the city only functioned in private when people leveled with each other. Away from microphones, a person's word was expected to be his or her bond precisely because in front of the microphones it was not. A lie to a colleague's face was considered a greater transgression than a wrong vote or a hypocritical press conference.

More than once, Rena had heard a senator say venomously about another, "That man lied to me. To my face. He's a liar."

As if lying in Washington were so rare.

What kinds of lies or truths are they being tasked to find now? What is the real point of this furtive meeting, away from the White House entry logs and staffers' eyes? Has it been arranged to persuade Rena and Brooks to sacrifice their own reputations to protect a public lie? Or is it plausible Nash does *not* know what happened in Morat and is asking them genuinely to find out? And how would they know?

"How many apple carts can we topple?" Brooks asks.

She addresses the question to Carr, the chief of staff who would have their backs but might be holding a knife in one hand.

"Topple goddamn all of them," he says.

The black Cadillac drops Brooks home first, then Rena.

He makes a drink, heads into the den, sheds his suit jacket, and eases into the chocolate-brown leather Morris chair he uses for reading. The small room is lined with books on three walls, mostly history. In the years since he became an accidental advisor to people in power and in trouble, Rena has tried to make a study of both those subjects. There is a lot of ground to cover.

Nearly everything that happens in Washington, he has found, has happened before, somewhere. Before the Internet, before television, before airplanes. Even before democracy. The rival siblings of honor and vice, power and ambition, public spirit and private envy seemed to Rena largely unchanged by time. And some sense of the outcome of every encounter between them could be glimpsed in the expanse of the past. Rena found that having even some small understanding of history was an enormous tactical advantage in Washington. It was the capital of a country without much history of its own, filled with impatient bristling people who had little interest in anyone else's. It was a country of amnesiacs.

Rena puts on Sarah Vaughan, the song "Mean to Me," and picks up the biography of Grant he'd been reading, but in a minute he is recalling a conversation he had with Randi Brooks in the car driving back from seeing the president.

She hated the assignment they had just been asked to take on. "It feels like a pile of shit in a paper bag," she had said. "And we're holding the bag."

That was when Rena had pushed the button closing the soundproof divider between the backseat and the driver.

"Look at the options," Brooks had said. "Option one is Nash is telling us the truth: he really doesn't know what happened in Oosay and he wants us to find out. That implies his own national security people won't come clean to their boss. If that's true, then the palace intrigue in the White House is worse than we know and the place is dysfunctional."

"What's the other option?" Rena had asked, trying to sound funny.

"That Nash *does* know what happened. He's just lied to us. And he's hiring us to pretend he doesn't know, to create the illusion of distance. Then this is a fiction. And you and I are a couple of tools."

During the Madison nomination, Rena had been skeptical of Nash's sincerity about wanting to put a moderate on the Court. Brooks had believed him. Now their roles were reversing.

"You really think it's possible the president doesn't know what happened?" Brooks had said.

It was not just possible, Rena thought. It's more common than people imagine. In a military operation, you plan for every contingency you can imagine. The fact that people died here—including a general—means the planning failed, or someone didn't do their job, didn't follow the plan, got scared, was in the wrong place; something wasn't installed right or malfunctioned. Whatever it was, it was the kind of mistake that ends careers. So was it possible someone wasn't telling the president everything? Certainly.

"Yes, I do, and the bigger the screwup, the more likely it is people are holding things back."

They both knew the other reason the White House was reach-ing out to them. It was because they were genuinely bipartisan. They didn't just have Republicans and Democrats on their staff who worked with separate clients. They all worked both sides, and they chose their clients not according to party, but by something harder to define: whether they trusted them. It made them reviled in some circles, but it also made them independent, and when things were really bad, that made them useful. Sometimes indispensable.

"If you get a reputation for candor in this town," Brooks had said in the car, "people start hiring you so they can rent your reputa-tion. If you're not careful, pretty soon your reputation is gone."

A month from now, when the presidential campaign began to take on a more public form and the pandering to the far edges of the two parties began in earnest, some would call Oosay a scandal and others a witch hunt regardless of the truth. Nash was putting them squarely in the middle of that.

Sarah Vaughan finishes, and Miles Davis takes over, "'Round Midnight," the first collaboration with Coltrane.

A part of him is drawn to this task even if they are being used. One element of America's decline, he thinks, is its divisions at home over how to act abroad. Politicizing incidents like Oosay, shrouding them in distrust and accusation, only alienated people more, from their leaders, from each other, and from their soldiers.

He should call Vic—Victoria Madison, the daughter of the Su-preme Court justice he had helped confirm. They began seeing each other after the confirmation. She lives and practices law in Califor-nia, and Rena is supposed to visit her for Christmas and stay through New Year's. It is his first serious relationship since his divorce from Katie. Canceling will be bad, but now, he thinks, he has no choice.

He takes a long drink of Grey Goose vodka and Dolin vermouth.

Vic was the emotional center for them all during the confirma-tion fight. Her father, Roland, is a brilliant but difficult man. Vic managed to help Brooks and Rena understand her father, and Madison to understand them. He might well not be on the Court without her, and she had almost died for her trouble. The man who'd been stalking Madison in the end attacked Vic instead, as well as Hallie Jobe, Rena's friend and employee.

"Guess who called tonight?" Rena says when he phones her. "Your friend James Nash."

"What did *he* want," Vic says with a laugh.

"For Randi and me to investigate the Oosay incident."

A moment's pause. "Isn't there some official procedure for that?"

"Yeah. And now an unofficial one."

"What does that mean?"

"I wish I knew."

He begins to walk through the conversations he'd had with Randi about the risks. Then he realizes this may be the last time he can have a conversation about this subject over an open phone line. They will have to turn to secure double-encrypted phone communication technology, and perhaps use an encrypted messaging channel. He wonders, too, how much he will be able to share with Vic. The answer is not much.

"I think you and Randi are looking at this the wrong way," Vic says.

"How so?"

"The issue isn't whether Jim Nash is trying to use you to protect himself. It's whether you and Randi can get the answers you need, the whole country needs. You want to know what happened in Oosay, right? So it can't happen again? If you can do that, you are making a contribution. You should do it."

Even from three thousand miles away, he thinks, Vic often seems to see things more clearly than he can close-up.

## TEN

## MONDAY, DECEMBER 9, 9:15 A.M.
## 1820 JEFFERSON PLACE,
## WASHINGTON, D.C.

When the investigative staff of Rena, Brooks & Toppin assembles the next morning, most of them are no happier with the assignment than Randi had been the night before.

"They're using us as a fig leaf," says Walt Smolonsky.

At six foot five and two hundred fifty pounds, Smolonsky, a former cop and Senate investigator, resembles a tank more than a fig leaf.

"What does this mean, *fig leaf*?" asks Arvid Lupsa, the young Romanian immigrant who is one of the firm's two digital experts.

They are gathered—four lawyers, a former cop, two ex-military officers, and two digital sleuths—in the fourth-floor attic of the firm's town-house office.

"A fig leaf in this context means a loincloth," says Ellen Wiley, Arvid's boss and mentor. Wiley, the former *New York Times* head librarian in Washington, looks like a Berkeley grandmother who buys her clothes at craft shows and has reading glasses hanging around her neck from a gold chain. But she is one of the most effective Web hunters in the world, a legend among hackers and even early developers of the Internet. "You know," she adds, "to cover the naked parts?"

"So we are being used to cover the president's naked parts?" Lupsa says, thickening his accent to pretend to be confused.

Maureen Conner, the prim lawyer and former Senate Ethics staffer, makes an unhappy face.

The firm has grown large enough now—eight professionals and four support staff—that the attic is the only room where all the investigators can fit. The town house at 1820 Thomas Jefferson Place, spread over four not-quite-level floors, isn't all that practical a headquarters. But "1820," where Theodore Roosevelt once lived during the Harrison administration, has another charm for people who uncover secrets for a living. Located on the shortest street in Washington, halfway between the White House and Dupont Circle, it is hidden in plain sight. Even Google has trouble finding it.

Raymond Toppin, a former "wise man" counselor to various presidents, had founded the firm but retired a year after Rena and Brooks joined him. His name remained in large part because Rena, the lover of history, insisted on it.

"We *could* tell them to go to hell," Smolo says.

"That would only make the White House look worse," says Jonathan Robinson, another lawyer and the firm's political communications expert. "As if Oosay were so bad we didn't want to touch it."

"I don't want to touch it," Smolonsky says.

Rena raises a hand to quiet the room.

"I think we're looking at this the wrong way," he says.

"How else is there to look at it?" asks Smolonsky.

"I want to know what went wrong in Oosay. Our job would be to find out and not care about the politics. Who better to do it than us?" He is echoing Vic from last night.

"And what if they bury what we find?" asks Maureen Conner.

"Same rules as always," says Brooks, speaking for the first time.

She has come to her partner's defense. While last night she was reluctant, this morning, as they prepared to tell everyone else about their summons to Rawls's house, Rena had told her what Vic had said. She had simply nodded and said "that's right," and then they headed upstairs for this meeting.

"The best thing to do, the only thing, is dig up everything we can and hand it over," Brooks says. "The closer we get to the truth, the more likely the client will come clean."

The only person in the room who has not spoken is Hallie Jobe, a former Marine and the daughter of a black Baptist preacher from Alabama. Jobe rarely speaks in meetings. And rarely looks rattled.

Rena glances her way. She nods in support.

A few minutes later it is settled. They are taking the job—as if they ever had a choice.

**LATE THAT AFTERNOON,** the White House will issue a press announcement on the events in Oosay. Buried near the bottom will be a reference to "the president's counsel directing an internal inquiry on the incident in Morat and the loss of life that ensued as a result." The counsel's office, the release will say, "will be aided in its work by the firm Rena, Brooks & Toppin." The statement will describe the consulting firm as "a respected Washington research group with a reputation for independence and bipartisanship." The statement will go on to say only that the inquiry will "help the White House assist any subsequent probes by the FBI, Congress, or others that might follow."

Most in the press will pay no attention to the two paragraphs, a disclosure required because public funds will be used to pay the outside firm. Not all in the press, however, will miss the item. The *Wall Street Journal* will call the inquiry an "unusual and curious maneuver," given the laws in place for other agencies to investigate the death of Americans on U.S. soil overseas. The conservative magazine *Week Ahead* will speculate that "the White House Counsel conducting its own inquiry on Oosay raises the specter of a taxpayer-paid cover-up," adding that the phrase "reputation for independence" to describe a group of D.C. fixers "strains credulity even in Washington." The FBI will offer no comment. Nor will State. But some members of Congress will quickly affect a tone of high dudgeon. Senator Richard Bakke of Kentucky, chairman of the Committee on Homeland Security and Government Reform, will tell a friendly cable channel, "there may be the need for a congressional investigation of this so-called investigation."

**BY THE TIME** these skeptical notes are raised the following day, however, Rena and Brooks's team would be headlong into its work.

After the brief debate over whether to turn the White House down, the group had spent the next several hours making plans about how to conduct its investigation. They began by outlining the players who might be most responsible for what occurred in Morat—and the degree to which any of those people might mislead the president.

This list included Diane Howell, the president's national security advisor. A former college professor who was drawn into politics by Nash, she was controlled and careful, and a political outsider. They imagined she would be loyal.

There was Daniel Shane, the maverick former Republican and military veteran who had switched parties to join the Nash administration as secretary of defense. Committed to finding new ways to fight the war on terror, he also had presidential aspirations of his own. He was a wild card.

There was Owen Webster, head of the CIA. Webster was a career spy and a political survivor. Nash had appointed him to his job, though Webster might well try to distance himself from Nash to protect the Agency.

There was the secretary of state, old Arthur Manion, cautious in all things, a corporate lawyer from the West Coast and then UCLA law professor but not close to the military contingent or to General Roderick. He often operated independently of the rest of the cabinet and was viewed as not being fully in control of his department.

And there was Admiral John Hollenbeck, the chairman of the

Joint Chiefs. General Roderick had died on Hollenbeck's watch. On the other hand, from what they knew of Roderick they imagined the late general was taking risks Hollenbeck might not have sanctioned.

That is the inner circle for national security. Who were they missing?

"We could be missing any number of people," Robinson had said. "There are something like seventeen or eighteen federal intelligence agencies. And each of them has tentacles."

"Maybe the Defense Intelligence Agency," said Maureen Conner.

The DIA was the spy group inside the Pentagon. It did less original intelligence collection than the CIA or NSA, but it used what it collected and what it curated from others to direct *special ops*—the military term for secret military operations. A longtime military intelligence man, army general Frederick Willey, was director.

"Put him on the list," Brooks had said.

And who had the most to lose from Roderick being killed? The army, the CIA, State, other intelligence agencies? What if any private security contractors were involved? There were a number of companies now deeply enmeshed in our national security, with less oversight than traditional military.

They would work from the bottom up. Start with people they knew personally, the most junior people first.

"By the time we talk to anyone who is an undersecretary of anything," Brooks had said, "I want to know when we hear their answer if they are lying."

The first move would be to send Smolonsky and a team of forensics consultants they would hire to the scene in Morat. Wiley and Lupsa would collect all public documents, and everything that had been written about the incident, plus develop dossiers on the key players. Rena and Jobe would track down the two survivors of the security detail and find out if there was anyone in that compound that night who could tell them anything.

All of it would be posted to "the Grid," a digital system Lupsa had built to track their work. The Grid broke down all the key elements of any investigation into categories that could be easily sorted and compared and put everything the team learned into one document.

In the case of Oosay, the protests the night before would be one category, the breaching of the gates another, everything known about the security detail a third, the death of Roderick a fourth. And so on. There would be channels for each person they wanted to know about.

The Grid helped them share information faster and spot contradictions between conflicting accounts, and protected them against falling in love with a single theory while ignoring dissonant facts later.

"I'll curate," Rena volunteered, meaning taking on the task of monitoring the contents of the Grid. Whoever had that task was deemed the Curator.

"Let's meet back here at three P.M.," Brooks had said.

This pattern on the first day of a job—to organize quickly, pushing intensely for hours to gather everything they could and then reconvening to take stock—was a core technique of Rena and Brooks's. They believed these first few "magic hours" done right, with eyes still fresh and everyone involved, usually revealed many of the answers as well as the gaps in an investigation, and created a road map for the rest of the way—before anyone had taken a first step out of the office.

They hoped the Grid would help them stay ahead of everyone else. It wouldn't.

\* \* \*

At the *Washington Tribune,* reporter Jill Bishop is one of those who had not missed the small announcement of the internal White House counsel inquiry into Oosay and the hiring of Rena and Brooks.

That next morning, when editor Will Gordon arrives in the

newsroom, Bishop makes the long walk over to his office and leans against the doorjamb.

"You see the White House has asked your old friend Peter Rena and his partner to look into Oosay?"

Gordon looks up at her. He *had* seen the skeptical *Wall Street Journal* piece last night on social media, he tells her. He had even made a note for himself about it.

"I think maybe the *Wall Street Journal* has it wrong," Bishop says. "Rather than a cover-up, maybe the White House isn't sure what happened out there and doesn't trust their own people to tell them."

"Funny," Gordon says. "I had the same thought."

He hunts for something on his desk.

"And I have a Post-it note here I wrote to remind myself about it."

"What's it say?"

He lifts it up. Written on it are the words "See Jill Bishop."

PART TWO

# *THE ROTTEN ONION*

## ELEVEN

## THURSDAY, DECEMBER 12
## WASHINGTON, D.C.

Rena can sense at once that they are in trouble.

As with any crime, they need evidence from the scene, and they sent Walt Smolonsky to Oosay with a forensics team to examine the damaged compound. Even that devolved into controversy. The FBI is angry about an outside group fouling its crime scene. The State Department is angry about jurisdiction in general. The CIA is worried about anyone being inside the new secure American building called "the Barracks." The trip turns into a group tour—Smolo and two forensics consultants they've hired, an FBI team, plus monitors from State, CIA, and DIA. They fill two vans.

After only a day, Smolo sends an encrypted message saying there are serious questions about the administration's account. The compound's gates were clearly detonated by some explosive device, not overrun, which suggests a level of premeditation to the attack.

They are still trying to track down the Liberty Brigade guards who vanished into the countryside. The five people who had been staffing "the Barracks" that night are also gone. They are private military contractors, and now they are "on leave" in Europe—which is as suspicious as it is frustrating.

Morat and Washington both teem with rumors—everything

from the attack being an accidental U.S. drone strike now being blamed on the Moratians to the attack being a fake, a so-called false flag, to create sympathy for U.S. policy. There are also varying reports of a mysterious "man on the roof." Some witnesses described the figure as someone with binoculars who appeared to be monitoring the compound before anything began and remained on the roof throughout. Who was he? Had someone found him? There were more questions than answers, and before long the mysterious figure would fade from interest.

Wiley and Lupsa have assembled all of it, everything they could glean from public records about the incident into different digital files—one each about the protest in Oosay, the political situation in Morat, extremist groups in the region, and the key players who might be hiding something from the president. In the firm nomenclature, these background dossiers are called "Wileys" and are so thorough and nuanced they are considered a unique asset of the firm.

"Wileys" also fit with Rena and Brooks's own approach to investigation. At West Point, Rena's favorite professor was a man named Stanley Atkins, a civilian historian and a Napoleonic scholar whose orations were closer to sermons than class lectures. "To survive in battle," Atkins would tell students on the first day, "I don't know if it helps to believe in God. But I know you should believe in preparation."

As they prepare for this investigation, Rena and Brooks believe the key is understanding the late General Brian Roderick.

"There is a good deal known about the general, a lot more than about most one-star brigadiers," Wiley says, handing out printed copies of her file on the third day of the investigation. "Journalists loved him. He was a prominent character in two major books on the wars in Iraq and Afghanistan."

"Our man was brave," Brooks says as she reads. "Roderick was deployed in the Middle East longer than any other officer in the U.S. military, much of it on the front lines."

"Two and a half years in Fallujah," Rena says, reading.

Fallujah was an Iraqi hellhole—the site of a bloody years-long operation to hold the city, taking it, losing it, retaking it, and trying to hold it.

"And he was a renegade," says Brooks. Wiley and Lupsa's file describes how Roderick preferred to stay near the battle's edge rather than in a commander's tent and disliked the new method of officers watching battles from drone cameras.

When he visited primitive combat outposts, he avoided staff officers, who Roderick thought were too eager to please and hence inclined to varnish the truth. He gravitated instead to kids whose body armor bore the insignia of lance corporal, the second-lowest rank. These were the everyday soldiers who did the inglorious work of war and nation building, understood the war better, and were more inclined to honesty.

He had similarly unusual views about getting close to the local residents whose countries he was trying to liberate or rebuild, the file says.

Roderick was often out of uniform, in plain clothes or native garb. He spent hours with civilians close to the ground, sitting in cafes and the homes of ordinary people—not high-ranking local officials.

"He argued we couldn't help rebuild countries whose people and cultures we didn't understand," Wiley has written. Roderick forged widespread relationships with these people, and from these hundreds of hours on the ground began developing his own thoughts about what was wrong with U.S. policy.

He began to believe both party orthodoxies about the war on terror were wrong. Conservatives—and many Pentagon officials—tended to advocate massive troop presence and staying the course. Roderick thought those policies were doomed to inspire more terrorism.

Liberals tended to favor keeping a small footprint for as short a time as possible. Roderick thought that would leave the region in chaos.

He finished a Ph.D. at Johns Hopkins while on active duty. In his dissertation he argued that the data proved American policy was failing in the Middle East and Africa. In 2004 there were 21 Islamic terrorist groups in 18 countries, he had written. By 2017, there were more than 40 operating in over 30 countries.

Roderick began to develop a new theory on how to fight the war on terror, which he gave the clinical name "Multidimensional Global Security."

It was built on four ideas. The first was that the United States needed to replace what looked like military occupation to root out extremists with intensive nation building at the local level that would win over local populations. This work should be done painstakingly, he argued, thoroughly reestablishing civil society in one city or area at a time before moving on to the next. "Establish a deep and functioning society in one place. Prove our concept and our sincerity. Then repeat. It will begin to develop its own momentum. Right now we are failing in many places and proving our own inability—however good our intentions," he wrote.

The second concept was that this work should be done largely out of uniform. It should look civilian.

The third concept was about length of commitment. Roderick felt the United States needed to convey to the countries where it was involved that it was there for the long haul, a commitment of at least a decade, to prove we were serious. Anything less, Roderick argued, would be doubted by the people in these countries and worked to the advantage of the jihadists, who are playing the ultimate long game. "These people believe we will abandon them as soon as we can and that the extremists will return and retaliate."

It was an impossible commitment to make politically. That was precisely why, Roderick argued, it was so vital a commitment to communicate. "We did in it Europe. We did it in Korea. Why can't we do it in the Middle East and Africa?"

The final element of Roderick's approach was in some ways the most controversial: it leaned heavily on global covert special ops rather than conventional troops on the ground. In effect, at the same time we were building civil societies from the bottom up, Roderick advocated we use those local contacts to engage in an intense campaign of assassination to cut off the heads of terrorist groups worldwide. His plan for daily military presence was fairly small. He didn't like carrying on low-level civil war everywhere.

What some thought paradoxical was that Roderick had come up through special operations—the military euphemism for classified and often brutal secret warfare. In some circles, that background gave his nation-building theories added credibility. In more Machiavellian quarters at the Pentagon, Roderick's background as a secret soldier raised questions about whether he had gone over a cliff—or whether his civilian nation-building ideas might be a cover story for what was a massive covert war in Africa and the Middle East.

For all that Roderick had his detractors, however, he was universally acknowledged for his courage and his battle acumen. He was considered one of the bravest leaders in an American uniform and one of the single best leaders of frontline troops and of special operations—a rare combination. That had made him immune to being ignored or entirely put out to pasture.

"What do you think he was doing in Oosay?" Brooks asks Wiley.

"He was on the ground. Talking to local people," Wiley says.

"But according to the public reports, he was meeting high-ranking Moratians in the Manor House. Not going undercover in cafes."

"Maybe those days were over," Wiley says.

Rena knew Roderick by reputation. "Or maybe not," he says.

## MONDAY, DECEMBER 16, 3:10 P.M.
## ELYRIA, OHIO

It was Hallie Jobe who found the first survivor.

Media reports usually referred to Adam O'Dowd as a "private contractor." Jobe thought that made him sound like he worked construction.

In another era, he would have been called a mercenary. But with so much of the U.S. defense and intelligence budget now obscured through outsourcing to private contractors, O'Dowd was really just an American soldier paid at a higher wage to fight for his own country—with the money harder to trace.

After meeting him, Hallie Jobe thinks he would have fought for free.

O'Dowd was part of General Roderick's five-man personal security detail, and one of only two who survived. He took automatic rounds to the back and shoulder, then picked up another man, Terry Halleck, and carried him across the killing zone to the safety of the Barracks. When he put his friend down again, Halleck was dead.

It is eight days since the Oosay incident. O'Dowd had spent three in a hospital in Germany and has been back in the United States for five more. Jobe found him through an old Marine contact, recuperating at his aunt's in his hometown of Elyria, Ohio. His mother, who lived a mile away, claimed she didn't know where he was. When Jobe finally gets him on the phone, O'Dowd agrees to meet her.

Elyria is west of Cleveland about forty minutes, down Interstate 80, just past the outer edges of the suburbs. Jobe flies to Cleveland and rents a car.

Ohio is gray, and the Great Recession clings to it like a smoker's cough. Off the interstate, there are industrial parks with "for lease" signs and ghostly shopping malls with most of the storefronts and parking lots vacant, save for the clusters of old-model cars outside the Applebee's and Olive Gardens.

O'Dowd had agreed to meet at Ruben's Deli, which turns out to be a coffee shop with faded Formica tables located in a mini mall across the street from a vacant lot.

He is waiting for her inside on a bench by the door, a bandana sling securing his wounded arm. He is African American, not Irish. He rises from the bench carefully, the shoulder and back still obviously painful. He has a running back's build, squat, about five ten, thick legged, and strong, with a gentle face that is easy to read.

They are shown to a booth, and she asks how he is mending.

"I'll be fine."

"It can take a while," she says. "I took a blow to the head eighteen months ago. More than a year before I was all the way back. But I got there."

"In country?" O'Dowd asks, meaning in the Middle East. He can sense she'd been military.

"No. I did two tours. Iraq and Afghanistan, Marine Corps, and never a scratch. I got hurt working as a private investigator."

Jobe had been almost killed by the man who had been stalking Judge Roland Madison, but she had probably saved the life of the judge's daughter, Victoria.

A pale teenage waitress arrives with water glasses and laminated menus. When she wanders off again, O'Dowd says, "I don't know how I can help you."

Jobe repeats what she'd said on the phone. She is working for the president of the United States. The president wants to know what happened out there. So he hired her firm to find out, outside the usual channels, outside politics.

O'Dowd gives a quarter smile—maybe he believes a quarter of her story.

"That's a lot of investigations," he says warily. "White House. FBI. I'm sure they got one at DOD, DIA, CIA coming. My first debrief was in hospital in Germany."

He is a man caught in the middle of something he wants no part of. But he has agreed to see her.

"The more complete we make this interview, maybe the fewer of them there can be," she says, trying to reassure him. But seeing him now, Jobe is eager to be as thorough as she can with this. Memory degrades. The more time passes, the less accurate and useful O'Dowd's accounts will become. Rather than the event, he will be remembering his recollections. And he is already afraid of something.

"I need to have a record of this conversation," she says apologetically. "I can take notes. Or I can use my phone to record as we just talk.

"The transcript will never become public," she adds.

O'Dowd is unsure.

"Look, Adam, we work for the White House Counsel's Office. Which means the president's lawyer. Which means no one can subpoena this. Not Congress. No Freedom of Information Act. No one." She wonders whether this promise would hold up in court.

"Okay," he says in surrender.

Jobe slides the phone between them and touches the recording app to "on."

She starts with easy questions. "Tell me about the compound in Oosay. What was it like inside?"

He explains they were pouring money into it, upgrading it.

"They built a special facility on the property. A Barracks. That's what we called it. A green zone, you know. A secure space."

He is relaxing some.

"I thought this compound was an old French manor house surrounded by land. Some distance from the city center."

Jobe knows better, but she has learned from Rena to suggest confusion over innocent details as a way to get a reluctant witness to open up and begin helping.

"That old Manor was a soft target. Too close to the outer wall. So they built this new place. They were separated by a little more than one hundred yards of open space in the compound. The Barracks, the new place, was a hard target, very well protected, with its own interior wall."

"But Roderick, General Roderick, he died in the Manor? Right? Trapped there when the compound was overrun?"

"Yeah, that's where he met with any Moratians. It was like a diplomatic setting."

The waitress reappears and O'Dowd orders a Reuben, Jobe a chicken salad. The waitress takes the order on an old-fashioned paper pad. Jobe can see sheets from the pads clipped on a wire that slides in front of the cook, same as it probably was in the 1960s.

They walk through more easy details, the people on-site, the five contractors who staffed the Barracks—O'Dowd never knew their names—and the five-person security detail with Roderick.

Then, slowly, she begins to push. Why was Roderick's security detail so small, just five people?

"General Roderick wasn't one for pomp. He liked things low profile." Jobe doesn't press the point.

Did they stay in the Manor all day?

"We went back and forth between the Manor and the Barracks. Like I said, they were about a hundred yards apart."

Jobe nods sympathetically. "Let's get to that night," she says. She starts slowly. When did they first hear about the protests? Where were they when they began? She is trying to get a chronology of the final minutes.

"Why was Roderick still in the Manor at midnight? He didn't have meetings that late, did he?"

"No. Last meeting probably finished around eleven. Maybe a little before. I guess he stayed making notes, thinking the protest would die down. It was unlucky. We were in the wrong place at the wrong time."

In Jobe's experience, good soldiers aren't *that* unlucky. They find safe ground instinctively. Unless there is a good reason to stay where you are.

"Why didn't you head to the Barracks when the protest began?"

"I don't know exactly when the protests began," O'Dowd says. He is getting tired. The food arrives, giving him some reprieve.

Men tend to be either drawn to Jobe or intimidated by her. She is a tall and dark-skinned African American woman with high chiseled cheekbones and a strong chin—beautiful and exotic but also imposing.

"Tell me about your getting wounded. And getting Halleck, Phelps, and Ross back over to the Barracks."

Now she has come to the most difficult part.

O'Dowd takes a deep breath. "Like I said, the Ali Baba breached the zone."

He has slipped into soldier slang for Islamic fighters. "Ali Baba." A pejorative for Middle Eastern combatants. But this was North Africa.

"They're inside the wire. And they're shooting at anything that moves."

"Were there fighters on foot in the compound?" Jobe wants to know if all the shooting had come from trucks or if men had come as infantry as well. If fighters were on foot, it was a sign they were trying to track down and kill everyone they could find. Maybe they were even looking for Roderick.

If there were only trucks, it was more likely they were just trying to shoot the place up, scare people, and flee.

"I only saw trucks. Machine guns mounted in back. Guys with Kalashnikovs buzzing from the cabs. And it was dark. We didn't have a lot of interior lights inside the compound. Not in that ground between the Manor and the Barracks."

Jobe lets the next question breathe a little, staring at O'Dowd, as if she is puzzled by something.

"One thing I don't understand. If you were pinned down in the Manor, why didn't you stay there? Why head back to the Barracks?"

O'Dowd stares back at Jobe as if searching for an answer.

"We thought we could make it."

Jobe has learned how to use silence from watching Rena: people in interrogations tend to fear it. If they are lying or being evasive, they often will try another answer if you say nothing at all.

O'Dowd eventually adds: "The Manor got hit. It was no longer safe. So we headed back to the Barracks. And we didn't make it."

Two of them had made it. Four had not.

O'Dowd winces from shifting his weight. "Look, Ms. Jobe . . ."

"Hallie."

"You served, Hallie."

"Yes, sir."

"So you know you're doing the best you can, right? Just reacting."

"Just tell me what happened, Adam."

"We got trapped at the Manor when the gates were breached. We were keeping the general secure. Then the Manor got hit and caught fire. We tried to save Roderick, but we couldn't. Phelps, Halleck, Ross, Franks, and I tried to get back to the Barracks. Phelps, Halleck, and Ross didn't make it. Neither did Roderick. That's what happened."

The answer feels rote. Jobe looks at O'Dowd sympathetically.

"Adam, I'm sorry. I'm having trouble picturing it. Can you draw it for me? The Manor, the Barracks." She pulls out paper and a pen. He draws a crude sketch.

"Walk me through it one last time."

"No," he says.

"One more time. Then we're done."

O'Dowd's drawing is more vague than his telling.

A few minutes later Jobe watches O'Dowd get up, walk outside to a white Sierra pickup, and drive away.

She dials the office on the new secure phone lines they have acquired.

"He has two different stories. He's lying about one of them," she tells Rena and Brooks. "Or maybe both."

## THIRTEEN

## WEDNESDAY, DECEMBER 18
## FALLS CHURCH, VIRGINIA

Ten days in, things feel as if they are becoming murkier rather than clearer. Every formal request for an interview has to be made twice—and often requires a call from the White House Counsel's Office to vouch for them. Even old friends are slow to respond. It is as if working for the president of the United States has made them anathema.

Jobe's interview with the private contract soldier in Ohio, O'Dowd, only makes them warier.

Then George Rawls summons them to the White House.

"The FBI would like status reports from you," he says.

"Status reports?" Brooks says.

Rawls's substantial gray eyebrows point upward, as if they were saying, yes, it is an interesting term, isn't it. The old lawyer has learned to communicate in ways that can never be recorded.

Sitting in Rawls's office that morning, they note, is Diane Howell, the president's national security advisor. The concession to the FBI, Rena thinks, must be her idea.

A trip to the FBI's headquarters across town, with Rawls in tow, introduces them to someone named Vince Harper, a young man with a serious expression, a trim military-style haircut, and a night degree from Georgetown Law Center. Harper's boss, a deputy director of some division of the FBI, explains to them it is imperative the Agency be kept aware what information the counsel inquiry is gathering. They should brief Harper every few days, they're told.

"The White House was getting too much grief," Brooks says when she and Rena are finally alone. "The idea of the White House counsel having its own investigation just sounds too suspicious."

"Maybe it will help us," Rena says. "Maybe we can use the fact that we have to report to the FBI as leverage."

Brooks looks doubtful.

"Did you notice the presence of Diane Howell in our meeting with Rawls?" Rena asks.

"Hard to miss," Brooks says.

"I wonder if that was another kind of subtle Nashian message. Whatever fissures exist inside Nash's national security team, he wanted us to know he still trusts Howell?"

Howell has gotten more grief than anyone for her statements the morning after the Oosay incident for suggesting it was a more minor incident that had simply spun out of control. That misstatement, as much as anything, has fueled suspicion the administration is hiding something.

"Then she should goddamn sit down and tell us what she knows," Brooks says.

But it will have to wait. That afternoon, perhaps by chance, they find the second survivor of the Oosay attack. Sergeant Major Garrett Franks has just returned to the United States and is back at his home in Virginia.

They take Rena's ancient Camaro, he and Jobe, and drive the forty-five minutes west of Washington to Falls Church. Brooks suggested Jobe join Rena for the trip: she had talked to O'Dowd, and Franks might be more open to two former soldiers rather than a lawyer.

The house is a whitewashed brick rambler with a gray concrete slab front porch and black iron lattice railing built in the late 1940s for veterans returning from World War II. They probably went for about $5,000 then, bought with GI loans, and sold for $600,000 now.

Sergeant Major Garrett Franks meets them on the front porch with a scowl.

He looks past Rena at the Camaro.

"Sixty-seven?"

"No, 1969," Rena says. "Last year of the first generation."

The Camaro, Chevrolet's answer to the Mustang, was introduced in 1967; the first-generation Camaro, often thought the best, was produced for just two seasons. The second generation, produced from 1970 to 1981, was less beautiful and less valuable.

Franks nods in appreciation.

"Not a ZL1, is it?"

"In my dreams," Rena laughs.

The Camaro ZL1 was the rarest production car in General Motors history. Only seventy were ever built. A ZL1 would have cost Rena more than all the cars he'd ever owned. Franks is a detail man, Rena thinks.

"It's just a run-of-the-mill Z28," Rena says. But a 1969 Camaro Z28, Rena thought, was still the best-looking of the old Camaros, before they made them ugly, then bad, then stopped making them at all, and then brought them back pretty well.

Franks swings open the door to let them in.

He is a huge man in his late thirties whose stare and massive body look sculpted from marble. His head is shaved save for a tiny flat landing strip on top.

General Roderick had an aide-de-camp, a West Point lieutenant named Joseph Ross, who died in Oosay—all brigadiers get second looies. But Franks, who'd been with Roderick longer, would have been the trusted man.

The sergeant major leads them through a small family room addition to a screened-in porch overlooking a backyard. Franks's wife—Wiley's background brief told them her name was Charlotte—leans against the kitchen counter, a boy and his younger sister wrapped around her legs. She glances at the visitors suspiciously with the look of a protective lioness. Jobe stops, says hello, kneels, and admires the baby. Charlotte Franks's eyes soften only a little.

"Charlie, we're gonna talk back here," Franks declares.

"I'm taking the kids to Talley's," she answers sharply.

The backyard has the chaotic feel of young children—a toy kitchen, its utensils strewn about, two toy trucks abandoned during some apparent playacted rescue, a plastic log cabin under a tree with toy spatulas stabbed into the windows.

Jobe, Franks, and Rena sit in white plastic outdoor chairs, the kind you buy at Target for fifteen dollars. Franks offers them nothing other than his impatience.

Rena always prefers to watch and listen at the start of interviews—better to "read" the person they are talking with. So Jobe begins. She offers the same explanation she'd given O'Dowd two days before. We're here from the White House. The president wanted a direct line to the truth, unfiltered. This is not a formal interview. There are no signed affidavits.

"Have at it," Franks says.

Jobe asks him to reconstruct the day. Easy questions again. When did they arrive?

"Early."

Who did Roderick meet with?

"Moderate leaders in Oosay. But take *moderate* with a grain of salt. Everyone there is out for themselves."

Franks is giving the shortest answers he can.

"Why were these meetings classified?"

"Not my call, ma'am. I can't answer that."

"Sure you can, Sergeant Major," Rena says coolly.

The sergeant major has a habit of looking directly at whoever asks him a question. He looks now at Rena.

"The meetings were secret, frankly, to protect the Moratians. It was bad mojo to meet with American devils. That's why our detail was small. And Roderick's presence in country was low profile."

"Why didn't you use the new building, the Barracks, for these meetings if it was more secure?"

"That old house was a well-known landmark in Oosay. It was comfortable. And the new building, frankly, is off-limits."

Franks looks at Rena a moment longer. "When do you plan to ask me questions you don't already know the answers to?"

Rena had learned interrogation in the army, most of it from a U.S. soldier named Tommy Kee, a Korean American kid who had grown up in Seoul and East L.A. and who had been interrogated himself by cops as a teenager. He had learned the hard way what worked and what didn't. Tommy called his own method "careful listening." It didn't involve intimidation tactics or good-cop, bad-cop routines, the use of false incriminating evidence, other scare tactics, or legal deceptions. Tommy didn't believe in wearing your subjects down or forbidding them the use of bathrooms or a lot of other techniques some police use because a lot of suspects are stupid. Tommy's careful listening involved asking a lot of questions that overlapped, taking careful notes, listening for contradictions and holes. It took patience and care. You let the subject fill the silences—a lot of silences. And add pressure at the right time.

"Why was a general holding these meetings and not someone from State? Why wasn't the ambassador to Morat there?"

"Good question," says Franks, eyes locked on Rena. "Not mine to ask."

"Who arranged the lineup for each meeting? Roderick? Or someone else?"

"Again, not my line of authority."

"When did the last meeting end?" Rena asks.

"Twenty-three hundred."

Eleven o'clock.

"And you were spending the night in the Manor?"

"No, the plan was to bunk in the new Barracks building. The Manor was being phased out for all activities except for these kinds of day meetings. Most everything had been moved over to the new building."

"Then you went back to the Barracks?" Rena says. "After the last meeting?"

Franks pauses. "We got caught in the Manor," he says.

"When was that?" Rena asks.

"Twenty-three hundred," Franks says again.

"No, that was when the last meeting ended. When did you realize the compound was overrun and you were caught in the Manor?"

Franks searches Rena's gaze. "Sometime around midnight. Look, we were in the wrong place at the wrong time when things went down. We were unlucky."

Franks is the kind of guy, Rena thinks, the army likes and promotes, jut-jawed, broad shouldered, a guy who knew the book—the parts to honor and to ignore.

The brief Wiley and Lupsa had prepared also made clear that Franks did not lack for guts under pressure. He had a record of running toward people in trouble. Soldiers gravitated toward him. And bad ones didn't last long around him.

But beneath the intensity, Rena senses something else. He felt it in the house, in the look of Franks's wife, and in Franks's stare. The man is barely suppressing a rage. He is standing near the edge of an abyss. What is down there? Too many deployments? A tormenting father? Something at home with his kids or his wife? Or a secret in Oosay?

They press him for ten minutes more. When their questions push him too close to the edge, Franks catches himself. A couple of long four-second breaths in, and four-second breaths out. It is an old Special Forces trick. Soldier yoga. Calm yourself when you begin to panic.

"We're just trying to get a timeline," Jobe says.

"Yeah, well, there is no effing timeline when you're in it. You're just reacting. Timelines, ma'am, if you don't mind my saying so, are twenty-twenty hindsight for clerks."

"Yep," Jobe says. "But the clerks are all over this now, Sergeant Major. There's going to be nothing from now on but clerks."

"Yes, ma'am," says Franks. "Roger that."

"I need to ask you something else about the timeline," Rena says. "Something we need to understand. And the record doesn't fit."

"What is it?"

"That protest going on out there, outside the gate, you stayed in the Manor rather than going back to the Barracks during it. Why was that? Why would you do that?"

Franks stares at Rena longer this time. "You know, when I was around six, I liked taking things apart," Franks says. "I had a little tool kit. Everything I saw, I would unscrew, unbolt, see how it was put together. I could never put anything back together again the right way. My father called me 'Inspector Break It.' He told me if I undid an electric plug in the wall, I would get a shock so big it'd kill me. 'That's what curiosity will do to Inspector Break It,' he'd say. 'If you're not careful and you don't know what you're doing.'"

Franks gives a sergeant's stare to the West Point man. "You know what you're doing, sir?"

"What happened between one A.M. and two A.M., Garrett?" Rena asks.

"Men died. Their names were Joseph Ross, Alan Phelps, Terry Halleck, and Brian Roderick. And they are heroes."

"No doubt, soldier. Where were they when they were hit?"

"In the line of fire."

Rena takes the drawing O'Dowd made for Jobe and puts it in front of Franks.

"And where was that?"

Franks touches his finger to the drawing four times, but he doesn't name anyone.

"Where was Ross exactly? Where was Phelps?"

"Wherever you want them," Franks says.

Then Franks stands. "You got what you need? Because I have no answers for this administration. Or anyone else."

**THEY DRIVE IN SILENCE.** Franks has made them feel like intruders. He was also hiding something, and he wanted them to know he was doing so.

Jobe and Rena say little about all this until they get back to 1820 and are sitting in Brooks's office and can add her intellect to the puzzle.

Jobe begins by scanning her notes. "He used the same words as O'Dowd," she says. "Almost verbatim. 'They were in the wrong place at the wrong time.'"

She flips more pages.

"And 'Timelines are for clerks.' That seem odd to you?"

"Like they rehearsed," Rena says.

"Why would they do that?" says Jobe.

"Because they're afraid they might tell different stories," Rena says.

"And why would they tell different stories?"

"Because they can't tell the real one."

They have found their first major clues about Oosay.

"Let's do the math," Rena says. "Rawls told us this had to be an interagency investigation. That suggests more was going on in Oosay than just political meetings with moderates. It implies this was a classified covert action. One where something went wrong. The president calls us in because he doesn't know what it was. Or doesn't want to know. Or doesn't think his own people will tell him.

The two survivors from the security detail are hiding something; one of them is afraid; the other is angry. And the other five people, the ones in the Barracks listening post, have vanished in Europe somewhere."

"What's all that tell you, Peter?" Brooks says.

"We are investigating a cover-up."

*FOURTEEN*

## WEDNESDAY, DECEMBER 18, 2:35 P.M. OFFICES OF THE *WASHINGTON TRIBUNE,* WASHINGTON, D.C.

Jill Bishop watches the pen in Jack Hamilton's right hand.

As he reads, he spins it between his thumb and middle finger with enough force that it makes a full revolution, a feat that requires ducking his index finger at just the right instant to clear a path. Then he regrips the pen and repeats the maneuver.

Hamilton, the national editor of the *Washington Tribune,* had obviously perfected the pen trick long ago, probably as a child in school, to the irritation of scores of teachers. He performs the feat now without thinking about it, a way of burning nervous energy.

Hamilton is leaning back in his chair and concentrating on Bishop's memo.

Then the pen stops moving.

He's reached the third paragraph, Bishop thinks.

Bishop, the *Tribune*'s national security correspondent, learned long ago how to pitch her stories to editors. She informed them of what she was working on only in memos that she printed out and delivered in person. That allowed her to see an editor's reaction for herself—have it on record, you might say. There could be no deniability if someone was enthusiastic at first and got cold feet later. That could happen, Bishop knew; if by chance there was resistance from above, or sideways, or some other direction—not all of which were on the official organizational flow chart.

Hamilton keeps reading. The pencil begins circling things in the memo.

Bishop has another rule about pitching investigative exposés. She writes her memos only after she has actually written her stories. She isn't the best writer in the world. She is good with facts. No, she is awesome with facts. But she struggles sometimes showing people less adept at facts what they add up to. And she has some pretty awesome facts here.

Ken Stewart, Hamilton's deputy and Bishop's direct boss, sits next to her. He had finished reading Bishop's memo and story an hour ago. They'd made some changes, and he'd agreed to go to Hamilton. That was their deal. She would show Stewart first—but only a little bit—and he didn't talk to Hamilton without her.

Stewart agrees to these terms, which would have been absurd for almost anyone else, because it is the only way Bishop will work and because, in reality, there are only about five reporters in the country who have the sources to consistently break major stories about national security. If you want to be precise about it, Bishop maybe has only one real rival she admits to, Roland Garth at the *New York Times*.

"How long will it take you to write this?" Hamilton asks.

"Already done," she says.

"Of course," Hamilton groans. "And don't tell me: you wrote in a Word document, not in the system, right?"

"Of course," says Bishop.

She hands him a flash drive.

Along with offering her memos only printed in hard copy, Bishop doesn't believe in writing inside the company's computer system. In the system, data administrators and other meddlers can violate the rules and access her stories and notes. The Chinese, Russian, and Korean governments had also hacked the *Tribune*'s computer system.

She wouldn't put it beneath NSA, either. She also doesn't believe in using the company email. That is reserved for minor editing at the last minute.

You could go all the way back to Clark Mollenhoff in the 1960s, or for that matter Nellie Bly in the 1880s—Bishop's personal hero— and find great investigative reporters all agreeing about this: don't tell your editors what you're working on until you have so much evidence it is hard for them to stop you. Bishop just took it a little further. Okay, a lot further. But it was the freaking digital age. The Web is a cesspool. Privacy took a lot of work.

Even then, the *Tribune* has screwed her over a few times during her twenty-plus years at the place. It almost knuckled under to Jim Nash's predecessor, Jackson Lee, over publishing revelations of the government skirting domestic surveillance laws. Then the story won a Pulitzer—her third if you didn't count the two that went to the paper because they were team projects. The *Tribune* failed her, again, when it parted ways with her on legal strategy defending the surveillance series. The judge offered her a compromise to get her to testify "just a little"—not identify her source but describe him in general terms. The paper, under previous management, had considered the deal worth taking. Bishop thought it was Orwellian. She found new counsel who worked her case pro bono for seven years. She kept the *Tribune*'s disgrace private—mostly. But there weren't many places to go if this is what you do for a living, and she didn't feel like having to break in a whole new group of idiots somewhere new.

Things at the *Tribune* were better now. The Lord family had sold a 51 percent interest in the paper to the Ralston brothers, two tech geniuses who thought the *Tribune* a data gold mine and media an interesting business problem. If they couldn't solve it, they could afford to lose $50 million a year for a decade and never notice. That isn't their plan apparently. Maybe they will figure it out. Here's hoping. Raise a glass.

But they'd hired a new editor, Will Gordon. Some different folks had been promoted. Stiffer spines. As for Gordon, Bishop thought he believed in news, was twice as smart as most people she knew, and had the biggest balls of anyone still left in the business.

"Give me an hour to read your full story," says Hamilton.

"But I get to be there when you talk to Gordon," Bishop says.

An hour later, they are in the executive editor's office. Gordon, who looks to Bishop like a tree that bent over for years to find sunlight, is sitting behind the same scarred, wooden desk every top editor at the *Tribune* has used from the 1940s to 2000. Gordon found it in storage when he arrived at the paper and brought it back. Nice instincts. Gordon's long body seems to be draped from his chair and spilling under the desk.

Hamilton and Stewart sit on a fading black leather couch. Bishop sits in one of the tattered visitor chairs across the desk from Gordon. The shabbiness of the place is attributed to the fact that the *Tribune* is moving offices in six months—too much of the space is empty, and the real estate is worth almost as much as the paper itself. But in truth no one had spent money on the interior since 2005.

Gordon glances at Bishop's memo and then holds out his hand. "Can I see the novel rather than the CliffsNotes?"

Hamilton hands him a printout of Bishop's full story.

Gordon spends several minutes on it, a combination of reading and scanning. Then he stretches his long legs out to the side of his desk and narrows his eyes. You can't tell if they are open or closed.

"So we're saying the following," Gordon begins. "The *Tribune* has unearthed evidence from intelligence sources that the deadly attack in Oosay appears to have been more serious, more premeditated, and possibly more preventable than the government has let on." He looks up over his reading glasses. "So far so good?" He resumes his summary. "The particulars are as follows: The whole incident may have been a planned attack, not the outgrowth of a protest spun out of control, contrary to what some in the administration have suggested. There is some reason to think there was advance warning. And Roderick had an unusually small security detail for a general in a danger zone. In addition, the perimeter outer wall of the compound had not been strengthened, in violation of congressional instructions to do so at all U.S. installations by last September. Put it all together and it raises questions about whether the Nash administration did everything it could to be ready for and to stop what happened or was negligent and now whether it has leveled with the public."

It is a better summary than Bishop had written.

Gordon looks up again to see if there are any objections. Then he continues.

"Then comes the Nash administration's reaction to what happened. We don't know if the president's team intentionally misled people to obscure apparent mistakes or if the misstatements it made the next day were from lack of information. But the misstatements haven't been corrected."

Gordon pauses again. More silent assent.

"Then we have the following evidence to back up our thesis. First, you've got evidence from forensics tests that the gates at the Oosay compound appear to have been blown up, not overrun by a mob, as initially indicated.

"Second, there were substantial warnings in the intelligence traffic that something might happen in Morat and even in Oosay. Those warnings, some in the government say, anonymously, were ignored.

"Third, some intelligence sources think the protest that occurred outside the gates may have been staged as a diversion and not spontaneous at all, again anonymously.

"Fourth, a five-man security detail for a brigadier general is the bare minimum.

"Fifth, the height and width of the perimeter wall of the compound had not been upgraded.

"I miss anything, Jill?"

"That's about it. But it took me four thousand words. You did it in about four hundred."

"Is this Oosay facility CIA, State, army, or what?" Gordon asks.

"Not clear," says Bishop. "The U.S. government bought the property, which was a colonial mansion, but recently built something new there. Maybe CIA. There is some speculation the new building was some kind of interrogation site. The fact that some of Roderick's security detail were private contractors also suggests some kind of special op or intelligence thing. Straight military would be all uniforms. And officially we don't have troops in Morat and that compound is a diplomatic mission."

Bishop had done a series on the effects of outsourcing military functions to outside contractors.

Gordon's eyes narrow again, a signal of his concentration. "And how do we know all this?"

Bishop regards him cautiously. He is asking about her sources.

"Interviews with people inside government conducting the after-action inquiry on the incident, access to some of their investigative materials, and evidence from people outside government who were in Oosay that night."

"I can read that much, Jill," Gordon says. "I mean where'd you get it?"

She stares at Gordon longer this time.

She understands that editors need to know something about their reporters' sources. But Will Gordon has insisted on knowing more about them than anyone for whom she has ever worked. And you have to be careful who you trust in this town. Too many people in Washington like to go to cocktail and dinner parties and make themselves look important by running their mouths. In this town indiscretion is a parlor game and a power trip.

How much could she trust Gordon? Or Hamilton and Stewart? In general, she has found it better to trust no one.

"If I don't know the sources, Jill, I can't publish the story," Gordon says. "That simple."

"No names," she says. "Then we don't have to share a jail cell."

Gordon gives her a grin.

"I was allowed to read sections of a draft intelligence report on the incident. It was based on the interviews with people on scene. I was allowed to take notes, but I was not allowed to read the whole report or to make a copy. I have two other intelligence sources who are 'familiar' with the investigations going on in other agencies. The fourth agency source is not involved in the investigation but has spent a lot of time in Oosay. I have an NGO worker who was in the city the night of the attack and can talk about what she saw."

"Where was the first tip?" Gordon asks.

Christ, Bishop thinks, this feels like a proctology exam.

She shifts in her seat and gives Gordon a look that makes clear she thinks this is enough.

"I heard thirdhand about evidence that the gates were detonated, not overrun. There was early forensics evidence on that, which I was able to confirm, after a joint trip with FBI, State, and those investigators from the White House—the Rena and Brooks team. Then I figured, if this was planned, there might be advance intelligence traffic. And there was. I leveraged that to get a look-see at sections of the debrief report of people who talked to people on the scene. Most of the rest of it is corroboration of the debrief report findings I saw."

Bishop has worked the story the way good reporters always do, Gordon thinks. A piece of string here and another there. Press investigations are rarely "leaks" in the sense the public imagines. Usually a source offers a fragment that is little more than a tip and hopes someone else will provide the rest. Rarely does anyone offer a whole story. That's how sources protect themselves and keep their jobs—by giving reporters only fragments of a story. Reporters then weave the pieces into stories like patchwork quilts. And you never print anything you can't substantiate. The way you screw up is by publishing what you *know* to be true, even if you can't quite prove it.

The hell of it is if you make a small mistake, you get caught, and that is hung around your neck for years as proof you are fake news.

"I think we've got a hell of a lot," Ken Stewart, the deputy national editor, says in defense of his reporter. "Especially two weeks in."

The man isn't wrong, Gordon thinks. But having "a lot" isn't proof of anything. You can have a lot of nothing.

"What's the weakest part of the story?" Gordon asks.

The national editor Hamilton looks down at his copy of Bishop's story and at the points he'd circled.

"Well, 'they were warned' is always soft," he says. "There are warnings before any incident, all kinds of intelligence traffic—specific and general—and all kinds of reasons some of them are ignored."

Bishop nods her agreement.

"But the bombing of the gates," Stewart adds. "That's solid evidence."

"From what we report in our own paper, everybody in Oosay is armed all the time," Gordon pushes back. "The idea that someone might show up to a protest with a hand grenade isn't far-fetched."

No one has an answer.

"And what about the guy with the binoculars, the so-called guy on the roof?" the editor asks. "Any more on that?"

"No. He seems to have vanished, if he was ever there at all. Three different groups have taken credit for the attack but none is considered credible."

Gordon gives Hamilton a look saying the article needs some rewriting.

"Jill, go back to your sources, and see if you can get any more on the intelligence traffic. And let's see if Suzanne Koble can work any of her diplomatic sources."

Bishop tenses. Suzanne Koble is a foreign policy blogger turned reporter who has a large following and appears frequently on television. But Bishop thinks Koble is in the bag for the Nash administration. Many of these new kids, who make their name writing point-of-view analysis online and then get hired because they bring an audience with them, lack what Bishop thinks is the most important quality in a journalist: the cold eye to distrust everyone equally.

Gordon does seem to be able to weave these different types of reporters together by making them work collaboratively. And she has to admit Koble has good contacts—"a good Rolodex" in the antique parlance of having good sources. Her only worry is Koble tipping the Nash folks to their exposé.

"Is this competitive?" Gordon asks Bishop, meaning does any other news organization have any of it.

"Not yet."

"Then let's revisit Friday morning," Gordon says. "It is Wednesday afternoon. If it can hold, I'd love to break Sunday night." That would land in the print edition Monday morning.

"Not Sunday morning?" Hamilton says.

"Sundays suck in digital," Gordon says. "And Saturday night is worse. If we break Sunday night, everyone starts their workweek chasing us. That means, Jill, ask for reaction from the administration Sunday midmorning," Gordon adds. "All that will put the administration at a disadvantage, making it less likely that Nash's team could act swiftly and try to preempt or blunt the story with some press conference of their own. I hope no one had plans for the weekend."

The editor's usually arid smile has widened into a delighted grin.

## FIFTEEN

## SUNDAY, DECEMBER 22
## WASHINGTON, D.C.

Randi Brooks saw the *Tribune* news alert on her phone a half hour before George Rawls called her.

It wasn't as if they weren't warned. The machinery of the Nash White House began to move that afternoon when Jill Bishop called to ask for comment. But you never know what a story really is—or how much damage it might do—until you see the whole thing.

Brooks thinks the story will be a full-on disaster. Apparently Rawls's thoughts are similar. "I think we better meet in my office tomorrow. Be there at eight thirty." Even through the phone, Rawls's deep staccato voice reminds her of gunfire—aimed in her direction.

In the Oval Office, the president is sitting on a floral sofa across from them, White House Counsel George Rawls next to him, and Chief of Staff Spencer Carr in a chair just a bit apart—as usual.

On a sofa facing the president sits National Security Advisor Diane Howell, another signal that, if Nash distrusts some of his national security team over Oosay, he still trusts Howell.

Spencer Carr, the president's disciplinarian, speaks first, in a voice as welcoming as a traffic cop over a loudspeaker.

"We hired you two to stay ahead of this. Ahead of the press, ahead of Congress, ahead of leaks. You haven't done that." Carr's narrow, angular face is in full glower, and he has glower down pat.

"Did your people leak to Bishop?"

Rena looks back defiantly.

"No."

They exchange Washington power glares.

If Rena is wrong—if someone in their shop did leak—this moment will haunt Rena and Brooks. Carr, who derives much of his power from being both suspicious and retaliatory, will assume he has been lied to knowingly, and he will make her and Peter pay for it for years.

Is Rena sure no one has leaked? Brooks can't imagine anyone has, but it's hard to know with certainty. During the Madison nomination, someone had leaked from their office, a new hire working as Peter's assistant, which they discovered only at the last minute.

Bishop's story, however, suggested the president had a bigger problem than a leak from Rena and Brooks's office that didn't happen. Bishop's exposé appeared to come not from a single leak but from many sources interwoven throughout the intelligence agencies and military, from people unhappy with their bosses, including some who didn't like the president.

That, Brooks knows, is the real issue—and Carr's larger fear. The administration is springing leaks in too many places at once. Relations between the White House and FBI, in particular, had soured considerably in the last year, and it is no secret that Carr thinks sources in the FBI have begun to leak to Republicans in the House and Senate. FBI director Phil Hoskins is having trouble keeping control of his people.

If there are multiple leaks from different agencies, it is a sign of an administration fissuring from within. Unless it stops, Nash's capacity to govern will be greatly diminished.

"I'm reading about preliminary investigations by my own agencies in the newspaper before I have them on my desk. And I'm learning in the media that my own aides may have lied to me and the public. Do you know why that happens?"

The voice is President Nash's. He has unfolded his legs and is leaning forward, staring at them with those dazzling blue eyes.

"Our politics has become cannibalistic. We are so divided as a country, each party now engages in tactics that are slowly dismantling the system of government in which they serve. Once a party has power in Congress, it throws out the old rules to get what it wants because the other side won't cooperate and the parties won't compromise to get them to do so. When power changes hands again, there is no peace, only revenge, more rules tossed out. Once all the rules are gone, there will be nothing left to stop the devil. We are destroying our government from within. And our enemies abroad, whether they're terror groups or formal states like Korea or Russia, are watching in delight."

The president is standing now.

"That is what is at stake in Oosay. That is what people inside our government do not understand. Oosay may feel like just another terrorist incident. But if we use attacks by outsiders against the United States as a way of attacking ourselves, rather than rallying together, the incidents become part of an infection that is more dangerous than our enemies could ever be."

The president has moved behind his desk, the one from which he commands the free world but apparently not his own federal domain.

"This isn't about this incident. It's not even about how to win the war on terror. It's about whether we can govern at all."

The words, coming from Nash himself, normally so confident, silence the room.

The president looks out the windows. There has been December snow, a rarity in Washington. On the other side of the country, there are winter fires threatening Los Angeles because the temperatures are so hot. The government is imploding from within. And the seasons no longer make sense.

The president turns and leans over his desk, as if the weight of it were pulling him down.

"It's a symptom of the same political schisms you see everywhere in the country and on the Web. Those same divisions are now dividing coworkers in their cubicles at the FBI and the NSA. Everyone feels it's okay in America if their private feelings and political allegiances color their jobs. I've got nests of Common Sensers running the New York FBI office. And liberals at the CIA who hate the FBI. I have a memo telling me the Texas office of Immigration and Naturalization is 'BakkeLand.' And the vice president is already telling Democrats he would be a different kind of president than I am."

Brooks knew from years in Washington how much leaks infuriated leaders. People you had confidently assumed were on your team, who had nodded to you in meetings and said "yes sir," had betrayed you. Nash's anger, however, seems different.

"Tell us where your investigation is," says Rawls.

Brooks isn't sure how to answer him. Tell him their investigation is a mess and the president is correct that people are hunkering down with something to hide, and that this isn't the worst part? The worst part is they think they have discovered a cover-up.

Fortunately, Peter coolly answers for both them.

"As we know them so far, the facts in the *Tribune* story are accurate," he begins.

He walks through the details of what they know—that Walt Smolonsky in Oosay found the gates were blown up, not overrun as Howell had suggested on TV. That the compound walls had not been made higher and more secure, as Secretary of State Manion had suggested on TV a few days later—another unnecessary misstatement. That Roderick's security team had indeed been minimal.

There was more the *Tribune* didn't have, Rena says: The survivors of the Oosay attack are clearly hiding something. And the five men who had been in the highly secure Barracks that night have disappeared somewhere in Europe or Asia.

They would be able to work faster, Rena tells them, but they are getting little or no cooperation from the president's team. The CIA, State, NSA, and Pentagon are all dragging their feet in answering questions. That includes Diane Howell, Rena says, looking directly at the national security advisor.

"Diane will cooperate fully," the president says.

"I will tell Virginia to call you to set it up," Howell says. Presumably Virginia is Howell's scheduler.

There was another story the *Tribune* didn't know and couldn't be told. The night of the Oosay incident was one of most successful in history in stopping terror. Western allied governments, in sharing their monitoring of chatter on the radical Dark Web, had successfully thwarted planned attacks in France, the Netherlands, Belgium, Tunisia, and England. But none of that could be made public. Doing so would reveal too much about the most precious power rings of all spydom, "sources and methods." That's why the stories of spy war successes were often secret, like the exploits of the fallen heroes whose stars were marked on the CIA wall.

"George, we need you to lean on people to get us more access," Brooks adds.

Spencer Carr answers, not Rawls. "You should know, I got a call from the Senate majority leader last night. Senator Dick Bakke called her at home shortly after the story broke. He's demanding hearings."

Bakke, who chairs the Senate Committee on Homeland Security and Government Reform, is just a second-term senator. But as the Common Sense movement, which began as a middle-class revolt, merged with a more blue-collar and even fiercer anger in the country, Bakke quickly emerged as a national leader. He was given the committee to appease him. Now he wants to run for president. That would make his chairing a special committee on Oosay a nightmare.

"What did she tell him?" Brooks asks.

The Senate majority leader, Republican Susan Stroud of Mississippi, the first woman to rule the Senate, is someone Brooks respects but is also frustrated by. She feels Stroud has failed to live up to her promise to govern, not just obstruct, and in the end has only enabled the right wing that now threatens to overtake the GOP, giving in to them too often. Stroud would argue she has done what she had to and kept them at bay.

"She put him off, for now," Carr says. "Not even Susan Stroud wants Bakke chairing hearings on this."

This last remark seems to tip the president past some point he has been holding at. "Do you appreciate what's at stake here?" he says to no one in particular.

The president leans over and touches a pen on his desk.

Brooks has heard the story of this pen. A Wisconsin woman found it in a box in an attic when her father died. Inside the box, along with the pen, was the Congressional Medal of Honor. The medal had been awarded to her grandfather posthumously for his courage in France during World War II. The grandfather had deployed before his son was born and died without seeing his child. The medal had been given to the son, and he had kept it a secret all these years. The woman had no idea her father had it, or that her grandfather had even won the Medal of Honor. But when her own father died, she found the box with the medal inside it, along with the pen President Dwight Eisenhower used to sign the order awarding her grandfather the medal and the note about it from Eisenhower to her family. Though she hadn't voted for him, the woman had sent the pen to President Nash, she said, because she wanted whoever sat in the Oval Office to think about the impact of war down the generations. That story had never leaked to the press.

"People today seem to think they will find freedom in their own selfishness and own separateness. We have a whole new digital economy built on it. They're wrong. We find freedom in tolerance and common purpose. That's what is at stake here."

The president leans over his desk and says without looking up, "I need you to go faster. Stay ahead of this. Whatever you are doing, it isn't enough."

* * *

When they return to 1820, Peter and Randi assemble their team in Rena's office to review the case. Enough people are out or on the road that they don't need to retreat to the attic conference room.

They summarize what they know one more time. The administration had clumsily and inaccurately described the attack in Oosay the first day on television. Either that was bad intelligence or they were hiding something. National Security Advisor Howell in particular seemed poorly briefed.

The evidence on the ground quickly established those first statements to be flawed—there were various signs in the explosive forensics that the attack was carefully organized.

They don't know what advance warnings the team in Oosay had about an attack because the NSA was withholding from Rena and Brooks the classified traffic that night.

The men in the Barracks were being hidden. Smolonsky had gone from Africa to Europe to try to find them. So far, he had had no luck.

The two survivors of the Oosay attack were both clearly hiding something.

They'd been hired because Nash didn't entirely trust his generals and his spies to tell him the truth. Those same generals and spies were hiding from Rena, Brooks, and their team. Even Diane Howell was dodging them.

General Roderick almost certainly was on a secret mission in

Oosay. If they could find out what it was, they were convinced that they could begin to unravel the mystery.

"And we were moving too slowly," Brooks says. "Spencer Carr warned us about this, and he was right."

"I think we should lean on Howell," says Maureen Conner.

"We shouldn't lose track of those men from the Barracks. They're missing for a reason. They know something," says Robinson.

As they continue to debate, Rena gets up and starts dialing his new secure cell phone, which he takes into the hallway for privacy.

"Please have him call me when he can on this number," he is saying as he returns.

They stand around a few moments more until they recognize the meeting is over.

**AT HOME A FEW HOURS LATER,** Senator Llewellyn Burke returns Rena's phone call.

Burke, the senior senator from Michigan, is Rena's old boss, but neither description is adequate. When Rena, then a rising army officer, refused to ignore a pattern of sexual harassment by the general slated to take over Central Command, it was Burke who rescued him by giving Rena a job on the Senate Armed Services Committee. And it was Burke who later encouraged Rena to create the private consulting firm with Brooks. Though Rena had not known it at first, Burke was also behind him and Brooks being hired by President Nash to steward the nomination of Judge Madison to the Supreme Court.

With an unseen hand, Rena had come to realize, Llewellyn Burke guided a good deal of what occurred in Washington. If anything remained of what Senator Daniel Patrick Moynihan once called "the vital center" in American politics—people still trying to find some common ground by which American democracy could govern—Burke was part of it. This governing center had no formal shape or institutional presence anymore. There were no meetings or members. There was only a fluid and informal network, made up of those handful who understood real power—former presidents, some cabinet members, a few members of Congress, and some presidential advisors—people who, whatever their party, at one point had felt the frightening weight of being responsible for millions of lives and the safety of nations. To the degree the vital center existed at all anymore, it operated in the shadows, in private, even covertly, out of sight of press or party, for in the twenty-first century bipartisanship and compromise put one at risk of political suicide. But in odd moments here and there you could glimpse flashes of the vital center's presence, in a huddled session in the corner of a banquet room, in an impromptu conversation after a chance meeting at a party, occasionally at White House dinners, in moments at social gatherings. And sometimes, as with the Madison nomination, the center changes things. Compromises that matter are forged. Problems are unstuck.

Burke managed in this role, privately crossing party lines, because he was a political rarity, a northern Rust Belt Republican who kept winning the support of voters who generally agreed on little else—white elites, religious conservatives, people of color, and the so-called white working class. They saw something in Burke they didn't see in many others.

Whatever that quality of character was, Burke, the heir to a Michigan auto dynasty and a successful high-tech investor, also had no higher ambition than the U.S. Senate. So he moved with almost unprecedented freedom, guiding the actions of friends in both parties and acting as a bridge in a city where most other bridges had crumbled.

"Peter, how are you?" Burke says.

"A challenging day, sir. I was at the White House."

"Oosay?"

"Yes, sir."

Though he cannot prove it—and there would never be any traces or footprints—Rena suspects Burke had a hand in his having this assignment from Nash as well.

"May I help in some way?"

"I need someone in the intelligence community to guide us, sir. To act as our sponsor. Our protector. To vouch for us."

Burke and Rena both know that people who operate in the covert world, the fearful space of hidden knowledge and secret plans, tend to distrust everyone unless they have been otherwise assured someone is a friend. Paranoia is survival, trust temporary and conditional.

Burke is quiet for some time, and says at last, simply, "Yes."

*SIXTEEN*

## THURSDAY, DECEMBER 26, 11:10 A.M.
## BIG LAKE, WASHINGTON

The drive from Sea-Tac Airport takes ninety minutes. It rains most of the trip. Mount Rainier, shrouded in clouds of gray linen, appears and disappears like some kind of Indian spirit in the sky. Brooks, driving, asks more about the man they are going to see.

"Anthony Rousseau," Senator Burke had told Rena on the phone four days earlier. "He's your rabbi."

It took Burke three more days to persuade Rousseau to see them, including two calls yesterday, on Christmas.

"He'll be wary," Burke had counseled Rena. "But if you can persuade him to help, he knows everyone. And if you push the right button, Tony can't keep a secret." After a pause Senator Burke added: "I know, ironic for a spy."

Rousseau had retired to a little town in the Skagit Valley north of Seattle called Big Lake.

With the possible exception of Bill Donovan, who created the CIA, and Allen Dulles, who directed it under two presidents, arguably no one had left more of an imprint on the Agency than Anthony Rousseau, though he never became director.

When the planes hit the twin towers, Rousseau had been the leading voice arguing that Al Qaeda and Islamic extremism were the next great threat. In the aftermath, he helped shift the Agency's focus away from cloak-and-dagger spying to paramilitary operations, thus reviving the Agency's budget at a time when some in Congress wanted to slash it. Ellen Wiley's background file on Rousseau said "he helped transform the CIA from secret agents to a secret army."

Brooks had asked what "secret army" meant. Rena explained that in the hot war zones of the Middle East, the CIA's supersoldiers, specially trained military personnel, armed with the best weapons and high-tech intelligence, ran military operations that were entirely covert.

"I was Special Forces," Rena had explained to Brooks. "The CIA recruited its secret army from the best of that group. They were more special. We called them Captain Americas.

"In six weeks, Rousseau's secret soldiers, working with northern rebels, swept most of the Taliban out of Afghanistan before the bulk of U.S. troops arrived. It didn't last, but they did it."

As the ground war cooled and troops were withdrawn, Wiley's brief explained, Rousseau innovated again. He became an early champion of arming drones. That was when the Agency budget really started to grow. "Seventy percent of the intelligence budget is now outsourced to contractors and other services," the brief said.

"Jesus," Brooks says.

Then Jim Nash chose Owen Webster to be his CIA chief over Rousseau.

"Why?" Brooks asks.

Rena ponders the question. "I have two guesses," he says finally, "but that's all they are. Rousseau was an innovator. Inevitably making change means making enemies."

"And?"

"As prescient as he was for so many years, Rousseau in the end missed the rise of ISIS, the whole second wave of radical terrorism we're facing now. For all he got right, maybe some people thought he had lost his mojo."

Rousseau worked for a while under Webster as number three in the Agency, director of Operations, the division in charge of collecting intelligence. A different division, Analysis, decides what it means. But soon Webster wanted him gone. When Rousseau left, three years ago, he moved back home to Washington State and this small, isolated lake.

"You've met him?"

"Only briefly, Iraq in early 2004. I was pretty green still. Then a couple times through Senator Burke."

"What's he like?"

"Burke warned he's sort of haunted. He used the term *Shakespearean*."

"Haunted by what?"

"He didn't stop 9/11, couldn't stabilize Afghanistan, was part of a war in Iraq that obviously was a mistake, and didn't anticipate the next wave of jihadists."

"That isn't exactly all his fault."

They see a lake appear below them not long after they leave the interstate. The lake is smaller than they expect, given the name of the place, and it is surrounded by a mix of late 1950s fishing cabins, 1970s ranch-style suburban houses, and a few modern multimillion-dollar mansions.

They stop in front of what was once a small cabin that had grown over the years into an impressive modern vacation home. At the door, Rousseau greets them in blue jeans and Patagonia flannel.

"Look at you," he says, taking Rena's hand. "Out of uniform and in politics. What has happened to us?"

Now just past sixty, Rousseau has the looks of a James Bond kind of spy—broad shouldered, thick black hair, and deep wary eyes—but the impression is deceptive. Rousseau was a Senate staffer and National Security Council aide before joining the CIA. A suit, not a spook. A minder. A purse keeper. A man who knew appropriations and how to please overseers—necessary skills in the quaint days after the Cold War when the Agency was contracting.

Few expected him to become a visionary spy.

He leads them to a back deck overlooking a lake the color of dried basil. He brings coffee, warm cider, and cookies, and they sit, three figures around a teak table, bundled in jackets against the chill of a clearing storm.

He has owned the house since college, Rousseau tells them, when it was a one-room cabin. He knew the lake as a boy, bought the place "for nothing, with money I'd saved from a paper route, literally. Now there are houses here worth five million dollars."

It is Rousseau, when the small talk slows, who says, "Tell me why you're really here."

"You know why," says Rena.

Rousseau warms his hands on his coffee. "Tell me anyway. I'll learn from what you leave out." He aims an impish glance at Brooks, then stares stonily at Rena.

They explain it all again, the charge from the White House to stay ahead of Congress and the media, the shock of the *Tribune* exposé. They leave out their suspicions about O'Dowd and Franks and the awkward meeting at the White House this week.

"What the hell you gotten yourself into?" But it is only half a joke.

"That's what we came to ask *you*," Brooks says.

"A mess," Rousseau answers.

"Then we need an annotator."

It's a term Rousseau liked to employ, Burke had said. "Tony liked to say most people look at the world and see only the outlines. Never the context. Never the meaning. They need an annotator. Especially presidents. 'The CIA,' he would tell them, 'is the annotator.'"

Rousseau smiles at Rena's use of the term.

But they hope Rousseau will be more than that. Nash had

passed over Rousseau and chosen Webster to run the CIA. Now, through Rena and Brooks, the president in effect is reaching back and offering Rousseau a chance to be in the game again. That is their real offer. That is what he can annotate.

"You would have made a good goddamn spy, Peter," says Rousseau.

"No," Rena says. "I'm too direct."

"Who knows you're here?"

"No one."

The answer seems to irritate Rousseau.

"Bullshit. You think you're just regular citizens anymore?"

"What happened in Oosay?" Rena asks, trying to stay on track.

All at once the former spy is out of his chair and walking to the dock. He stops at a boatlift, pushes a button, and a large motorboat hanging fifteen feet in the air begins to lower into the water.

He returns to the table. "Let's go on the lake," he says. "I'll get us warmer coats."

Without another word he heads into the house and comes back with two heavier coats, which he hands to his visitors. In a few minutes they are in the middle of the lake.


**ROUSSEAU DROPS ANCHOR** and flips a switch and music begins to play, a Bach cello concerto, coming through scratchy boat speakers. He scans the horizon, then makes his way back to where Rena and Brooks are seated in the back of the boat.

"You are into the shit," he says.

"Why?" Brooks asks.

"The intelligence community hates Nash," Rousseau says.

"And why is that?"

Brooks knows her role here is to play the innocent, the uninformed, which would pull Rousseau to reveal more.

"Because Jim Nash only trusts certain kinds of information and certain kinds of people."

"You need to explain that to me," Brooks says.

Rousseau glances at Rena in recognition he is being handled.

"In intelligence, Ms. Brooks, there are three kinds of information. There's the kind that comes from people on the ground. Spying. The acronym is HUMINT. Short for 'human intelligence.' There's intelligence from imagery—cameras and satellites. IMINT. And there is machine and signal intelligence—from picking up specific signals from fixed objects, listening, hacking, and electronic monitoring. MASINT, or machine and signal."

Rousseau scans the lake and the shoreline.

"I always hated the acronyms."

His head swivels to the other shoreline. An old habit—always monitor your surroundings? Or does Rousseau think they are being watched?

"Over the last decade, the United States, and especially the Agency, has leaned more heavily on image and machine intelligence—cameras and eavesdropping. And then, in fighting the war on terror, on drones."

"It's a shift you started," Rena says.

Rousseau smiles ruefully. "Those who make changes are always more mindful of their risks than those who inherit them."

He examines their faces for understanding.

"It was inevitable really. When you're losing a war, you want new tools. Technology seems safer. Better. More accurate."

"Why does that make Nash's national security team distrust him?" Brooks asks.

"Because over time the president and Diane Howell have come to trust only the intelligence they can see for themselves and to doubt the advice they get from their team of generals and spies. Nash has struggled to find a defense secretary he trusts. He's squabbled with the Joint Chiefs. He isn't close to Webster at CIA. He just fired his director of national intelligence, the person who is supposed to coordinate everything. He also fired his first national security advisor and brought Howell down from the United Nations."

"Is he wrong?"

"Imagery and machines aren't enough," Rousseau answers. "You can't win this war with drones and imagery. It's a war of ideas. We can't kill our way to victory here. Nash knows that, but he doesn't know what else to do."

Rousseau stares at Brooks.

"And it has made the feuds in the family worse."

"What feuds? What family?"

"Look, Ms. Brooks. Spies want to spy. Soldiers want to fight. If drones can do your killing, and CIA contractors your fighting, your soldiers become obsolete. So do you. So does your knowledge. You're being outsourced and replaced by machines."

Rena, who has been listening and watching Rousseau, finally speaks.

"What does this have to do with Oosay?"

"Morat, and all of Africa, they're another place to watch the same movie again," Rousseau says. "Another country in chaos. Another place where DOD vies with CIA to see which service leads, which has the president's ear, which has control. The army wants to play a bigger role in Africa because it thinks the CIA's role is too big in the Middle East. My guess is that's why Brian Roderick was in Oosay. Trying to put the army in charge. Not the CIA or other agencies. If Africa is the next great battlefield, try it the military way."

They have gotten part of the way. Now Rena and Brooks know they have to go further.

"Something happened out there and Shane, Webster, Hollenbeck at the Joints Chiefs, they're hiding something," Rena says. "Maybe hiding it from Nash. We've talked to the survivors. They're hiding something, too."

Rousseau stares at Rena.

"We need to ask you about Roderick. Shane. Webster. Howell. We need to know what Roderick was doing out there. That is the key to what happened, and what is being covered up."

Rousseau smiles. Then he stands, moves to the center of the boat, hoists the anchor, and pushes a button to restart the engines.

## SEVENTEEN

The two big outboard motors begin to moan. The boat shimmies in anticipation, and they feel their weight shift back as Rousseau accelerates and pushes the boat full throttle to a distant part of the lake.

He slows in front of a marshland with high reeds, where there are fewer houses, and then eases the boat into an inlet that makes them nearly invisible.

He turns off the motor, lowers the anchor, and flips another switch. The Bach cello concerto resumes through the scratchy speakers, and Rousseau sits down, closer to them this time.

"Why would people be lying to us about Oosay?"

Rousseau sighs as if exasperated, but Rena knows he is thrilled they are here.

"I don't know what Roderick was doing in Oosay that night," Rousseau says. "But I know what we're trying to do in Africa. Avoid the mistakes we made in the Middle East."

"Which means what?" Brooks says.

"The CIA has been very focused on Iraq, Syria, Afghanistan, Pakistan, and Iran, and if you do that largely with technology, everything ends up being about resources and geography. Where do we fly our drones? Where do we put our listening devices? But technology misses the deeper issues. Who *are* these extremists? How do they think? What motivates them? What might they do next?

"To know that, you need human intelligence. You need to understand your enemy as people. You need to be with them. Inside them.

"That's what Dan Shane believes is wrong with our approach to the war on terror. He wants to rebuild HUMINT. And when he became defense secretary, he saw Africa as a chance for the DOD to do it, in the new theater where the CIA had little influence. And he saw the Pentagon's own intelligence agency, the DIA, as a way to do it, to build human intelligence for the military and the DIA into something of a rival to the CIA—at least when it came to spies on the ground."

"Was that what Roderick was doing in Oosay? Recruiting spies?"

"I don't know Roderick. I don't know what he was doing there."

The look on Rousseau's face is final.

"Tell us about Diane Howell," Brooks says, changing the subject. Brooks thinks Howell may be a pathway to the truth, but so far she has avoided them.

"She's damned smart," Rousseau says. "Especially for an academic." The former spy smiles mildly at his own joke. "But she's a skeptic about nation building in the short run. Thinks democracy in the Middle East is a joke. Pretty hard-line for a liberal."

"Would she have known what Roderick was doing?" Brooks asks.

"I wouldn't underestimate her knowing everything. But she and Roderick wouldn't have been close. She keeps her distance from the other members of the national security team. That's partly her personality. Partly experience. Partly gender. There's a lotta boys around."

They ask more questions about Howell but get few answers they don't already know.

"What about Webster?" Rena asks.

"Owen won the job of running the CIA. I lost."

"Why'd he win?"

"You are direct, aren't you, Peter?"

"That's why I was a better interrogator than your CIA torture boys, Tony."

"Now I see you're a kind of torture all your own."

"Tell us about Webster."

"He's always in favor, you might say, of whatever is likely to happen." Rousseau lets that linger, a line, apparently, he has used before. "It's a convenient position to have. You're almost always on the winning side."

"Tony, what does that mean?" Rena is tiring, too, of Rousseau's way of circling around subjects.

"It means he tends to tell his bosses, including the president, whatever they want to hear—and he rationalizes that it will be good for the Agency because it will grow the budget. Whether it is good for the Agency or not. Whether he agrees with it or not. Whether it is good for the country or not.

"If the president wanted to fight the war on terror with drones rather than soldiers, Owen would give him drones. Robot killers from the sky, like something from science fiction. We are creating more new Islamist fighters out of terrified civilians than we are killing radical leaders."

Rousseau leans back and looks up, as if he expects a drone overhead.

"I've seen this lake change over forty years. It felt like a secret place when I was young. There are no secret places anymore."

"So Webster is an enabler," Rena says, trying to refocus Rousseau. "He tells the president what he wants to hear."

"It's not that simple. He is a spy. He will tell everyone what they want to hear, and then do what he feels he needs to."

"Would he lie to the president about Oosay?"

A smile, briefly. "Lying and keeping things from the president are two different things."

Now Rousseau seems to recede into himself, into his secrets, into his wounded memories.

They ask more questions about more people involved in Oosay. But the answers are no longer helpful. Finally Rousseau signals to them he is done by moving around the boat. "I don't envy your task," he says. He pulls his jacket collar over his neck and then looks at them hard. "There will be a witch hunt over Oosay but it's all bullshit."

"What's bullshit?" asks Brooks.

"The whole thing. Take any country where Islamic terrorism is mixing with liberation. Syria, Iraq, Libya, Morat, Tunisia. I could name a half dozen more. You have three choices as a policy maker. You can take sides and get involved militarily. But you will have involved the United States in another war the American people don't want. And, most likely, Islamic terrorism will grow anyway.

"You could do nothing. But doing nothing feels immoral. You'll be condemned for it. And Islamic terrorism will grow anyway.

"Or you could do something in between, some careful policy of air support, targeted drones, no-fly zones, sanctions, and aid. Pick whatever you want from the kit. Then you can say you did *something*. But your enemies will say it was the wrong thing. And Islamic terrorism will grow anyway."

Rousseau looks at his visitors to see if they understand. He has begun to perspire in the cold.

"Will you help us do this? Annotate?" Rena asks.

"I don't have much on my plate," Rousseau says.

"Then can we go back now?" Brooks says. "Because I'm fucking freezing."

Rousseau, however, doesn't get up to restart the engines just yet. He gives them a look to convey that he has one more message to deliver. "You guys need to understand something. This is life and death. Not politics. People know you came here. People who watch other people for a living. Lethal people. You remember, Peter?"

"You telling us we're in danger? On American soil?" Brooks asks.

Rousseau's look suggests she is naïve to ask. Then he gets up from his seat and begins to repeat his ritual of pushing buttons, hoisting the anchor, and starting the motors. He steers them out of the high grass and back into the lake and then drives the boat hard back to his dock. He ties up the boat and carefully does the work of cleaning up, putting the seats away, raising the boat from the water, washing it, and putting on its cover. It is midafternoon when they are done. Rousseau makes them a late lunch of eggs and sausage. He doesn't like to go out much, he says. He is the town's most famous resident, and people pay him too much attention. He doesn't ask where they are staying or their plans. When they finish, he wishes them good luck and sees them to the door.

* * *

"It comes down to Webster, Shane, and Howell," Rena says, guessing, as they drive back to Seattle. "One of them knows what happened. Or all of them."

Brooks isn't listening.

"What the hell were we doing in that goddamn inlet?" she asks. "Hiding from snipers? You really think people know we came here?"

Rena has been wondering, too. Instead of answering her, however, he hears himself defending Rousseau.

He has seen it too often, the unspoken, secret scars of defending your country. It was part of the tragedy of fighting our wars off the books, with all-volunteer armies and private contractors. The war on terror is all but invisible to most Americans, an inconvenience that is mostly put out of mind.

People wave their caps to veterans at the ball game, pay minimal attention to stories in the news about deployed soldiers, and watch with frozen familiarity the videos of the next attack on civilians in Europe.

"Rousseau was the most brilliant intelligence agent of his generation," Rena says. "He spent nearly thirty years in it, more than twenty at the Agency. And when he was through, the world was so much worse than when he started."

"Then by all means, let's get *his* help," Brooks says.

Instantly, she regrets her sarcasm. She is quiet a moment and then has one more thing on her mind.

"David Traynor called again," she says. "He wants to know whether we will work for him, do that opposition research on him so he can run for president."

Rena had nearly forgotten. It was the night of the Oosay attack, of that dreadful White House correspondents' dinner.

They had been distracted by Oosay and had never had a chance to talk about Traynor.

"What do you think, Peter, about helping him?"

Rena is quiet. He didn't like the man, though he was more impressed by Traynor than he expected to be. He also didn't want to be pulled into work for a Democrat. Republican friends warned him that after working for Nash, and with an election coming, Rena would eventually have to choose sides. Everyone did now. It gnawed at him. The city of Washington, the whole system, the idea of a large country that could still be a democratic republic, all were founded on the notion that that was not true.

"I worry that working for Traynor violates our promise to each other," Rena says.

When they'd become partners seven years ago, he and Brooks had made a pact that they would not work election campaigns. They would take work from politicians of both parties, to help them govern and solve problems—if they trusted and believed in the people involved. But no campaign work; that was too purely political.

"We wouldn't be working to elect him," Brooks says. "We'd be doing a scrub, just like we do for companies. We'd be finding out if he is clean to run."

A lot of their business was commercial, corporations asking

them to check the backgrounds of potential CEOs, even pro sports teams occasionally hiring them to scrub potential draft picks about whom there were difficult rumors.

"It's not the same," Rena says. "We're not endorsing those companies."

"We're helping them. And we choose who we work for."

It's not out of character for Rena and Brooks to debate like this over work. Randi is quick to share her feelings, and her candor makes people trust her. Her outspokenness is also a useful balance, Rena knows, to his own reticence. They make better decisions because Randi wants to argue those decisions out.

"I don't like Traynor," Rena says at last. "I don't trust him."

"He's crude," Brooks admits. "But Peter, think: a Democrat who would actually take on entitlements, who wants to shrink the bad parts of government, not just defend them, who says he'd help reelect Republicans who work with him?"

She turns her head and looks at her partner. "Isn't that what you say you want?"

"Do you think he'd make a good president?" Rena asks.

"I think he's a paradigm shifter. And we need to try something. Because the paradigm we've got isn't working."

Rena is quiet.

"Peter, if we say no to him because we never get involved in elections, who are we fooling? What are we doing for Nash right now? Don't you think Oosay will influence the next election?"

But Rena has no answer for her.

## EIGHTEEN

## THURSDAY, DECEMBER 26
## SAN FRANCISCO

Brooks spends the night in Seattle and flies to Washington the next morning. Rena takes the late flight from Seattle to San Francisco to see Victoria Madison and grab what remains of their Christmas plans, interrupted by the deaths in Oosay and the summons from the president.

At the arrivals curb at the San Francisco airport, a Porsche Boxster pulls up next to Rena. The car window eases down and a woman with a freckled upturned nose and sun-streaked hair leans over from the driver's seat.

"My Christmas present to myself," Vic says. "I finally decided it was insensible to drive a sensible car in California because you're in it too much for it to be dull."

"You get wiser and wiser," Rena says.

He drops his bag in the tiny trunk and slides in beside her. He is reminded all over again of his first impression of Vic—a girl on a Beach Boys album all grown up. She smiles and leans to him. Her smoke-gray eyes, flecked with gold at the irises, do not close until the last second before they kiss.

"Hi," she breathes. "Merry Christmas."

Rena feels a wave of peace wash over him, at least for a moment.

"Hi."

A longer kiss, grateful and reacquainting.

If he is honest with himself, he is a little apprehensive about this visit. His and Vic's lives fit into each other at long distance. Vic is his refuge from D.C., his faraway life, almost a dream. They talk or text most days and sometimes have long calls at night—which can be very late in Washington.

Rena wonders how long this state of easy grace can last. At what point will Vic say they have to move further along or stop? She is about to turn thirty-seven, four and a half years younger than he, and, like Rena, she has already been divorced once. He hasn't asked if she wants to become a mother, and Vic hasn't brought it up. That conversation means talking about something else. His own marriage ended after a series of miscarriages and his emotional distance. Does he want to try to have children with Vic Madison? Where would they live? How would their lives blend together in the same place? In which place? In some ways, they hadn't spent enough time with each other to know the answers. In other ways, how much time do you need to spend? What does it imply that he is not eager to have this conversation?

Vic is an attorney in California, unconnected from politics, living in the world of technology and law and the outdoors. He, by contrast, lives in a city built as political compromise between the southern and northern states, a compromise that has never really settled.

They head south down the Bayshore Freeway toward Vic's house in Palo Alto, and Rena talks, but only carefully, about the assignment that has interrupted their Christmas vacation.

She'd read the *Tribune*'s exposé, Vic says, and the accusations afterward that the administration might be involved in a cover-up.

Out the window they pass a lighted life-size replica of Mr. Peanut in his monocle and spats standing atop a small factory building.

"How could anyone seriously think this is anything more than just a tragic accident?" Vic says. "Terrorists killed these men. Not the administration. Why does everything have to be turned into something you can use to your political advantage?"

Of course she is right, Rena thinks. Vic had been an important and calming influence during the sometimes surreal political theater that enveloped her father's confirmation fight. She was the one person to whom the prickly judge would always listen, and Rena and Brooks never would have understood Roland Madison without her. Now, for Rena, she often provided a sane counterbalance to the hothouse atmosphere of the events in his life.

But in Washington no one thinks twice about James Nash being blamed for Oosay. Everyone expects it—that whatever happens in D.C., the calculus will quickly turn to how different factions can exploit it, or be hurt by it. Even foreign attacks by terrorists. Being surprised by that, or unprepared, only makes one vulnerable. Lamentation is a luxury no one can afford.

It's taken Vic only ten minutes to remind him how people outside the city might see that as perverse.

When Vic was hurt by the killer who was stalking her father, Rena blamed himself for not anticipating the threat sooner and protecting her. As their feelings for each other deepened, Rena worried Vic would suspect that his feelings for her were mixed with that guilt, and such suspicions would scuttle their relationship, the first of any consequence for him since his divorce.

He'd confronted her with this fear, a rare instance of his articulating his feelings, particularly with women. But he can't seem to bring himself to raise the subject of where their relationship is headed now. Especially, he tells himself, in the middle of another crisis.

Vic lives on a hidden street near the Professorville section of Palo Alto, not far from Stanford University. The street is called Community Lane. A hundred years ago, the land had been part of a compound for a utopian boys' school. The boys lived in cabins, as did the teachers. Vic had bought one of the old cabins and rebuilt it into a Frank Lloyd Wright–influenced two-bedroom house with floor-to-ceiling windows that opened to a rock and water garden on all sides. She had spent time in Bali, and she re-created that environment in the garden. All of it, the house, its rock, fern, and water gardens, all hidden by a tall wall from the houses around it, made Vic's home feel like a sanctuary.

Inside the house, Vic takes Rena's hand, pulls him gently toward the bedroom. "I made a bet with myself regarding something."

"Will I be let in on it?"

"You might say that," she says, closing the bedroom door behind them.

**THE NEXT MORNING,** Vic tells Rena she is taking him to a place for lunch called Duarte's Tavern. "It's over the hill on the ocean side in a little town called Pescadero. And then I have a surprise for you. A Christmas present."

Pescadero turns out to be a small ocean town halfway between San Francisco and Santa Cruz. It has two street lights and a one-block main street. In the center is a plain-looking barn-red storefront with an L-shaped neon sign announcing DUARTE'S TAVERN and a smaller one underneath that spells out LIQUOR. Inside are two rooms with tables and a grand old wooden bar. Photos of the Pacific coast going back one hundred years hang on the walls. The owner, Ron Duarte, lives upstairs, Vic says. His grandfather, a Portuguese fisherman, started the place. "The three things to get here are the fried oysters, cream of artichoke soup, and pie."

The weather is cool but sunny, something close to what it would feel like in early spring in Washington, though it is two days after Christmas.

She eats delicately, a tiny spoonful of soup at a time, and as she tilts her head her bangs dangle into her eyes.

"The best artichoke soup ever, right?"

"I've never had artichoke soup before."

"Then that's a yes."

He has missed her.

"What was this man like, the one you visited in Seattle—this Russell, or Rousseau?" she asks.

Rena pauses over this. There are things he cannot tell her—indeed he can tell her almost nothing. But he knows he also can't fly out to visit her and then say he can't discuss anything about his life.

"He's haunted."

"By what?"

What can he say to her?

"I think serving his country over this whole period we've gone through, fighting terror and making the mistakes we've made, it's scarred him. The job is too big. We're not throwing enough of the country into it. We borrow the money to fight, and ask most people for no sacrifice; the war only divides us."

This is ground they have covered before. Rena thinks U.S. citizenship comes at too low a price. He believes the country should require two years of universal service of everyone at age eighteen, male and female, in some form of civilian or military work. Among other virtues, it might be the only time people of different cultures and classes will ever mix anymore in America. Vic has made counterarguments for which Rena has no good answers. Compulsory service hasn't unified Israel, has it? she says. Why would it work here?

She is watching him now, and Rena wonders if she, too, is thinking about how different their lives are, she the liberal from California and he the soldier, even if he was no longer welcome in uniform.

"You should move here," she says suddenly.

Rena takes her hand.

What would he *do* out here? Security consulting for technology companies run by people who just turned thirty?

"Would you consider it?"

Washington is a disaster, but it's what Rena knows. And though he and Randi make most of their money working for corporations, not politicians or public interest groups, they know the commercial work mostly pays the bills so they can afford clients engaged in public affairs.

"Yes, I would consider it. Would you consider Washington?"

"I would," she says, but Rena can see doubt behind her smile.

They are reaching that point, he knows, that neither of them is entirely ready to confront.

They finish and pay. They have another stop to make, Vic says. She has a surprise for him.

They drive north to Half Moon Bay, a much larger town up the coast that is beginning to get discovered by city people. The old part of the town, away from the highway, still has fishing boats and an old main street and coastal charm. Vic pulls her new Porsche into a space in front of an old Victorian house.

The sign out front says TABBY'S PLACE and has a picture of a cat on it.

"My friend runs this," Vic says. "He made one hundred million dollars in a start-up before he was forty. When he cashed out, he decided he wanted to create a place to rescue cats."

It is like a luxury hotel inside. The cats live in suites. There are enormous parklike common spaces, with runs and hiding places and climbing structures. Scores of cats lounge about and play. Rena thinks of an all-inclusive resort he stayed at once in Mexico—Cabo San Lucas for cats.

"What are we doing here?"

"You'll see."

They stop in front of one of the cat suites. Sprawled inside, looking out, is a large charcoal-gray cat with dense short fur. It has startlingly bright golden eyes, an upturned Myrna Loy nose, and an enormous triple chin. The cat, Rena thinks, bears an uncanny resemblance to Winston Churchill.

"He's a British shorthair," Vic announces. "They're very affectionate. And I've already made a large donation for him in your name."

"I live in D.C."

"I also bought you a carrier. So he can fly home with you. Only rule is they live indoors. I signed papers promising."

Rena looks at Vic with an expression that in an interrogation room had frightened suspects into confessing to crimes that put them behind bars for years.

She seems immune to the look.

"He will be your buddy, this little man," she says gaily.

She opens the door to the suite, picks up the cat, and hands him to Rena. The cat puts an arm on each side of his neck as if hugging him.

"It'll be good to have someone who appreciates you when you come home at night. He can keep you company in your den while you read."

Rena and the cat stare at each other.

"By the time we get back to my place in Palo Alto, I expect you to have given him a name."

Rena looks pleadingly at Vic.

"Look, pal, do I have to tell you the obvious?" she says. "Let's just say you might have commitment issues. Your mother abandoned you. Your dad died on you. Your wife divorced you. We need to work on this. We're gonna start with a cat."

Rena experiences the unfamiliar sensation of powerlessness—and the even more unfamiliar feeling of giving in to it.

**AS THEY WALK OUTSIDE,** Rena holding the cat in its carrier, he notices a black Ford Focus down the street. Two men sit inside.

He has seen the car before, he thinks, in Palo Alto. He is sure of it, though of course he can't be entirely sure.

He recalls Rousseau's warning about being watched. Would they be so obvious that he would notice them? Or perhaps that is the point? Or is he imagining all this?

"You okay?" Vic asks.

He puts his arm around her. "I'm great."

## NINETEEN

## THURSDAY, JANUARY 2
## 1823 JEFFERSON PLACE,
## WASHINGTON, D.C.

Even in the twenty-first century, people just didn't expect a woman.

Not to do this kind of work: surveillance, security, personal protection, and the rest.

As far as Samantha Reese was concerned, that blind spot only made women better choices for the job. People would look right past them, just a glancing thought, a reflex—"oh, a woman."

So you use that, every slight, every prejudice; it's all opportunity.

Reese has gotten to the restaurant early, watched it for an hour before it opened and then entered through the small French doors at 11:30 A.M. just after seeing the owner, Giovanni, open up. She sits at the bar drinking Campari and soda, deciding which table she thinks would be best, then excusing herself and asking where the restrooms are. She goes the wrong way so she can scan parts of the place one can't see from the main room, and apologizes when she wanders into the kitchen and finds the back door to the alley, making amends in perfect Italian before she returns to the dining room.

When the man she is meeting arrives, she is seated at a corner table from which she can see the whole room. She watches him slip through the small front door.

She waits.

He looks the same, which is to say good, still lithe, strong. He always reminded her of a panther, quiet, watchful, dangerous. He isn't her type; he'd also been married until recently. Still.

"Thanks for coming, Sam," Peter Rena says when he gets to the table. He is wearing a gray suit and a formal wool overcoat, the Washington uniform of respectable anonymity. Reese is wearing blue jeans and a black T-shirt under a down vest, her only acknowledgment to the gray January cold.

"You only need to ask, Peter," Reese says. "You know that." She glances around the restaurant. "Good place."

It is called Trattu, a small Italian restaurant on Jefferson Place just down the block from the office at 1820. It is Rena's favorite restaurant in the city. Twelve small tables in the basement of another town house. Giovanni and his wife, Antonia, serve northern Italian food they learned to cook from grandmothers, parents, and aunts—*Mama Style Oven Fish Stew, Chicken Breast Stuffed with Roasted Red Pepper,* and *Corn Meal from the Pot.*

"What's so urgent I had to leave Colorado for?" she asks.

"I want you to keep an eye on Randi and me."

Reese raises an eyebrow.

"You think someone's watching you?"

"Anthony Rousseau thinks it's possible."

That raises the other eyebrow.

"You've seen Tony Rousseau? What are you into, Peter?"

She and Rena met in the army when Reese was doing a rotation in the military police. Rena had never met anyone so determined and disciplined, even in uniform. She came from a military and athletic family, her mother a talented triathlete, her father a decorated marksman. Her mother died young and in the open spaces of Colorado; her father taught her to hunt and track and shoot. In college she accomplished something her father had aspired to but never achieved, a spot on the U.S. Olympic biathlete squad—the hybrid sport of cross-country skiing and shooting. She enlisted in the army, like many Olympians, for the support and discipline required to help her train. Reese became one of just four female soldiers to successfully make it through the grueling nine-week Army Ranger school. When injuries set back her Olympic prospects, and the army failed to deliver on promises, at age thirty-one she resigned her commission.

She lives in Colorado near Snowmass, where she can train and work when she wants at a gym she co-owns. She keeps a low profile, and clients barely notice when from time to time Reese seems to vanish because she and a group of other military friends have taken a job doing surveillance or personal security, so-called body work.

Rena still hasn't answered Reese's question about why he had seen Anthony Rousseau.

"Don't make a show of the watching our backs," he says. "You don't need to be invisible. But I don't want to make Randi crazy. Or anyone else. Far enough away that most people would never notice you. Close enough that if someone really good were watching, they'd know."

"Why would someone be watching you?" she asks again.

"I don't know that they are."

"Why would Rousseau think so?"

Rena isn't sure how much to say.

Reese is a brunette with broad shoulders and the sculpted features of an athlete. Her manner is direct and eerily calm, something she refined from years of her father telling her to win men's respect by looking them in the eye and telling them what she really thought, not by looking away and winning their fascination. Often her expression is sardonic.

"Sorry, Peter. You need to tell me what this is about. Or my answer will be no."

Of course. He would demand the same if their roles were reversed. So he tells her what he can—the assignment from the president, their frustrations, their visit to the lake, and Rousseau's warnings. Not everything. Hopefully enough.

"You must think the threat is at least plausible," she says.

"Something went wrong out there in Oosay, and people don't want to talk about it—maybe not even tell the White House the full story."

Sam Reese has a refined sense of irony. The idea that people would be making mistakes and then panicking to cover them up seems to fit her worldview, which—as best as Rena can make out—is that if people thought harder about the state of their lives, they would be in a perpetual state of panic or despair. So most people don't think about it. Not that Reese has ever sat down and told Rena her worldview.

"How big a mistake was this in Oosay?"

"When we know, we'll be done with this."

"And you'd like to stay alive long enough to also find out what they're hiding."

"Not funny, Sam."

"Sure it's a joke?"

"If I were, I wouldn't be asking you to do this."

She offers the first shadow of a genuine smile.

"Okay."

And they eat their lunch in peace.

**RENA HAS BEEN HOME** a few days from California. He has made little more progress on Oosay than he has with the cat Vic gave him for Christmas.

The animal has spent his first days in Washington hiding behind the dryer in Rena's row house. The only evidence the animal has moved is when Rena returns home from work and there is a little less food in a dish that now sits on the floor in the breakfast nook. Even the litter box is inconclusive. The cat still has no name.

## TWENTY

## FRIDAY, JANUARY 3, 3:15 P.M.
## TYSONS CORNER, VIRGINIA

When Jill Bishop arrives at the restaurant, the woman she calls "Talon" is already seated at the usual table in the back. She's nursing a Thai beer and ordered one for Bishop.

Talon is a nickname Bishop uses in her notes for a senior CIA officer from the intelligence division. The name is a reference to the long fingernails Talon once mentioned she wore in graduate school, a small indulgence in her otherwise utilitarian approach to personal grooming. When she joined the CIA after getting her master's, an instructor at "the Farm" where the Agency trains new recruits ordered her to cut the nails short. Back then she did everything she was told.

The story is obscure enough that Bishop thinks "Talon" would be a safe alias if anyone ever got access to Bishop's notes—by hacking them, stealing them, or, God forbid, by court order. The woman's real name is Katherine.

Talon slides the beer toward Bishop. The reporter in turn leans down to her bag, picks out a box, and puts it on the table. "Merry Christmas," she says. "From Peru." Talon unwraps the box and admires the scarf inside.

"I got something for you, too." Talon gives Bishop her own box. Inside is a set of three monkeys carved in ivory.

The reporter grins. "I love it."

A year ago Talon helped Bishop break a story about three men in Iraq who had peddled bad intelligence to the U.S. government. The faulty intelligence connected a well-known militia leader to Islamic radicals. Many at Talon's level in the Agency doubted the information but were overruled from above. The militia leader was killed in a drone strike, destabilizing that part of the country. At the Agency, the Iranian men who'd peddled the bad intelligence were known as "the three monkeys." Such fuckups need to be reported so they don't get repeated, Talon thought.

She is tiny and dark haired, with thin, delicate features that have taken on a harsher look over the years from the stress of her job. She is in her midforties, about five years younger than Bishop, and has reached a point in her career where she is highly skilled and has already made many of the compromises women confront in the covert world. Katherine has lost one marriage and is weighing how much she wants to fight to save her second. She mostly worries about the effect that would have on her two daughters.

"Well, you've got the whole freaking U.S. intelligence community in lockdown right now, Jill," Talon says.

"Oh?"

"The investigation into Oosay has basically slowed down to nothing. The excuse is the holidays."

"Maybe it is the holidays."

Talon offers Bishop a doubting look.

A waitress approaches but keeps some distance. The two diners are regulars, and the waitress, an older Thai woman, knows they like their privacy. Talon nods for her to come to the table. The CIA agent orders pad thai, as she always does. Just as she always insists they come to the same Thai restaurant.

These meetings of reporters and intelligence sources are not like the ones you see in the movies. You don't meet outside, on the street by the Washington Monument—good for a location "wide shot"—or at a secluded park or in a parking garage. Being outside makes surveillance too easy. It is also, to be honest, too campy, and it makes sources self-conscious.

So Bishop usually suggests a restaurant, someplace not too crowded, a place with booths where you can talk and expect some privacy. You go late afternoon or early evening or sometimes late—whenever there aren't a lot of people around. Someplace innocuous. Somewhere in the suburbs. Somewhere that neither Bishop nor the source is likely to bump into someone they know.

When you cover the intelligence beat, you also don't wear a press pass around your neck that gets you access to a building. You don't have a cubicle at CIA headquarters or attend press briefings. You don't get official statements and press announcements sent to your "in" basket. You have to develop your own clandestine network of people in national security who put their careers in your hands. You earn their trust, and you pay it back by protecting them—even going to jail to do it. These are relationships, friendships. Bonds. They take time. Sometimes years. Ninety percent of the job, Bishop estimates, is spent finding people and earning their trust. Only about 10 percent is spent actually reporting and writing stories.

"People are sheltering in place," Katherine says. "Hiding under their desks. You touched a nerve."

Bishop and Talon have known each other three years. They were introduced by a retired Agency source of Bishop's who was a mentor of Talon's. Retired spies were critical to covering intelligence. They felt freer to talk, and if they were retiring early, as many did, they usually had grievances. That's why they were retiring early.

In time, former agents introduced you to their own network of friends still on active duty, people whose information is more current and who can track things down for you, be your guide and your sounding board.

For reasons Bishop could never quite figure out, most of the introductory meetings at which trusted sources brought along a friend to meet Bishop occurred at the same one or two places. The favorite one was an espresso bar at the Hotel Royale near Tysons Corner, Virginia, not far from CIA headquarters. The coffee bar, with the absurdly ironic name "Ronde-voux," is a favorite of old spies, many of whom went on to work for defense contractors after leaving government. A lot of arms, matériel, and technology got sold in Ronde-voux. Not all of it legally.

Bishop never understood why spies liked to behave so daringly in front of each other. Maybe, having lived in the secret world, they felt safer doing their business where they could watch one another.

After their own introduction at Ronde-voux, Bishop and Talon spent months talking—sometimes every week—usually at the same Thai restaurant they are in now. "Tell me about your career. Tell me about your kids." Katherine had earned a master's in international relations at Wisconsin. She wasn't recruited to the Agency through some talent spotter. That sort of thing was rare now. She'd seen the job opening at the CIA online, like she was applying for a job at IBM.

"You'd think spies would have more backbone than to be frightened by one newspaper story," Talon says.

"Depends on the story." Bishop smiles.

"They're like frightened little boys."

The two women got together nearly every week for six months before Bishop ever pulled a notebook from her bag. She set it on the table between them. Wordlessly. Ceremoniously. The motion deliberate—the message unmistakable: *Here is a notebook. I'm now going to ask you questions and take notes. I am becoming a reporter. You are becoming a source.* The crossing of the Rubicon. She had engaged in the same ceremony with a number of spies over the years.

Bishop and Talon crossed that Rubicon two and a half years ago. Since then, Talon has helped on a half dozen stories.

People in the secret world talk to reporters for various reasons, but none do so without getting something out of it. Sometimes it's violent disagreement over policy—trying to stop the government from making what a source thinks is a terrible mistake. Sometimes it's moral outrage over something the government intends to do that a spy thinks is wrong. Spies oddly tend to be idealists. Sometimes the motives are more personal, trying to exact revenge or vent frustration. Nearly everyone Bishop knows in the intelligence world is unhappy about something. Sometimes when spies talk to reporters they are simply playing a dangerous game of office politics, one faction vying with another using the *New York Times* or the *Washington Tribune* as leverage. Sometimes people just want to feel important. Usually it isn't one reason alone.

Reasonable people can disagree about whether any one leaker's actions are noble or traitorous, Bishop thinks, but the more senior someone gets in the world of intelligence, the more likely that at one time or another they have been a source. You don't survive near the top, and almost never rise higher, without having allies in the press.

Through all her years at it, Bishop has learned one lesson that is constant. You never judge a confidential source by his or her motives. You judge them by the information they provide. Period. Is what they are telling true? Can it be verified? Should the public know it? Or is it better kept a secret? Everything else is quicksand.

"Tell me, Katherine. What do you mean by lockdown?"

"After your story ran, there was an order to expedite a full draft of the internal Agency report on the Oosay incident. The section you saw and others were put together and sent up the line. Then it was supposed to be sent back down for one last review. But now it's vanished."

"What do you mean vanished?"

"The people who were working on the report can't find it anymore. It's gone from the system. Or they no longer have access."

This *was* a story—if Bishop could get more:

*An internal intelligence community review of the events leading up to the attack in Oosay that left four Americans dead has been pulled back from distribution.*

But Bishop would need more. She'd need to talk to someone who'd seen the report and knew for certain what was in it, someone who could confirm that it had now disappeared.

What Talon has told her is only a tip.

When did the report go up the line? What day? When did someone first notice it had vanished from the system? How many people have tried to look for it? Did the report have a title? What department was responsible for it?

Before she finishes eating, Talon says, "I have to go."

"Meet in a week?" Bishop suggests.

This is how almost every encounter with a national security source ends. Bishop always meets her intelligence sources face-to-face. You avoid electronics as much as possible. No phone calls. No text messages. No email. At the end of each meeting, Bishop makes a verbal plan for the next one. It isn't only safer. If someone wants to back out, they can just fail to show up. But then they would be ending a relationship that was usually as valuable to them as it was to Bishop. And they'd have to hazard electronics all over again if they wanted to reconnect.

"I could do next Friday," Talon says.

Bishop nods.

Talon looks at the calendar on her phone. "I could do two o'clock. Then I have a field hockey game."

"See you here, two o'clock next Friday. A week." Bishop writes it down in a small Filofax notebook she keeps. She still has one. Pen and paper are more secure. Katherine keeps one, too. One Bishop gave her.

Katherine rises. "I gotta go." They hug and kiss and Katherine leaves the restaurant for her kids and the husband she isn't sure of.

Bishop wonders how she can confirm the story of the missing report and what it contained that people at the highest levels of the CIA wanted to keep hidden.

## TWENTY-ONE

## THURSDAY, JANUARY 9
## WASHINGTON, D.C.

Dick Bakke had been waiting for something like this, something from the outside to trigger hearings on Oosay. When you mix power and ambition and foolishness—and they are always part of the mix in Washington—you never had to wait too long.

It comes in the form of a phone call from a man named Lester Winley. Winley is the legislative director of a conservative foreign policy think tank called the National Security Institute, which is famous for filing copious numbers of federal Freedom of Information Act requests designed to expose the government as bloated and dysfunctional. And he hates President Nash.

"Senator, I come bearing a gift," Winley says in his ornate way, as if they were citizens of ancient Rome.

The gift, Winley explains, is a four-page memo written by a press aide to Arthur Manion titled "How to Discredit the President's Critics on Oosay."

The memo's author, Aaron Rubin, was a friend of Diane Howell, who had been sent to State to help Manion with communications.

It argued, "The only way to defend the president on Oosay is to play offense."

The memo even offered "talking points" to attack anyone curious or critical about what happened in Oosay.

While cynics might not be shocked that the administration was trying to organize its political defense on Oosay, a paid government staffer using his time and official capacity to do so went too far. It seemed proof that the administration did not want anyone to really know what happened that tragic night in Morat; it even raised the possibility that the administration's so-called internal probe into the incident by Rena and Brooks was a sham.

Bakke thinks the talking points themselves aren't half bad—if you played for the other team.

- "Denounce anyone attacking the president over Oosay as disgracefully exploiting the death of American citizens for political purposes."
- "Say these critics are emboldening our enemies by sowing division at home."
- "Note that Oosay critics are weakening the United States by presenting a conflicted face to the world."

"How'd you get this?" Bakke asks.

A year ago, Winley explains, he submitted an FOIA request to the State Department demanding all documents relating to improving security at U.S. foreign installations abroad—everything from Jim Nash's inauguration to the present. Yesterday, that request was approved. Among the ten thousand pages Winley received was this memo.

"An oversight, I suspect," Winley says.

Bakke leans back in his high-back red-leather senatorial chair and thinks there are times when you have to love the incompetence of the federal government.

After Winley emails the memo over, Bakke thinks that if it isn't exactly a smoking gun, it would still make news. Friendly cable hosts would call it "explosive," and even newspapers, which Bakke thinks are so liberal now they don't even recognize it, would call it "controversial."

But he doubted it would be enough to finally persuade Senate Majority Leader Susan Stroud to allow him to hold hearings. He'd tried twice before in the month since Oosay, and the Senate majority leader had resisted: "Too soon . . . we're on recess . . . we should wait for a public clamor."

Mainly, Bakke thought, Stroud didn't want him to chair hearings about the current president because she didn't want Richard Bakke to become the next president.

For all Dick Bakke disliked liberalism, with its elitist disdain for the idea that America had been anointed by God to be a beacon for the rest of the world, his most dangerous enemy, he knew, was the old guard in his own party. And that meant people like Susan Stroud.

Bakke had entered politics with a purist's vision. The country had been on a long slide toward faded glory since the 1960s, he believed, and the main reason was the government had swollen in size like a cancerous tumor. America had become basically a socialist nation. The federal debt had exploded and, with it, our vulnerability to foreign powers that held the notes, especially Chinese, Russian, and Middle Eastern powers that backed radical Islam. The only way back was to return to the vision of small and efficient government that predated Lyndon Johnson's Great Society and even Woodrow Wilson's activism—a true belief that the best government was one kept off people's backs.

Susan Stroud, Bakke thought, was not only from a different time—at seventy-three she was twenty-five years his senior—but she also came from a whole different world. She came from a world of privilege, political dynasty, country clubs, and her daddy's car dealerships all over Mississippi. In Stroud's world, conservatism was about conserving what you had.

That was emphatically not Dick Bakke's world. He came from nothing and spent his life making his own hole to climb through.

He didn't like to complain or even talk much about it. But with his mother largely absent and his father dead, he was raised by grandparents and recalled his childhood now as a growing realization he was smarter than most of the people his grandparents described as "above" them. They ran a failing roller rink in rural Kentucky, and "their Richie" worked every humiliating job in the place, taking tickets, working the concession, waxing the floor, even serving as "Roll-ee the Raccoon," the rink mascot, adorned in a giant, wool, sweat-soaked raccoon suit on roller skates. A worker, a watcher, angry, envious, and driven, he learned that resentment could be a kind of fuel. He also learned as he got older that he was not the only one who felt the way he did, and he could use that fuel to outpace nearly everyone who had all those advantages he lacked. Bakke was the first in his family to go to college, lived at home through law school, finished first in his class, and later was picked to be a Supreme Court clerk. Roll-ee the Raccoon.

Susan Stroud will still say no to hearings if he calls her.

"Les, you give this memo to anyone else?" Bakke asks.

"I went to you right away, Senator," Winley says.

"And I'm mighty glad you did, Les. Mighty glad. But to be fair, though, why don't you give a call to Curtis Gains in the House, too."

Curtis Gains is a relatively junior congressman from Florida who through good luck and retirements had become chair of the House Foreign Affairs Committee after just two terms in Congress. Gains, too, has been clamoring for hearings.

"Do you think I should?" Winley asks.

"If we want hearings on Oosay, Les, don't you think pressure from two places is better than one?"

"Very wise, Senator."

"Well, that's fine."

* * *

It was actually Curtis Gains's chief of staff, a man named Tom Beyers, who had been urging the congressman to become the most vocal member of the House calling for hearings on Oosay. He needed an issue to stand out, Beyers kept telling Gains. Getting your chairmanship was just an opportunity, Beyers advised him. Now people need to see what you will do with it. Beyers was shrewd and aggressive and Gains was grateful to have him, someone so naturally political.

After getting the call from Winley, it was Beyers who persuaded Gains to call the Speaker of the House immediately and ask for an audience. If you can get here in ten minutes, the Speaker has an opening, Gains was told.

Gains and Beyers speed-walk from the Rayburn Building across Independence to the Speaker's "private" office in the Capitol just off the House floor.

In the inner office, Gains hands over a copy of the memo, walks through the basics, and announces he would like his own committee, Foreign Affairs, to hold hearings on Oosay.

The Speaker, a pear-shaped, disheveled man, doesn't know Gains well. But he generally considers anyone in only his third House term a neophyte. He tapped Gains to fill the vacant chairmanship of Foreign Affairs because he needed to mollify, once again, the Common Sense wing of the party.

Take it all together—a baby House member, a hard-liner, and a lawyer—and the Speaker, who doesn't much like lawyers, isn't thrilled.

He weighs all this in a few seconds.

"Curt, we're gonna get to the bottom of what happened in Oosay. You bet. But I don't want to look like we're just going fishing. You run out on a lake in a boat without the right tackle and all you come back with is an empty cooler, a hangover, and a sunburn."

If the Speaker isn't sure what to think of this young House member, Congressman Curtis Gains has no doubt what he thinks of the Speaker. He considers him weak, suspiciously moderate, and maybe dull-witted. But he recognizes the old Ohio relic has friends in every quarter of the House GOP caucus, something no one else in the leadership can say, and that is how he maintains power.

"Mr. Speaker, if we hesitate, I understand Senator Bakke has this memo, too. The Senate may act before us."

If Gains knows one thing for sure, it's that the Speaker hates Senator Dick Bakke, who spent two terms in the House scorning the Old Man before jumping to the Senate.

"Whaddya think, Mitch?" the Speaker says, turning to his chief of staff, Bobby Mitchell.

The Speaker and his aide aren't rookies at this, for goodness' sake. They know the Winley memo is circulating and that it might be why Gains was coming by.

"If Senator Bakke has this memo," Mitchell says, "it might be wise to consult with Susan Stroud. See what the Senate majority leader has in mind."

"Aw Christ, Mitch, we run our own chamber here," the Speaker replies, as rehearsed. "Let the Senate delay. We should act."

"And we can, Mr. Speaker. But why not know what the majority leader has going on first?"

Among other virtues, the Speaker hopes, this little dance will remind Gains of all the complications and nuances the Speaker has to consider.

"He has a point, Curtis," the Speaker says to Gains. "Sit tight. We'll be back to you."

"Mr. Speaker, even if you create a special committee for this, I'd like to chair it," Gains says.

It is an absurdly audacious request. But then Gains had always been quick on his feet.

The Speaker drags his palm down the lower half of his face, a habit when thinking that brings unfortunate attention to the flesh on his neck.

"Let me talk to Stroud, Curt."

## TWENTY-TWO

An hour later, the Speaker and his chief of staff have traversed to the north side of the Capitol—a trip that requires crossing under the Capitol Dome—and are sitting in the ornate suite of the Senate majority leader. Susan Stroud's ceremonial office in the Capitol makes the Speaker's own ceremonial Capitol office look meager.

Everyone knows the nicknames. The Senate is now "House Stroud." The cautious inscrutable majority leader is "the Southern Sphinx," and "Wake Up, Lil Susie," when she is slow to respond. Nicknames attach themselves to politicians like gum on the floor of old movie theaters. And for a woman, the whispered corridor sobriquets often involve misogyny, sexism, physical slurs, innuendo, and every kind of harassment imaginable. In her rise to the top, Stroud steeled herself to it and gained strength from overcoming it. In one of her early local races, an opponent had dubbed her "Madame X," a reference to the famous portrait of a mysterious young woman whom the artist depicted as undeniably pretty but perhaps empty-headed. The painting, on loan from New York at the time, was on posters all over Gulfport and Jackson under the title *Who is Madame X?* Stroud, initially furious, had turned the phrase to her advantage and won. Now, during her fourth decade in politics, that nickname could instill fear in her enemies over her unpredictability: What would Madame X do?

They sit in facing chairs, their chiefs of staff with them. Stroud stares at the Speaker, the frumpy man whom she considers a kind of cut-rate Columbo, smarter than he seems but not as smart as he thinks.

With them is a fifth person the Speaker has not expected. Senator Llewellyn Burke of Michigan, chairman of Armed Services. Not formally a part of the Senate leadership, Burke is a member of Stroud's more informal "kitchen cabinet." Burke, it seems to the Speaker, is an informal counselor to nearly everyone in this goddamn town. He is even friends with the president and is the former boss of the Oosay investigator, Peter Rena.

"Les Winley is peddling this memo around," Stroud says. "Which means he has given it to the press, too."

"I assume," says the Speaker.

"So let's consider the details."

It is something Stroud says often. She is always careful about "the details." About protocol. And timing. To whom she is talking. About appearances.

And if she had any core political philosophy, it was probably purely practical: *Always play the long game.* That's why she likes the Senate. Senators run every six years. Presidents run every four—and they're out after eight. The long game is the whole point of the Senate.

"I've got chairmen chomping at the bit," the Speaker says.

"We all have people chomping at the bit, Mr. Speaker. I just got off the phone with Senator Bakke. He wants to hold hearings, too."

"Lew, what's your gut tell you?" Stroud asks Llewellyn Burke.

"Well, if the Speaker has people who want to call hearings in the House, and you have people who want to call hearings in the Senate, why not create a joint committee of both chambers?" Burke says.

"Joint. House *and* Senate?" Stroud responds.

"You and the Speaker could handpick the members," Burke suggests.

Stroud rubs her index finger against her thumb, a habit she has when thinking. The high-gloss red polish on her nails catches the light. She smiles.

"A joint committee could both contain this and empower it," Burke says to Stroud.

She nods and glances at her chief of staff.

"Be careful who you put on it, Susan," the aide says.

"Mr. Speaker?"

The Speaker is unsure what to think of this idea. It is confusing and unusual, but it would at least give the House equal billing. "Let me sleep on it," he says.

**AFTER THE SPEAKER AND HIS AIDE ARE GONE,** Stroud and Burke spend more time mulling over who should be a part of the Select Joint Committee on Oosay.

There would be fourteen members in all, eight Republicans and six Democrats. To get there, they begin with the so-called Gang of Eight, the members of Congress to whom the CIA has already granted special access to classified intelligence. The eight include the highest-ranking Democrat and Republican on the House and Senate intelligence committees, plus the highest-ranking member from each party in the House and Senate—the Speaker, the Senate majority leader, and the two minority leaders.

To that, Stroud adds a Democrat and Republican from the Senate Committee on Homeland Security and Government Reform. That would give that little creep Dick Bakke a seat. Then a Democrat and a Republican from the House Foreign Affairs Committee, to accommodate Curtis Gains in the House. Added to that, she names two more Republicans to give the majority party two extra members of the committee.

As a member of the Gang of Eight, Stroud herself would be part of the formula. But being on a committee investigating Oosay would both dirty her hands and tie them.

"Lord knows, I can't be on this. Nor, I dare say, can the Speaker. Would you sit for me?" she asks Burke.

"You don't want an old dog like me, Susan. I'd send the wrong message. How about Wendy Upton?"

"Why her?"

"If Dick Bakke has thoughts of using this committee as a presidential launching pad, why not give Wendy a boost, too?" Burke says.

Wendy Upton, the junior senator from Arizona, is a former army attorney who'd been groomed by the ageless and legendary Judiciary chairman Furman Morgan to enter politics. She was the intellectual leader of the GOP on Judiciary, and on her other committees as well, with a kind of prosecutorial independence and sense of right and wrong that made people around her seem to be their better selves. She is being pushed by some in the party as the future of mainstream conservativism, and many are urging her to consider a run for the White House.

"Don't make her chair," Stroud's chief of staff advises. "You don't need the grief with the Common Sense Caucus."

**THAT NIGHT,** the Speaker's home phone rings at 10:30 P.M. He has just fallen asleep.

The caller ID announces it is Susan Stroud.

"Goddamn it," the Speaker growls. He's being played.

The Speaker is famous for needing his nine hours a night—an early-to-bed, early-to-rise man. The Senate majority leader is calling him late, hoping he'll be impatient, maybe even asleep, and agree to anything.

She isn't the first to pull this shithead stunt with him.

"Okay, I agree!" she chimes after he picks up.

She agrees to what, he wonders.

"Let's do a joint Senate-House select committee on Oosay," Stroud says.

The Speaker tries to focus. He is sitting up now, feet on the floor off the side of the bed.

"Here's what we propose," Stroud explains.

She goes through the numbers—how many Democrats, which committees to draw from.

"So your boy Gains gets a seat," she says. "And you and I each get to pick one more member of our choice."

The Speaker hates getting rolled, and he hates the House always getting shit on by everyone—the Senate, the press, everyone.

"Gains is chair," he hears himself say.

It is the first thing he can think of. Gains had suggested being named chair this afternoon, and he said he'd consider it.

Yet he likes the idea instantly. A House chair. A Common Senser. No doubt Stroud will think she can control him anyway.

"Be serious," she says.

"I am. Gains got the memo. And I'll have hell to pay if I give this over to the Senate to run. We could have done a committee on our own, Susie."

*Susie.* She will hate that.

He could screw with her head, too.

"Bakke got the same memo," she says.

"You won't let Dick Bakke chair this in a month of Sundays any more than I would."

"I get to advise on your other House member who serves in your stead," Stroud says.

She's making him eat it, too. He couldn't pick his own surrogate without her managing it.

Oh, what the hell.

"Done. But the goddamn press release is produced jointly. And not till we have all the names. Or the deal is undone."

"Sleep tight, Bill," Stroud says. But she is reminded again that the slovenly old man is maybe not the fool he seems.

The next morning there are the usual eat-shit-and-die phone calls with the Democrats in both houses. But by midmorning there is a deal.

As if the Democrats had any choice.

## TWENTY-THREE

## FRIDAY, JANUARY 10
## WASHINGTON, D.C.

On the Washington Richter scale, the seismic magnitude of any event is measured in the number and size of reactions in other offices across the city.

At Rena and Brooks's firm, that event begins with Walter Smolonsky appearing in Peter Rena's doorway. Smolonsky is back from Europe. He failed to locate any of the five men who had been monitoring communications in the Barracks in Oosay. They know they will have to send him back, but for now they need him here.

"Our lives just got a lot worse," says Smolo.

Rena looks up from his desk.

What now?

"Congress just announced it's holding hearings on Oosay. A joint committee. House and Senate."

Rena regards the giant former police detective.

"Who's chairing?"

"Curtis Gains."

"The House guy? Foreign Affairs?"

"Yeah. Little guy. Buzz cut."

A hard-liner, Rena thinks. It is a bad break for them.

"We knew it would happen," he tells Smolo. Smolonsky has

hated this job from the start. No need, Rena thinks, to make him feel worse by sounding alarmed by congressional hearings. "That's basically why the president hired us—to be ready for this."

"We ready for this?" Smolonsky asks, moving into Rena's office and sitting down.

Now Brooks appears in Rena's doorway.

"You hear?"

"About Congress? Yes, this scary man just told me."

"So, we ready for this?" Smolonsky repeats.

"You keep asking that," Rena says.

"I'll take that as a no."

Rena looks at Brooks. She's been frustrated, too, about their lack of progress. Rena is also nervous but tends to ponder problems in the back of his mind, arriving at sudden intuitive solutions. Brooks is a list maker, a linear thinker, and a worrier. And right now, she thinks, the list stinks. The *Tribune* exposé came out more than two weeks ago. They'd seen Rousseau the day after Christmas to help them chart a new course. But to Brooks's analytic mind, they had made depressingly little progress since. They'd lost another week to the New Year's break. It is now January 10. They still haven't located the men who'd been in the Oosay Barracks that night. They've made little more progress moving up the ladder of seniority at State, the National Security Council, or the CIA. No senior administration officials had agreed to see them yet. "The holidays," they were told. She'd also received another phone call from David Traynor's people pressing them to do work for him. She hadn't told Rena about that, either.

"Maybe the announcement of hearings will buy us time," Rena suggests. "If they want to do it seriously."

Rena and Brooks know a good deal about congressional hearings. They had met as Senate investigators preparing for one and they had recruited some of their team, Conner, Robinson, and Smolonsky, from Senate ranks. Good hearings can take more than a month to prepare. Bad ones can be rushed in days.

"I figure George Rawls will have our asses over at the White House before lunch to demand what we know," Brooks says wearily. "What do we know?"

"More than we think," Rena says.

**IT IS CLOSER TO 3:30 P.M., ACTUALLY,** when Rawls demands their presence. The meeting is held in his auxiliary office in the Old Executive Office Building, where most of the White House counsel staff is located, away from annoying reporters who monitor meeting schedules in the West Wing. Carr is there, but says nothing. Rawls listens to their status report.

"You need to lean harder," the old lawyer's typewriter voice bangs at them. "The point here is to stay ahead of a congressional inquiry we knew was coming."

"Then we need your help," Rena says.

"What do you need?"

"Webster," Rena says, referring to the director of the CIA.

Brooks wants to run at Diane Howell first, but Rena worries she will be too careful. He wants to try Webster. If the old CIA hand is the bureaucratic survivor who is always in favor of what will happen, he would be a good read, Rena thinks, because he will yield, bend, somehow, if only to shift the blame. They just need to have their eyes open to recognize it.

"We'll see what we can do," Rawls says with a glance at Carr.

Rena looks at the chief of staff.

"Owen is a difficult man," Carr says. "But I'll call him."

\* \* \*

When Will Gordon calls her, Jill Bishop is looking for her car somewhere in the labyrinth of the Tysons Corner shopping center.

"Where are you, Jill?" Gordon says.

"Lost."

"What?"

"I'm at Tysons. I don't remember which garage I parked in." She has just been meeting with her intelligence source, Talon.

Gordon lets it go without comment that the nation's most famous investigative reporter can't remember where she's parked.

"Congress just announced hearings on Oosay," he says. "A joint Senate-House committee, no less."

"That's pretty rare, isn't it? A joint committee? Who's on it?"

"Eight Republicans. Six Democrats. And get this, a House chairman. Curtis Gains."

She doesn't know him well. A hard-right guy. Somehow he wrangled the chairmanship.

"Who else is on it?"

He walks her through the names.

"Dick Bakke?" she says, referring to the chairman of Homeland Security and Government Reform. "Christ. We'll have a presidential campaign run from the hearing room."

Gordon doesn't laugh.

They go through the other names. Fred Blaylish of Vermont, the only openly gay member of the Senate, will be the ranking Democrat since he is the ranking Democrat on the Senate Intelligence Committee. He is joined by Jonathan Kaplan, the senator from New Jersey who had once been a comedy writer but had studied classics at Yale and turned out to be one of the more thoughtful members of the Senate. He was from Senate Foreign Relations. There are three left-wingers from the House, including a Hispanic congresswoman from Los Angeles who is an Iraq War veteran and the daughter of illegal immigrants—Nina Gonzalez.

And Democratic senator David Traynor, who was also on Homeland Security and Government Reform. The Democrats had named him largely as a counterbalance to Bakke, since he, too, was an outsize personality considering a run at the presidency.

"Every committee needs a dot-com billionaire," says Bishop.

"And another potential presidential candidate," says Gordon.

"Blaylish says he hopes the committee will be 'a genuine effort to search for the truth, not a political sideshow,'" Gordon says, reading from the *Tribune* story on the announcement.

"Good luck."

They have fallen into the journalists' habit of being amused by the spectacle they cover.

"Listen to Traynor's quote," Gordon says. "'I'm gonna be watching these guys. And if I see bullshit, I'm calling bullshit.'"

"You gonna put the word *bullshit* in the *Tribune*?" Bishop asks.

"Every day now is a new frontier."

"Why are you calling me, Will? I coulda read this myself. If I ever find my car."

"We need whatever you have on Oosay. ASAP."

Bishop hates this. She hates being pressured to *have something*. You can't rush investigative stories. It is a recipe for screwing up.

And what did she have, anyway? Bits and pieces. A report had gone missing—but she doesn't know why or what was in it. From sources she can't use.

You might be able to build some speculative TV talk show segment around such bits and pieces. With a chyron label at the bottom of the screen: "More Questions for Nash on Oosay?"

But a story written in words, in black and white or even in digital ones and zeros, for that you should have more, she thinks—facts, vetted, verified, edited. Not some shit you'd say in a bar . . . or a tweet.

"All I have are fragments," she says.

"The news is made up of fragments now," he says. "What can you pull together? And how quickly? Let's stay ahead on this story."

"I don't want to publish speculation," she says. "No one ever gained anything by being first with a story that's wrong."

She is throwing one of Gordon's favorite aphorisms back at him.

"So get it right," he says. "What do you have?"

Maybe because Will Gordon is Will Gordon, or because she can't find her goddamn car, or because the story really *is* fast moving, she says: "There might have been a drone that night. I'm not sure."

A drone meant there would be pictures of the Oosay incident. The whole event might be on camera. There might be photographic proof of what happened. That is not just *a story*. It is *the* story.

"How soon can you nail that down?"

She has just violated her own rule, the one where you don't tell editors what you have until you already have it. Don't say anything more, she thinks. Tell him, "As long as it takes, motherfucker. I'm not baking a cake here."

But she hears herself offering him the truth instead—or perhaps even being optimistic.

"Maybe a week."

"Go all out," Gordon says. "Let's find out what the hell happened out there." Then he hangs up.

Gordon does have a flair, she has to admit, a kind of gravitas—and such pure confidence in the cause of journalism—that is hard to say no to. In the next instant, however, she wonders if she will regret it. Stick to your rules. Don't promise. Never trust editors. Why had she not stuck to her rules?

And then there it was.

At the far end of parking level F. Her shit-ass gray Prius.

## TWENTY-FOUR

Rena dislikes running in the cold and at night, but events are controlling him again, and the only way he can ponder what to do next is by moving and being outside. He feels the pressure of the day slip away—at least for forty-five minutes.

When he arrives home again at the row house in the West End, the cat Vic had given him is lying on his bed. The cat opens his eyes—the surprising rich gold irises almost the same color as the flecks of gold in Vic's—and tracks him around the room, the eyes narrowing again as if suspicious. The cat yawns.

The animal emerged from behind the dryer yesterday and by evening had even begun to follow Rena around the house some. Last night, as Rena read, the cat slipped into his lap.

The phone rings. It is Matt Alabama.

"You okay?"

The question is personal, not professional, the TV correspondent calling as a friend, not fishing for a story. Rena wouldn't share his work anyway—even off the record—and the journalist doesn't expect him to. Rena's bond with Alabama is tied to something beyond their jobs. Both men are divorced, and Alabama, twenty years Rena's senior, feels protective of him in ways the younger man doesn't fully understand but is grateful for. A novelist who had moved to journalism to pay the bills, and to television to become famous—losing two marriages in the klieg lights along the way—Alabama at sixty-two had reached the age where his friends came before anything else.

"You mean are we ready for congressional hearings on Oosay," Rena answers.

"Yes, I imagine the worst thing and then double it."

Rena doesn't laugh. "I will strap in."

"How is that commitment experiment going?"

"The what?"

"The cat."

"Have you been talking to Vic?" Rena imagines them messaging about him.

"You name him yet?"

"You *have* been talking to Vic. No, I have not named him."

"Then the experiment isn't going well."

"Stop ganging up on me."

"We're helping you."

When they are done, Rena calls Vic.

"I've picked a name for the cat."

"What is it?"

"I'm thinking Nelson."

"I thought you said he looked like Winston Churchill."

"Nelson seems better."

"Why is that?" Vic asks, laughing.

"Churchill had cats—many of them over the years—but his favorite was named Nelson, after Lord Nelson of the Royal Navy. I don't know if he was a British shorthair or not. But this cat seems like a Nelson to me, in honor of Churchill's cat, rather than Churchill himself."

"How is Nelson?"

Rena glances down at the cat, which somehow, without his noticing, has climbed into his lap.

"Adapting."

"And how are you? I hear they've called for hearings."

"Adapting," he says. "Right, Nelson?" He strokes the cat's belly and Nelson gives out a soft purr, but Vic cannot hear it.

**OVER THE NEXT FEW DAYS,** Owen Webster does not call, and Rena's team looks at the Grid and tries, without much success, to fill in the many gaps.

They know little more than they did two weeks ago, despite everyone working their contacts.

Roderick was on a secret mission as well as a public one in Oosay. But they don't know what the secret mission was.

The survivors of Oosay are lying about something, but they have not figured out what.

The administration misspoke almost immediately about Oosay because someone in the intelligence community held back information from the White House, and from Diane Howell in particular.

The attack on Oosay was carefully planned and yet apparently the NSA, the CIA, and the National Security Council were caught off guard.

The communications team in the Barracks is still missing. They still do not even know their identities.

And people are leaking most of this to the *Tribune* while people at the top of the national security community are still dragging their feet and trying to avoid Rena's team.

Now the threat of congressional hearings is going to make their job harder.

Rena and Brooks have come to just one clear conclusion. The president hired them because he did not trust his own chain of command to tell him the truth.

## TWENTY-FIVE

It takes Jill Bishop about a week, just as Will Gordon asked.

At first she hadn't understood what Talon meant when she said, "There was a bird up there."

They were at the Thai place, the day hearings were announced, the day she'd been caught in traffic and arrived late at the restaurant. The day when later she couldn't find her car.

"A bird up where? What are we talking about?"

"That night in Oosay. There was a drone. Shooting video."

All this time and this freaking thing was on camera? Bishop had thought.

"Have you seen it?"

Talon had shaken her head no.

**FOR A MOMENT,** Talon had become irritable when Bishop asked what the video showed.

"I assume our people getting killed, Jill."

Then, apologetically, she had bent closer to Bishop and in a low voice said she only knew "bits and pieces" but apparently "the drone didn't get there right away." It had to fly from another country, maybe Tunisia. "They don't have a million of these things."

And, she added, "The one they sent wasn't armed. It only had a camera."

Talon seemed to recede into herself a little after that, as if she regretted mentioning it, as if Bishop had been too eager. She hadn't seen the video herself, Talon repeated. She couldn't get it for Bishop. She didn't know anyone who could.

Bishop had leaned harder on Talon that day than she had ever leaned on her before. When she saw the look on Talon's face, Bishop wondered if she'd crossed a line—and if Talon would begin to drift away as a source after this. It happened eventually with most sources. The risk becomes too stressful. Whatever sources feel they are getting from the leaking to a reporter begins to mean less to them; at some point they cancel a few times and then stop.

"I need you to find someone who can tell me about that video."

After a long silence, Talon had said: "Meet me at Ronde-voux in two days. Four o'clock. If I'm not there, come every day. If I'm not there after four days, the answer is no."

Talon appeared on the last day, and after twenty minutes she and Bishop were joined by a boyish-looking young man with sandy hair, ice-blue eyes, and the awkward demeanor of an intensely bright but shy teenager.

Talon introduced him as "Ken," and Bishop as "my friend Jill." Ken, she explained, had been her mentee when he came to the Agency. Now he was doing a rotation in video analysis.

Jill, Talon said, was a reporter interested in how video interpretation worked. Ten minutes later, Talon excused herself and didn't return. Whatever Ken would give to Bishop now was his business to decide. The handoff had been made.

Ken called video analysis "ant spotting," since the people in drone videos looked like ants until you zoomed in. He sat in an office in suburban Virginia, he said, and analyzed footage, identifying places and people, working with a tech who enhanced the images and helped make "intelligence out of pictures."

"Katherine said you were looking for a particular video."

It didn't usually go this fast. It usually took months to cultivate someone to the point that you were talking about something this specific. But Bishop didn't have months.

"I can't show it to you."

She hadn't asked.

"Have you seen it? Or just read something about it?"

It was a gamble to challenge a source on first meeting. But she had no margin here.

"I've seen it, but I can't show it to you."

She had no idea why Ken was here, what gumbo of motives might be driving him, or what anger he might have over U.S. policy. Edward Snowden was a child when he leaked, and even Bishop had mixed feelings about him. Most of her sources considered him a traitor who should be given the death penalty.

Whatever Ken's motives, he was here.

"Do you remember it pretty well?"

"I have notes," he said.

*Jesus. He made notes.*

"I don't normally do that. But when it came in, I knew it was hot."

"You don't have to show them to me," she had said. "But maybe we can meet again and I can ask you yes-or-no questions, and you can just confirm things."

"I have them now," he had said and pulled out his notes from the video. "I didn't know if I could meet you twice."

Over the next twenty minutes, Bishop asked every question she could think of. The boy was clinical, precise, and emotionless. She wondered if he had touches of Asperger's syndrome.

"I need some proof that I can believe you really know this. Some proof you have seen this video. That you didn't make this up."

Would he run off now?

"I have the serial number on the drone. It's registered on the video."

He read her the number. She could use it to verify his story. She knew someone else who would go that far to help her.

"Why an unarmed drone? Weren't there armed drones just as close by?"

"If you send an armed drone, you might have to fire it," Ken said. "And if you make the wrong decision . . ." He didn't finish the sentence.

"Can you see the Manor House burn?"

Yes.

"Did it catch fire or explode?"

This had become an issue. There were rumors the Manor caught on fire and help wasn't sent quickly enough to save Roderick and could have been—more culpability on the part of the administration.

"It all went up at once."

"And you saw O'Dowd, Phelps, Halleck, and Ross get hit?"

He nodded.

"And what else did you see?"

"That's not a yes-or-no question."

"I thought we were past that."

His eyes were beginning to move around the coffeehouse. She was losing him. By then, however, she had enough.

## TWENTY-SIX

## TUESDAY, JANUARY 21
## WASHINGTON, D.C.

The drone story posts Monday night and runs in Tuesday's paper—held while the city is off for Martin Luther King's birthday. The Oosay hearings are still unscheduled, a sign the committee was struggling.

Bishop's story reports that the Oosay attack had been captured on camera by an American drone flying above the U.S. compound. Not even Congress knew of the existence of the video, the *Tribune* story claimed.

"The footage, which observers told the *Tribune* is at times graphic, establishes with little doubt that the Americans were killed by militia gunfire, not mobs throwing rocks or other weapons."

The report noted that the drone, which was in Tunisia when the incident began and was redirected as soon as possible, does not include the beginning of the incident but does capture the period when the Americans were killed.

Senator Dick Bakke sees the story in a news alert from the *Tribune* on his phone. A moment later there is a text from his chief of staff, then phone calls from reporters. He implies the Oosay Committee may already know about the video. Curtis Gains is less nimble, or perhaps simply more honest, in his surprise.

Majority Leader Susan Stroud through a press aide crafts a statement that she hopes the video will help the committee in its work and expresses annoyance that Congress is once again learning something about Oosay from the media rather than the administration. But part of her, privately, has to hand it to that woman Bishop.

* * *

Randi Brooks sends her partner Peter Rena a text when she sees the news alert about the drone piece.

"What the hell?"

"Talk in the morning," he texts back.

She stews all night. How could they pretend with any semblance of credibility to be investigating Oosay without seeing that video? A video they learned about from a newspaper? A video they had even wondered about and hadn't been given?

The next morning she's in Rena's office before she puts down her briefcase in her own.

Rena is on his sofa smiling. The rat.

"Remember what you told me," he says, "the first day we got this assignment—that the White House was renting our credibility?"

"I remember. I wonder if we have any left."

"Well," he says, grinning, "I want to raise our rental price."

Brooks drops her briefcase on the coffee table and looks curious.

"Let's tell George Rawls that if he doesn't get us the drone footage, we quit," he says.

Brooks moves behind Rena's desk and sits in his chair. "I want to be the one to tell him."

When the White House counsel picks up the call, Brooks roars at him: "Goddamn it, George, we cannot do the fucking job *you* hired us to do if people are holding back from us. If you want us to be your goddamn patsies, we quit."

Rena cannot hear Rawls's response. But for the first time in weeks, his partner is enjoying herself.

Whatever Rawls says, Randi has not found it persuasive. "Why should we let the fucking goddamn White House ruin our reputation like this? Last I checked I wasn't the biggest dumb-ass in town. So maybe I should stop letting you destroy what is left of my frigging car wreck of a career."

The woman can curse, Rena thinks, she surely can.

She listens for several moments, then says, "What do I want? What the hell do you think I want, George?"

Apparently Rawls has guessed. "Correct. I want to see that damn drone video." After a moment she adds: "Well, here's how I see it, George. We're all supposed to be working for the same person, the commander in chief of the United States. Right?" She holds the phone to the air.

"Of course, Randi," Rawls's distant voice says through the phone.

"So I would think the commander in chief could demand the video, right?" Brooks asks. "Can he then send it to us?"

After a pause, "How soon do you want it?" Rena hears Rawls say with evident reluctance.

When she hangs up, Brooks leans back in Rena's chair.

"Sorry, I got a little sweary there."

Her face is flush with adrenaline. "You know, Petey, it's a lot easier doing that to a man when you're a woman. He was just immobilized." A sly grin lights up her face. "If you had done it, he would have gotten all macho and told you to screw off."

The video arrives by messenger late in the day. Rena is dazzled.

"Do you have any idea what we should do with this now that we've got it?" Brooks asks him.

"As it happens, I do," Rena says.

## WEDNESDAY, JANUARY 22
## COLUMBIA, MARYLAND

Columbia, Maryland, was supposed to be utopia—if utopia were a planned community imagined in 1967, halfway between Washington, D.C., and Baltimore, Maryland.

Fifty years later it has the feel of a pleasant but ordinary suburb, with only a faint echo of the hope urban planners once attached to the idea that mixed-income housing and village squares could change American life.

The man Rena calls "my video whisperer" lives in a midrange model, a one-story, three-bedroom ranch.

"That's a thing?" Smolo asks. "A video whisperer?"

"Wait till you meet Marty Wallace."

At the door, Rena and Smolonsky are met by a pale man in his late thirties with straight chestnut hair flopping into his eyes.

"Peter Rena," he says brightly.

"How are you, Marty?"

They had met when Rena was a military investigator working a case about U.S. soldiers running a drug ring in Asia. Marty Wallace was a corporal on the base, a kid obsessed with video and inventing a new job for himself helping base MPs cope with the swelling hours of human interaction captured on camera—everything from cell phones to surveillance footage to images from the sky. He and Rena used ATM imagery to break the drug ring.

"What's so urgent I had to drop everything?" Wallace asks.

He has a kind, square face, which lights up with interest when other people talk. But if you look closely enough, Rena has always sensed something held back behind the eyes, some doubting intelligence Wallace keeps to himself.

"I have a video to look at. I need to know what it shows and what it might mean." Rena is about to say more when Marty holds up a hand.

"No, sir. Don't tell me what to look for. Or I'll miss everything else."

"Don't 'sir' me, Marty."

"No, sir."

Wallace takes the thumb drive and disappears behind a door off the living room. Rena follows him inside and enters a kind of museum of moving pictures and a monument to the quickening pace of technology in the twenty-first century. There are video recorders of different formats, DVD players, film projectors, an Avid editing system, generations of computers and old monitors, machines with floppy disk drives and CD-ROMs.

"What a junk shop," Smolonsky says.

"Everything here is working equipment," Marty answers tartly. "You just need parts."

He boots up a computer, inserts the thumb drive, and glances up. "Peter, sir, please go. Sit on the deck. Or take a walk. I'll call you."

"Okay," Rena says, and smiles.

"I need coffee," Smolo says.

**AS RENA AND SMOLONSKY TRY** to figure out the espresso machine, Rena explains that all Marty wanted to do as a young man was work in television. But he was a fourth-generation army brat from North Dakota, and there was never any doubt he would serve. "He got out as fast as he could and did a little time in television news as a producer. But those jobs were vanishing. The correspondents were becoming their own producers, even shooting their own video."

"What's he do now?" Smolo asks.

"This," Rena says. "He makes a living telling people who own surveillance cameras what they are missing. Police. Corporations."

"And no one is allowed in his workshop."

Wallace's small house is tidy and masculine, largely void of mementos, save for three framed photographs of a girl playing softball and a trove of trophies from the sport, including a high school state championship. A daughter, Rena knew, who split her time between here and her mother's. She had just left for college.

Rena and Smolonsky take their second cups of coffee to the back deck. The utopian backyard is an exact square, about thirty by thirty. At the diagonal ends of the yard, there are worn patches on the grass where Marty and his daughter must have stood for thousands of hours playing catch. No grass would grow on those spots again.

More than two hours pass before Rena hears the screen door slide open and close, and Marty emerges from inside.

"You can come in."

Wallace leads them to a monitor that must be sixty inches wide.

"It's Oosay, obviously," Wallace says. "Thank you for putting me in the middle of something else I can't ever tell my kid about. It's hard enough to talk to teenagers."

"If it were easy, Marty, I would have gone to Ted with this," Rena says, referring to a rival video tech they both know.

"So what we're looking at," Marty says with a frown, "is probably footage from a Puma RQ-20. It's a relatively late model, based on the video quality. Pretty new. Pretty expensive. A fine example of a reconnaissance aerial vehicle."

"I thought it was a drone," says Smolonsky.

"The military calls them unmanned aerial vehicles."

"What does it show, Marty?" Rena says, trying to keep them on track.

"Well, you've got the redacted version here already, Peter."

"How do you know?"

"No establishing shots. With RAVs they turn the cameras on once they're anywhere near their destination. Or maybe they're on the whole time, depending on the battery. But once they got close to Oosay, this camera would be sending. These babies are five miles up, man. They can get the city, then zoom into the neighborhood, then into the building, then center the camera so you could get coordinates for something as small as a window. Right?"

Marty grins in sheer wonder.

"Imagine, really, shooting a whole movie that way. You've got like twenty drones, the actors are just moving in space, and you're shooting them from every angle."

Now Rena frowns.

"Yeah. Well, it would cost like a million dollars a minute to do that," Wallace says, turning back to the monitor. "So your footage picks up with a fairly tight shot, right? We're already over the compound."

"How much was cut?"

"Impossible to know, but it doesn't matter. I can get you what you need from this."

The video images reveal a ring of pickup trucks, not in any organized formation.

"You can plainly make out figures of two men in the back of each pickup. See, here and here." He puts the tip of a pen on the screen. "They're firing mounted machine guns. See?"

One man appears to be helping the other feed the gun. The second man is firing. You can clearly make out the recoil of the gun.

"They're shooting all over the place," Smolonsky says.

"Yes," says Marty, "it's chaos. They're moving those trucks around and swinging the guns at anything they can think of to shoot at."

"The whole point is to make a lot of noise," Rena says.

Marty slows the video and says, "Okay, now. Look here."

From the right side of the screen, four figures appear, moving haltingly, making their way across to the left.

"There are your boys. O'Dowd, Ross, Halleck, and Phelps, right?" Marty says. "I looked them up."

"Where is Franks?" Smolonsky asks. "Where is Roderick?"

"There is a fifth man, you'll see," Wallace says. "But not a sixth."

The four figures dash for two or three seconds at a time and then appear to fall down and crawl for a few seconds.

"Why are they like that? They hit?" Smolonsky asks.

"No, not hit. But they're under fire," Marty says.

Rena explains: "That's military training. It takes someone about four seconds to aim a long gun accurately once they have sighted a target. So you move for two to three seconds and then take cover. If there is no cover, you hit the deck and then move again."

"Dash and dive," Marty says.

One of the four figures appears to jolt suddenly.

Marty freezes the image and says, "He's been hit."

Marty moves the video in superslow motion. It is impossible to see what direction the shot came from, but you can see the clothing of the American move and the body absorb some kind of blow.

Marty moves the video a little faster but still below normal speed.

One of the other three figures stops, then turns his head to look back at the wounded man. He begins to crawl back in the fallen colleague's direction. A moment later, the wounded figure is jolted several more times.

"Shit," Smolonsky says.

"Yes, that man has been hit with three more rounds and is no longer moving," Marty says.

The figure heading toward him has stopped trying to get to the wounded comrade and turns around, resuming his dash and dive with the other two men in the other direction.

"That's Ross, I'd guess," Rena says, looking at the figure hit with four automatic weapon rounds.

"Yeah. He will take a few more rounds. But he's already dead," Marty says.

Marty reframes the video so that the dead figure of Lieutenant Joseph Ross is out of view and the remaining three figures are larger. "Let's follow the three still alive."

They continue their dash-and-dive maneuvering, occasionally finding cover, firing when they have something to hide behind.

"Now the drone camera operator pans out," Marty says.

"The operator?" Smolo says.

"There is a pilot on a joystick in Nevada flying the thing," Marty explains. "And there is a person sitting next to them who is operating the camera. They are remote-controlled aircraft, but they're being controlled from thousands of miles away. And at this point, the camera operator in Nevada pulls back so the pilot can see more of the scene."

It doesn't happen instantly, but in a few seconds the camera pans out and the figures of the three Americans get smaller. At the bottom left corner of the screen, a building begins to appear. The figures are heading toward it.

"Now there is another man," Smolonsky says, pointing.

Rena leans toward the screen. A new figure has appeared, standing on the veranda of the building in the bottom left of the frame. It is clearly the Manor House, the place where General Roderick would die. The man on the veranda is firing an automatic weapon in what appears to be the direction of the trucks, over the heads of the men coming toward him.

"Can you now tighten the image of that new man?"

"It'll get blurry," Marty says, but he does it.

"He's a big man," Rena says, looking at the image.

"Yeah. You can see by orientation to the railing of the veranda and the size of the doorway."

"Okay," Rena says, and Marty unlocks the screen and it returns to the wider shot.

Now they can see the trucks moving in different directions. To Smolonsky, they look like bugs, scattering after being hit with roach spray. Rena recognizes a more tactical design to the movement, action to make the trucks look more numerous, to attract attention.

"Now watch," Marty says.

One of the three men heading toward the veranda appears to be hit. His body is jolted. He staggers, then falls. He lies inert for a few seconds and then begins crawling behind a palm tree for cover.

"I think that's Halleck," Marty says.

Then a third figure heading toward the veranda is hit.

"That's Phelps getting shot," Smolonsky says.

"Yes," Marty confirms.

The fourth man begins to move, hands and knees toward the veranda. He is met there by the larger man who's providing covering fire. The bigger man pulls his colleague up over the side of the railing.

"That is Garrett Franks," Rena says, pointing to the larger man who has been firing from the veranda. "And that is Adam O'Dowd." Rena is pointing to the wounded man who had crawled to safety.

"Now, get this," Marty says.

The Franks figure leans over O'Dowd and they begin to move off the veranda together toward a small shedlike building between the Manor House and the second fallen body. They get to the shed and use it for cover.

"They leave?" Smolonsky exclaims.

"Just wait," says Marty. The video moves about fifteen more seconds. "Now."

The screen bursts with a flash and fills with smoke. For a few seconds everything is obscured. The screen clears momentarily, and then a second wave of darkness envelops everything.

"The building's going up," says Marty.

He points to the veranda, visible at the bottom of the screen. They can see flames.

The camera operator at this point has begun to pan out, apparently to get some orientation in the dark. The image continues to pan back until you can see the Manor House. It is half-obliterated, and the other half is ablaze.

"Christ," says Smolonsky.

"Where are our boys?" asks Rena.

Franks and O'Dowd are leaning against the shed some distance from the Manor House. The other two figures, the wounded Halleck and Phelps, are lying on the ground. Ross's body, farther away, is not in the frame.

Franks and O'Dowd now begin to make their way to Halleck and Phelps. They grab the wounded men and begin to drag them—but they are moving away from the Manor House.

"Peter, you get this?" Marty asks. "You know what you're seeing?"

He freezes the image, and they see the four figures staying low, two of them dying.

"Yeah, they're running the wrong way," Rena says.

"What?" says Smolonsky.

"Ross, Phelps, and Halleck didn't die defending General Roderick in the Manor House. They died trying to get *to* him."

"General Roderick didn't have a security detail with him. He only had Franks."

"Christ," Smolo says.

"Now we know what Garrett Franks and Adam O'Dowd are lying about," Rena says.

He looks at the frozen image on the screen.

As Marty lets the video begin to run again, Smolo says, "What the hell happened out there?"

## TWENTY-EIGHT

## WEDNESDAY, JANUARY 22
## WASHINGTON, D.C.

They call Randi Brooks from the car.

Stay late at 1820 and wait for them, Rena tells her. If Anthony Rousseau is right that they're being watched—and Samantha Reese, the security expert he hired, isn't sure about that yet—then their cell phones and movements are being monitored. The safest place to talk is the secure attic.

As they narrate the video in the conference room, Brooks is quiet. When they are done, she leans back in her chair and makes a declaration.

"You know, I'm damn tired of waiting for the gerbils to agree to see us." *Gerbils* is Brooks's new term for Nash's cabinet members, who have been dodging them. "It's time we took the game to them."

"Glad to have you back," Rena says in response to her new sense of energy. She gives him a look that goes from quizzical to vaguely disapproving, one that would make a perfect GIF. "What do you have in mind?" he asks.

"Diane Howell," she says. "She's the odd one out. The girl in the boys' club."

That much is true, and they have known it for weeks.

What did Howell know? It was her job, as national security advisor, to manage the team that conducted the war on terror. If Nash was being left in the dark by his national security team, was Howell in the dark as well, or keeping things from her boss?

Weeks after the Oosay incident, they still didn't have a definitive answer to that. Nash had invited her to meetings with them, signaling he trusted her. But she had still rebuffed their requests for an interview. Until now. Now they could insist.

**THEY SPEND THE EVENING PREPPING** for Brooks to pin her down.

What they hadn't known about Howell, Wiley's file fills in for them. That she was an émigré, an only child and age two when her diplomat parents fled Hungary after the failed revolution in 1956. She was raised in Texas, and grew up with a kind of double vision, an all-American blond cheerleader at school and the brainy multilingual Hungarian child of anticommunist intellectuals at home.

She began to move away from the hard-line Cold War views of her parents at Harvard, where she also married a cousin of the Lodges of Massachusetts. She moved to Washington for her husband's job at State and began a Ph.D. in political science at Georgetown.

There she became a protégé of Jeane Kirkpatrick, the former liberal turned Reagan advisor who was in the vanguard of neoconservative foreign policy intellectuals creating new justifications for American internationalism after Vietnam. One of Kirkpatrick's core ideas was that America *should not* try to force democracy on other countries. It took England and France hundreds of years to become democracies, she argued. It doesn't happen overnight, and forcing it can send an ally into chaos.

Twenty-five years later, Diane Howell rose to national prominence citing Kirkpatrick's thinking in her own arguments against the invasion of Iraq. President Bush's policies of preemption and pro-freedom interventionism, Howell had predicted, would destabilize the Middle East for generations and inspire decades of jihadist terrorism—a disaster all the more ironic because its architects were also Kirkpatrick protégés who had forgotten the lessons of history and America's own arrogant naïveté in Vietnam.

Howell had caught the attention of a young Nebraska governor named James Nash, who saw her eviscerate the outgoing chair of the Joint Chiefs of Staff at a Brookings Institution event. The admiral had just denigrated women, intellectuals, *and* civilian control of foreign policy in the same breath. Howell's rejoinder was so sharp, Nash would recall, "the poor man didn't know he had been fatally wounded, and, as his humiliation dawned on him, it was all the worse because Howell had been so charming twisting the blade."

When Nash ran for president, Howell became his foreign policy advisor. After his election he named her UN ambassador and finally national security advisor. She had a reputation for mixing "the charm of a Georgetown hostess, a gift for straight talk, and an ability to make diplomacy understandable without sacrificing the nuances," a *New York Review of Books* essay had said.

Lately the press had turned on Howell, as it had on Nash. One former colleague had written damningly in *Foreign Policy:* "While she can be an eloquent spokesperson for her superiors and a sharp and brutal critic of those who challenge them, it is unclear whether Howell has any views of her own or if she stands for anything other than her own ascent."

Ever since Brooks had read that line in the file she had been waiting for the right moment, and the right lever, to go to Howell hoping that doing so would help break their investigation open. "What utter sexist bullshit," she'd said after seeing that quote for the first time. "She's interested in her own ascent? Show me a man in the cabinet about whom that couldn't be said. But no one would say it. Or even think it."

It's not hard to track down a national security advisor. They're reachable twenty-four hours a day, if you know how. And it is easier to get their attention if you call after hours to say you have made a discovery damaging to the administration and need to speak to them as soon as possible.

Howell could make an opening at 10 A.M.

Brooks would approach Howell as a social acquaintance and a woman, she decided. They had a number of friends in common. Howell had even spoken to Brooks's book group when she was promoting the work that would eventually win her a Pulitzer Prize. Maybe, Brooks hoped, approaching her woman to woman, almost as a friend, would make a difference. The first clues aren't promising.

**HOWELL BRINGS HER COMMUNICATIONS ADVISOR** and a staff counsel with her. A studied move, Brooks thinks, and a signal to White House eyes that she is not revealing much in this interview. It reinforces rumors that some of Howell's aides may be reporting on her to former colleagues at the CIA and Pentagon. Such is the level of palace intrigue in most White Houses.

In the geometrics of Washington, the national security advisor has power because of proximity. Her office is in the West Wing, down the hall from the president, even if in the opposite diagonal corner from the Oval Office, as far by distance as one can get, the office next to the vice president's. But it is still the West Wing; you can just wander into the Oval Office—as long as Chief of Staff Spencer Carr doesn't stop you. That is a lot closer than State, blocks away at Foggy Bottom, or the Pentagon, CIA, or DNI across the river in Virginia.

Howell is dressed impeccably, as always, burgundy suit and cream blouse, the colors chosen to project strength but tastefully complementing her blond hair. Brooks feels pangs of recognition at the effort, the premeditation Howell apparently feels is required to level the ground in rooms of men. No male of similar rank would spend a fraction of the time worrying about appearances. Women in Washington talk often among themselves about the tactics and strategies required to be heard in meetings, to avoid being interrupted, to stop your points from being appropriated, to protect your ideas from being dismissed.

At sixty-two, Howell is imposing, slender and tall, with high cheekbones and striking gray eyes, the mature echo of the young European beauty from the high school pictures Brooks had seen in Wiley's file.

Brooks begins by asking about mutual acquaintances whose parties they had both been at and reminding Howell of her visit to the book group years earlier. But the national security advisor is formal in response.

"How is Amanda?" Howell says of the book group's well-known leader. "I haven't seen her in far too long. Please pass on my regards."

She and Brooks are acquaintances, Howell is suggesting, but not friends.

Brooks and Rena had war-gamed the night before what to do if the attempts at informality were rebuffed. They had agreed on a simple answer: level with her.

"We have the drone video, Diane," Brooks says.

Would she know already? Would Rawls have told her? Howell appears to wince slightly, and Brooks can tell at once this was one more thing the national security advisor didn't know.

"Are we on the record here?"

"We don't have to be."

If they are not, it means Brooks might get another chance at Howell later—if necessary.

Howell looks at her two aides, who promptly put their writing pads away. The writing pad held by Maureen Conner, who had come to take notes, also disappears.

"I have seen the footage," Howell says.

"When?"

More hesitation. "Yesterday."

Not until after the *Tribune* story broke.

It's an answer with several implications. It begins to distance

Howell from the mistakes of Oosay. But it also establishes her lack of influence over national security.

"Why were those men running toward General Roderick when they died, rather than already protecting him?"

Howell spreads her hands out to smooth a wrinkle in her skirt. The move gives her time to form a response.

"I don't know the answer to that yet."

"Have you asked?"

"Of course I have, Randi."

Now it is first names.

"And what were you told?"

"The people I asked have said they don't know yet."

"Do you believe them?"

A partial smile, appreciative and intelligent. "I don't believe that is a question I should answer. It would be conjecture on my part. It would not be relevant to your task, what you called fact finding."

"If I may, who did you ask?"

Another smile. "Fellow members of the Principals Committee of the National Security Council."

This is also a more revealing answer than it seems. The Principals Committee is a subgroup of the National Security Council, made up of just six people: the president, Howell, the secretary of defense, the CIA director, the chairman of the Joint Chiefs, and the director of national intelligence. Either none of these people knows what happened in Oosay, or one or more of them is lying to Howell. And without saying so explicitly, Howell has pointed a finger at them.

"When did you find out General Roderick would be in Oosay in the first place?"

Another hesitation. "The night he died."

This means Oosay was either too small an operation for the national security advisor to be briefed on, or it was an advance action, a special op about which the president was not informed because of its risk and the need to act in a timely manner. Over the last few weeks, Rena and Brooks have also come to know that advance action orders were being employed because Nash's generals and spymasters were frustrated by what they considered the president's growing meddling and micromanaging. As he became frustrated with them, they became elusive with him.

If the Oosay incident occurred during an advance action, then Roderick was meeting someone in Oosay, arranging something covert, and once he had died, the president had decided he did not trust the chain of command to tell him the truth.

"And what were you told about what General Roderick was doing there?"

"The same thing the American people have been told," Howell says. "Meeting with moderates."

"When did you finally learn the truth?"

This is pure bluff. Brooks and Rena don't know the truth about what Roderick was doing in Oosay. Brooks wants to discover if Howell knows.

The national security advisor takes too long to answer.

"Ask me a different question," Howell says.

Grudgingly, Brooks admires Howell's skill. She is dodging Brooks's questions but deftly. She has made it clear she didn't know in advance that Roderick would be in Oosay—exonerating herself from the planning of whatever he was doing there—but she has sidestepped nearly everything else, including whether she now knows the details of his mission. Howell's evasion accomplished two things: it avoided revealing just how isolated and irrelevant she had become inside the national security team, and it signaled to her colleagues, the boys, that she was protecting their secret.

In short, she was playing multidimensional chess at a White House level, which is like playing twelve different boards at the same time, and with your opponents moving pieces when you aren't looking.

"Why did you say on television the first day that you thought this was a protest that had spun out of control rather than an organized attack?"

Brooks is certain that the national security advisor was given poor intelligence before she went on camera. Brooks wants to know where it came from.

"I misspoke."

"That seems out of character."

"I wish that were true."

Brooks waits for more but there isn't any. "Why was the secretary of defense more circumspect the first day?"

"He did a better job." A gracious smile.

Brooks shakes her head. "You know the irony of all this, Diane?"

"I'm sorry, the irony?"

"Yes, of all this: what's happened in the Middle East and North Africa, it's just what you predicted. We've made a mess of the world with our hubris. We've bred terrorism with our impatience and our prisons. The men who make up the National Security Council were part of that. And you and the president have the job of cleaning it up."

To that, Howell says nothing at all.

Brooks is frustrated the national security advisor has given her so little. But she cannot help feeling some sympathy for Howell, too, and she is struck by the change in the woman in front of her. Missing is the graceful wit and bracing eloquence Howell displayed before she entered politics. There is only caution and precision now, and Brooks has the distinct feeling Howell is deeply unhappy: power is not what she imagined.

They go on almost another hour, covering details one by one. Why the failure to build up the compound? What has she seen since the night of Roderick's death about advance intelligence warnings about an attack in Oosay? What does she know about Roderick's chain of command? All of the answers are careful. Some are more informative than others. None gives Brooks more than incremental additional details she and Maureen Conner can add to the Grid.

"I'm afraid I'm out of time," Howell says finally. "It was lovely, Randi, seeing you again."

Howell's communications aide walks Brooks and Conner out through the Old Executive Office Building, where their coming and going would go unnoticed by journalists. When they reach Seventeenth Street, Brooks looks at Conner.

"She seems tortured," Conner says.

"Be careful what you wish for."

"And what did we learn?"

"That's what we have to figure the hell out."

## TWENTY-NINE

"She protected herself," Rena says.

"Skillfully," Brooks agrees.

They are in Brooks's office reviewing notes of the interview. Leaving the White House, Conner and Brooks sat on a bench in Lafayette Square and made the notes before their memory faded.

"She also pointed the finger, I think, at the boys," Conner says.

"Which doesn't tell us very much," says Brooks. "I thought we'd get more, frankly. I was wrong."

**NOT ENTIRELY WRONG,** it would turn out.

That night, after weeks of dodging them, CIA Director Owen Webster at last reaches out—in his serpentine way.

Rena is home trying to read, though Nelson the cat, coming out of his shell, has become insistently affectionate. He is competing with the book in Rena's hand. Lord Nelson, Rena thinks, is turning into something of a twelve-pound occupation force.

The call comes from Spencer Carr, the White House chief of staff. After asking, without much sincerity, how Rena is doing, Carr suggests that tomorrow Rena and Brooks might call Webster's office and ask again for an interview.

"Did you call Webster?" Rena asks, rubbing the sore spot that the White House has not done more to help them.

"Look, Peter, I know you're frustrated. We're asking you to get to the bottom of this and do it quickly, and we're not helping you. But we can't lay hands on your investigation and then call it independent. These folks need to speak to you on their own or everyone will say your inquiry is just White House spin."

"Then how do you know Webster will see us?"

"He called me."

"What changed?"

"I think congressional hearings concern him. And media leaks."

Those factors have been in play for more than a week.

What's changed, Rena thinks, is that he and Brooks have gotten their hands on the drone video, and they've told Howell they have it. Diane Howell, Rena marvels. She gave Brooks only what she wanted to, but she used what Brooks told her to apply pressure, subtly, to help them.

"Good night, Spencer," Rena says. "Thanks."


**THE NEXT DAY,** a young woman in a nondescript blue suit is waiting for Rena and Brooks in the gleaming white marble lobby of the CIA. She doesn't give her name, and it isn't readable on the plastic tag she wears around her neck. She leads them up an elevator, down an absurdly long hallway, and then around a corner.

Webster is waiting for them outside the door of his office. The CIA director's suite, tucked in one corner of the Agency's secret campus in Virginia, is a throwback to another era, a dark cavern of power and intimidation. The walls are mahogany. The secret CIA seal hangs on the wall. Webster's desk, which might have belonged to Allen Dulles in the 1950s, is a hand-carved wooden creature the size of a small battleship. To its left, in a space large enough to be a separate room, is a meeting table with chairs. To the right there are two enormous saddle-brown leather couches. The darkened room is so large Rena wonders if there are agents lurking in the shadows.

They sit on the leather couches on one side of the room. Someone introduced simply as "Alan Durson from our team" sits in, no job title or explanation for his presence. Rena assumes a lawyer.

"I'm glad we were finally able to make the schedules work," Webster begins.

Rena and Brooks are approaching the interview as they might a hostile interrogation with someone who cannot be bullied, someone who is nothing if not a survivor.

To counter that, they have decided to be as candid with Webster as they can, because he almost certainly will know if they are not. While Rena listens, Brooks begins by describing the state of their inquiries.

They have interviewed the two survivors, Franks and O'Dowd; they've sent their own scientific team to the site in Oosay; they've interviewed Moratian eyewitnesses; they've also done a forensic review of Web traffic that night on social media. And, she says, they have seen the drone video.

They have concluded the following: allied intelligence also had great success monitoring intelligence traffic that night, enough to thwart attacks in other countries.

But Oosay was different. The attack was premeditated, not a protest run amok. The gates of the compound were blown up, not overrun. Nor had the Manor House simply caught fire, as some had speculated. It was destroyed in an explosion. There appeared to be some effort to obscure, if not inhibit, any inquiry, including Congress's. Elements of an after-action report being compiled at the CIA had been modified, and parts were now missing. Potential witnesses that night from the Barracks were missing, off somewhere in Europe.

She leaves only one thing out. That they believe, from the video, that the men were running the wrong way and that there is a cover-up going on.

Now Brooks waits to see how her gift of candor will be received. Is Webster part of the cover-up, or will he help them untangle it—as they now think Howell is trying to?

Owen Webster does not look like a spy. He looks more like a sea lion. Over the years he has found escape from the boredom of dull meetings and the stress of a secret life in the pleasure of long and rich meals. His girth, though, is a deception. Webster played basketball at Princeton, was all-state in high school, an agile but undersize center who could play taller than his height. He had been a field agent once, too—and a good one. Covert operations are not the typical CIA path to rise as high as Webster had. Field agents, "the outdoor set," tend to resist authority, not become it. As is often the case with people who rise to the top, Webster is the exception to many rules.

He eyes his visitors now, but rather than rewarding Brooks's candor with his own, he explains his various constraints.

"I appreciate the position you are in, trying to conduct an independent inquiry for the president. But you need to appreciate my position, too. I have a responsibility to protect the lives of the personnel and agents and contractors who work for the Agency, and to maintain operational security."

The old spy, Rena thinks, has summoned them to say: Hey, thanks for accepting my invitation. I wanted to say, sorry, can't help you.

"You also have a grave disadvantage," Webster continues. "When the FBI interviews someone, as law enforcement, they have legal leverage you do not. It is a crime to lie to the FBI. It is not a crime to lie to you. I am not under oath. This is not an FBI interview."

"Is the Barracks facility in Oosay an interrogation site?" Brooks asks, pulling Webster's attention back to her.

Webster frowns.

This allegation—that the new building in Oosay is a secret detention center to interrogate Moratians—has surfaced in press accounts abroad and spread to right- and left-leaning obscure media in America.

"That is a myth and absurd on its face," Webster says with a great expulsion of air. "If we wanted to interrogate people in Morat, we wouldn't do it in the middle of the city, on a property that had frequent visitors and is known as U.S. soil."

The folds of flesh in Webster's face mask any tension or emotion. Corpulence as cover.

"So what is the Barracks?"

Webster glances at the mysterious aide Durson.

"It's actually a barracks," the director says. "We wanted some place safe, where our people could spend the night and not worry about mortars. Something modern, with proper communications. Something impenetrable, which circumstances have shown, I think, was a pretty good idea."

Garrett Franks had told them as much.

Rena leans forward to speak for the first time.

"What can you tell us about the drone video?"

"It doesn't belong to the CIA," Webster says.

"To whom does it belong?"

"I'd ask the air force. Or the DIA."

Yesterday Howell had told them she had only just seen the drone video the day before. Now Webster is distancing himself from knowledge of it as well.

"What is your understanding of what that video shows?" Rena asks.

"I haven't seen it."

"I didn't ask if you had seen it," says Rena coldly. He is surprised by his own sudden metallic anger. It is as if their frustration with all the clever evasions of the last few weeks has come to rest in this last one by Webster. "I asked what your thoughts are about what it shows. I can't imagine you would not have been briefed."

Webster regards Rena a moment, trying to decide how to react to his visitor's sudden change of mood. Two beads of sweat have appeared on Webster's wide forehead.

"But *you* have seen it," Webster says to Rena.

"Yes," says Rena. "I've watched it carefully. It shows that the men who died that night in Oosay were not with General Roderick. He was guarded by one man. Why was that?"

"I'd ask the DIA."

"The contractors who died, Phelps and Halleck, and the contractor who was wounded, O'Dowd, were they CIA hires?"

"The budget is classified."

"Why would Adam O'Dowd lie to us about his location when he was wounded?"

"Did he?"

Rena leans closer to the director: "Why won't you help us? Why won't you help the president?"

"I am helping the president."

"Then give us some idea of why Adam O'Dowd would lie about his location when he was wounded. Why was he not guarding General Roderick? Why was he running toward the Manor House and why, when he was wounded, were he and Franks then running away from the House, abandoning Roderick inside?"

Webster rises heavily from the sofa, with a great gasp of air, and walks in surprisingly delicate steps to his desk. He pushes a button and says into a speaker, "Can we get a pot of tea and some coffee?" When he returns, he settles back onto the sofa by shifting and easing his big body until he fits.

Then with a sigh, as if getting the lungs to work in the new position, he says, "Have you ever heard of the Office of Special Directives?"

"Should we have?" Brooks says.

Webster smiles. "Ah, yes, evasion may be government's highest accomplishment. I suspect that is a tendency of any great power. In a democracy, secrecy is often a rarity and in the modern world a concept we have almost entirely lost. WeLeaks has hacked our classified budgets, and the *Washington Tribune* has published them. Congress has investigated our past. Rather than a secret agency located on a campus we cannot admit exists, we sell T-shirts now at the airport that say 'CIA Langley' on them and we have a highway exit sign on the George Washington Parkway. What is the alternative when you operate in the secret world in an age when nothing is secret? The only alternative is evasion."

"You were talking about the Office of Special Directives," Brooks says.

"Yes, confusing name, isn't it. I believe it is part of the Defense Intelligence Agency." Webster pauses. "Do you know Henry Arroyo?"

"I've heard the name," says Rena.

"I think he and General Roderick may have been quite close. They are both, or were in the case of Roderick, very creative. Very bold warriors."

Webster's eyes move between Rena and Brooks.

"You might ask General Willey, the director of the Defense Intelligence Agency."

Webster takes a deep breath and is done. He has delivered the message he had summoned them to hear: Oosay was a DIA operation, or more precisely the operation of something called the Office of Special Directives, an office run by someone named Henry Arroyo.

Rena's face hardens.

"May I speak candidly, Director?"

Webster turns to Durson and smiles. "Are we in a secure location, Alan?"

"I believe so, sir," Durson says.

Rena has had enough. His voice becomes quiet, just above a whisper, and his words come slowly and with a kind of menace.

"Whether or not you had anything to do with the incident in Oosay, sir, you own it. It happened on your watch. If the president is damaged by it, the CIA will be, too. It will be part of your legacy. It may, if it all goes badly, define your legacy."

Rena pauses to make sure Webster is listening.

"In political terms, frankly, there really isn't any space here between you and Oosay, you and the DIA, you and this Office of Special Directives, you and the president. Or you and us. The best way to protect your agency is to be on the side of those who want to get to the bottom of this. When it's over, the only thing people will remember is who was trying to find out the truth, and who was covering it up."

Rena and Webster hold each other's gaze.

"I couldn't agree more," the director says at last. "I believe I have tried to do just what you suggest. Thank you for coming in today. I know how busy you must be."

The young female agent who greeted them in the lobby now appears through a door Rena didn't know existed. And she leads them all the way out.


**DRIVING BACK TO THE DISTRICT,** Brooks darts her BMW 535 in and out of traffic, accelerating and then braking, provoking a serenade of honks and shaken fists. Rena's feet move instinctively beneath him, as if there were a clutch and brake, but he is helpless.

"We're getting closer," he says, trying to calm his partner. His anger is spent and hers is peaking. "That's why Webster summoned us."

"You know this man, Henry Arroyo?" she asks.

"Maybe." Rena isn't sure.

"I'm calling Wiley and Lupsa to meet us at the office," she says.

They need only a few minutes to find a Henry Arroyo, a Marine colonel who four years ago was assigned to the DIA. His exact role is not listed. Nor, anywhere, is something called the Office of Special Directives.

And they begin to puzzle together some of the clues Webster has given them. If Oosay were a classified DIA operation, that would fit with the hints they had heard and perhaps not paid close enough attention to. Rousseau had told them the military wanted a larger role in Africa, in part because the Pentagon felt the CIA had usurped its role in the Middle East. They knew Roderick was an iconoclast and the DIA was the military's intelligence operation.

"Can we find him?" Brooks asks.

Wiley and Lupsa have gone home, and they are alone in Rena's office.

"It's easy to hide when you're funded by a black budget."

"I need to tell you something," Brooks says. "David Traynor called again. And I did something without asking you. I had Lupsa run a preliminary scan on him."

A preliminary scan meant Lupsa had done whatever initial deep Web check he could. It is something they would do if they were considering the job but hadn't yet agreed.

Rena gives his partner a stare. "And?"

"You mean what did it show? Nothing disqualifying. Less than I would have guessed."

"Maybe he is better at hiding it than most."

"We need to give him an answer."

Rena makes a grim face. "We need to find out about Henry Arroyo and the Office of Special Directives."

"And then," she says, "we need to give Traynor an answer."

# PART THREE

# HOW NOT TO GOVERN

## THIRTY

## FRIDAY, JANUARY 31
## WASHINGTON, D.C.

They concluded there was simply no alternative. They had to move up the date of the first Oosay hearing.

The chairman of the joint committee on Oosay, Curtis Gains, would have preferred more time. There were documents to read and witnesses to debrief—in effect a show to write and even rehearse. Good congressional hearings, after all, are a performance—one performed best without improvisation.

But matters had quickly slipped beyond their control.

The key witnesses were difficult to pin down. Through a phalanx of lawyers, the State Department aide who had authored the political attack memo had tried to set conditions for his appearance. Even more frustrating, the military and intelligence communities were claiming national security and stonewalling the committee about having anyone testify in public.

Then came the drone story. With that, Gains's committee had lost "control of the narrative," a phrase Gains had come to loathe the more he heard it out of the mouths of commentators on TV, hysterics in social media, and even some members of Congress. Washington, he sometimes felt, lived on overused catchphrases and borrowed ideas. The truth was more than "a narrative."

The morning after the drone story was published, Republican members of the Oosay Committee had gathered in a small conference room next to the Senate majority leader's office.

"I hope you have the taste of blood in your mouth, Mr. Chairman," Senator Dick Bakke had said. Bakke, who was becoming something of a mentor to Gains, was harsh about it. "Because I think learning about this drone from the newspaper is a punch to the teeth of Congress."

"That's enough, Dick," Majority Leader Stroud said.

"No, the senator's right, ma'am," Gains said. "We asked for any evidence the intelligence agencies had about Oosay, and we've received almost nothing."

"So we should hold the first hearing as soon as possible," Bakke had argued. "Put a marker down. While the public is watching. Deal with some low-hanging fruit. It'll help create pressure."

Stroud had worried aloud that "a poor hearing is worse than none at all," and then had asked for the thoughts of Wendy Upton, the Arizona senator she had asked to serve on the committee.

According to one rumor, Stroud had asked Upton to serve on the Oosay Committee so there could be "an adult in the room." Gains took that as an insult, though he knew it could also have been meant as a barb aimed at Bakke.

Gains didn't know Upton well, but her reputation was formidable. And she was nothing if not adult. The story was part of her political biography. Upton's parents had died in a car crash when she was sixteen and her sister just ten. Without any aunts or uncles to take them, the state intended to separate the sisters and put them into the children's services system. Still only a junior in high school, Upton had sued the state of Arizona to become an emancipated minor, taken the GRE, and begun running her parents' restaurant with the intention of raising her sister. When the younger Upton entered high school, Wendy finally enrolled at the University of Arizona in Tucson, graduating in two years. When the sister was old enough to go to college, Upton entered the army and went to law school.

Even Gains thought there was something about Upton, in the quiet way she carried herself—a sense of judgment and propriety—that was impressive.

"What do you think, Wendy?" Stroud had asked.

"I think bad hearings help no one, so rushing is dangerous," Upton had answered. "But I believe in this case Senator Bakke is right. We can hold an initial hearing, put a marker down, and it might give us time to get it right."

That had settled it, especially given that Upton and Bakke were considered to represent different parts of the party.

**AND SO TODAY THEY ARE STARTING.**

The lineup of witnesses isn't perfect, Gains knows. National Security Advisor Diane Howell had agreed to talk about her now-discredited public statements about a protest run amok. Secretary of State Arthur Manion would testify about the failure of the State Department to deliver on instructions from Congress to improve the perimeter security on all U.S. installations abroad. An FBI forensics expert would describe what he had seen in the aftermath of the bombing.

It isn't much. But no one wanted to launch the Oosay hearings with a closed session, which was the alternative. Senators and House members had statements they wanted to make, statements that would take up much of the morning. And a dull hearing, Gains told himself, might even signal to those who dismissed this as a political witch hunt that they were going to be serious in their approach.

That mattered to Gains. He aspired to be a serious legislator, just as he had been a serious prosecutor.

His young chief of staff, Tom Beyers, was by far the more political of the two. Beyers had urged him to press for hearings in the first place. And he had strong political instincts about how they should be structured now. One challenge was turning out to be the ranking Democrat on the committee, Senator Fred Blaylish, who seemed to ascribe only the worst motives to everything Gains did. It was Beyers who had told Gains it was better, as a result, to operate largely without informing Blaylish of his plans.

Gains waits a moment longer for the other members to appear. They are just a few minutes behind schedule. And now it's time.

## THIRTY-ONE

"Brian Roderick. Joseph Ross. Terry Halleck. Alan Phelps."

Gains speaks the names with funereal solemnity.

"American heroes. Killed by cowards in the night. Patriots fighting for all that we hold dear in America."

Is his microphone too low? Gains glances at Beyers, his chief of staff, seated in the row of aides behind him against the wall, and mouths the words "mike volume."

The sound acoustics are complex: he has to be heard in the room, and Dirksen G50 is a large space. But the sound has to work for television, too, through the mult box, given that all the cable news channels are carrying them live.

Beyers nods, and Gains continues: "Our responsibility on this special joint committee is simple. It is to honor these four American heroes by learning everything we can about how they died."

He's worked on the opening statement hard, trying to tell a story, one that would sway a jury back in Pensacola.

"What do we owe these men and their families? We owe them justice, justice that their killers are punished. We owe them the truth. The truth about what happened to them. The truth about how our government and the Nash administration are conducting the war on Islamist extremism. The truth about what our intelligence agencies knew and didn't know."

Watching in his office at the Pentagon, Secretary of Defense Daniel Shane cringes. He has worried about Curtis Gains chairing this committee from the outset. By reputation, the Florida congressman is a serious person. But the man lacks experience, and no doubt is getting more advice than is good for him. Gains had been a prosecutor in Florida, Shane knew, and this was a prosecutor's opening statement, but it was inappropriate at the opening of such a controversial congressional investigation. Were he still in the Senate, this rhetoric might have rolled off Shane's back. But he isn't in the Senate anymore. He is secretary of defense, responsible for the hundreds of thousands of people in uniform, and the thousands more who support them.

The more he hears, the more Shane bristles. In what universe, he thinks, should Congress air in public hearings what U.S. intelligence knows about America's enemies? With these grandstanding opening remarks, Gains is all but advocating treasonous acts without even knowing it.

Shane picks up the phone and calls Owen Webster at the CIA. Gains's rhetoric, he imagines, is probably making the spymaster's skin crawl. And he and Webster could use a little bonding.

"You watching this?"

"Do I have to?" says Webster.

"Yeah, Owen, you do."

"Well, I am."

"We owe these fallen heroes the truth about whether we provided all the protection they required," Gains is saying.

The chairman's list of "truths" is now at about twelve.

"We owe it to these fallen men to know whether our government has told the truth to the American people about their sacrifice."

In the public seating area, about halfway back, Randi Brooks is also surprised by Gains but less disheartened. She had worked on many congressional investigations in her career. That's where she and Rena met. And she knows melodrama doesn't suit the chair of a major committee. It is better left to others, to pit bulls on your side, so the chair can maintain distance and some decorum across the aisle. Like Shane, she wonders if Gains is in over his head. One way you can usually tell is when the person chairing a committee is not fully in control: they talk too much.

But a poor hearing works to their advantage. Perhaps, just maybe, the Oosay Committee will be less of a threat than she and Rena fear. They should be so lucky. They were less than five minutes in. It was way too early to even wish such a thing.

Gains finishes, and the ranking Democrat, Senator Fred Blaylish of Vermont, leans into his microphone. He pauses a moment, an old trick, to get the room's attention. Then Blaylish lets everyone know he is royally pissed.

"The chairman claims we're charged with pursuing this investigation 'on a bipartisan basis to get at the truth,' but I fear the facts suggest something else. I am disappointed to have to report that the majority has concealed witnesses from the minority, withheld documents in violation of Senate and House rules, and withheld details of its plans. It's hard to see how you get at the truth, or honor anyone, when you play fast and loose with the facts from the start."

He goes on for several more minutes, mostly outlining how he hopes the committee will run and what questions it needs to answer. But the message is unmistakable. Beyond even the most cynical expectations, the Oosay Committee after only a few minutes has become a partisan mess.

Dick Bakke is up next. Since the committee is newly formed, with no length of tenure on the panel, they've drawn lots on each side to determine the order of questioning. Bakke stares at Blaylish.

"Mr. Chairman, in response to the ranking Democrat, I feel we need to remind our friends across the aisle why we are here. I fear, Mr. Chairman, that the Nash administration is not only incompetent—which may be inferred prima facie from the death of General Roderick and his men. I am also here to find out if the Nash administration has lied about what happened and is now engaged in a cover-up to hide those lies. If that requires holding back some information from the Democrats, who in turn will leak it to the White House, so be it."

Senator David Traynor of Colorado suddenly twists in his chair to look at Bakke. The sound and the sudden motion, in turn, catch the attention of the network cameras. Several push in for a close-up on Traynor's expression, which is one of unmistakable disgust. In TV parlance, it is a terrific reaction shot.

Sitting in his studio across town, BNS anchorman Jack Anthem exclaims to his producer, "You see that? Make sure to mark that."

In the press section, a number of reporters begin to frame the day's story in their minds—Traynor versus Bakke, two men considering running for the presidency. Some older hands among them wonder if Traynor's reaction was spontaneous or calculated, and they are eager to hear what Traynor will say in his own statement.

They aren't disappointed. "Less than twenty minutes, Mr. Chairman!" Traynor snaps when it's his turn to speak. He pauses, waiting for every other member of the committee to turn his way. "That's all it took. Before these proceedings, the work of the U.S. Congress, went full DC Comics."

He pauses dramatically.

"You got senators here accusing the administration of murder. Others accusing the committee of being a fraud. And we haven't heard from our first witness yet."

Traynor shakes his head. "I may be new to Congress, but good Lord. I wonder what American citizens looking for us to help solve the country's problems think of us now?"

A pause. "What do we think of ourselves? We say we want to honor the dead. Let's do ourselves a little honor."

"Are we rolling on this?" Jack Anthem yells to his producer. The anchor is on set now, waiting to do a live shot during an expected break in the hearings. "Because I sure as hell want to play that tonight."

**THE NEXT STATEMENT IS FROM SENATOR WENDY UPTON,** the Republican from Arizona whom Stroud had begged to join the committee. Given that reporters already have begun to frame their stories, a number of them are not paying close attention.

"Mr. Chairman, I'll be brief. We are public servants. Our job on this committee is to learn what we can from this incident so that we can limit the chances of similar tragedies occurring in the future. The more we focus on politics, the less likely we are to do what citizens require of us. We honor the dead by doing our job. Not scoring political points, either by denouncing this committee or by abusing its power."

That was it. She yields the rest of her time and pushes the microphone away from her face, with just a hint of disgust.

One person who does not miss Upton's statement is Dick Bakke, three seats away. He is still smarting from what he considers the obnoxious antics of David Traynor. But he is surprised that it is Upton's remarks he will remember. They were impressive, even lofty, if as Upton suggested one were to remove politics from the equation. But, then again, what is the point of removing politics from the equation?

**THE HEARING WILL GO ON SIX HOURS MORE.** There will be testimony from the FBI forensics team about the explosion at the gates. Secretary of State Arthur Manion will testify about fortifications at the complex and the diplomatic situation in Morat. Diane Howell will carefully refuse to admit she did anything wrong, frustrating Republicans and delighting Democrats. But the story of the day is already written.

From his network TV office on Nineteenth and M Streets, Matt Alabama has decided to watch the hearings on his computer on Y'all Post Live, the way many Americans will watch it now. He sees emoji sweep by on his screen, the little hearts and evil faces as people worldwide register their instantaneous feelings about every word uttered by each senator, House member, and witness.

The universe, Alabama thinks, has become a Rorschach test.

**PETER RENA DIDN'T USUALLY WATCH TELEVISION.** While a lot of political Washington fixated on the story of the day, Rena finds it can often pull you off course. History suggests the news media's narratives are often ephemeral, a kind of misdirection driven by groping for public attention. Though it can be hard to do, he tries to look for deeper patterns and counsels his clients not to be distracted by what won't matter.

But today he had the hearings on in his office in the background, and he is nagged by clinging unease about national decline. The Oosay hearings were cartoonish and unprofessional, demeaning to the institutions of government and the public they are supposed to serve. He knows those institutions have operated in shame and chaos before and survived. They are designed to reflect popular passion, and it is a mistake to read too much into one event. But if you look hard and closely enough, history also teaches that no institutions made by humans last forever. And when change happens, it is rarely clear in the moment—only recognizable years later. Still, it is hard to watch the institutions of government function so poorly and not worry.

## THIRTY-TWO

That afternoon, still unsettled, Rena walks home, feeds Nelson, gets into the Camaro, and heads to Dulles Airport. Vic Madison is coming for the weekend.

Dulles International Airport was designed by the architect Eero Saarinen in 1959 to suggest the freedom of flight. The white steel and glass terminal, built at the end of a special access road deep in the Virginia countryside, was supposed to look like a bird gliding in the air. When people drove that road to their flights, or to pick up arriving passengers, Saarinen wanted them to see the serpentine lines of the terminal appear and disappear over the tree line and golden hills, like a bird in flight. It was a remarkable feat of engineering and imagination and a delight to see. But in the sixty years since, the land along the road has been fully developed. The tree line is gone, replaced by high-rise office buildings. And Saarinen's bird no longer flies.

One sees the terminal now only at the last minute, the bird perched motionless on a concrete slab.

Vic, tired from the trip, says she prefers to go to Rena's rather than out for dinner. He cancels their reservation. At the house, Nelson meets them at the door.

"You've grown in a month," she says, kneeling down to greet him. Nelson examines her and then nuzzles her face.

"I'm being vetted," she says. It is a reference to the job Rena and Brooks were hired to do on her father's nomination to the Court.

Rena carries Vic's bag upstairs and then makes them a quiet dinner. They eat at the small table overlooking Rena's walled brick patio. They talk about her work, a case where she is trying to protect a nonprofit client being sued by a Silicon Valley company for defamation.

"I know you can't talk about the Oosay investigation," she says.

"It depends. Some things . . ."

"Let's avoid it." She sounds irritable, and Rena is surprised. Vic is usually unflappable.

He thinks about bringing up the conversation he'd had with Brooks about working for David Traynor. He wants Vic's counsel about it. But he senses the timing is wrong, her mood off. Asking her advice, he worries, might seem patronizing. Or worse, she would think he was asking her permission to get more involved in politics when she wanted him to be less.

That night, they make love with a fierceness that is unfamiliar, passionate in a way that seems almost angry, and as he lies in the dark afterward, Rena feels even more unsettled. There seemed something urgent in their lovemaking, some insistence that he worries is a signal of farewell. He isn't sure. When it is quiet, Nelson arrives from downstairs, hops onto the bed, and settles in between them.

Saturday is the first true day off Rena can remember in weeks. He and Vic see Washington as tourists might, visiting city museums—the African American and an impressionist exhibit at the East Wing of the National Gallery—and presidential monuments.

They have dinner with Vic's father, Roland Madison, now in his second year on the Court. Brooks is joining them, but she is running late.

They eat at Kinship, a new place on Seventh, where boarded-up buildings and the homeless are not far from the newest, most interesting restaurants in town. They are seated in the back so Justice Madison will have privacy. But an anonymous diner buys drinks for their table, declining to be identified. Madison writes a warm note of gratitude on a menu and asks it be given to the secret benefactor.

"This doesn't happen to me a lot," he says. "Only a small number of people in the country can recognize a Supreme Court justice out of their robe. And most of them live within a five-mile radius of this spot."

Vic doesn't laugh. Her mother died when she was a child, and she and her father are unusually close. He had raised her, a single parent and an only child—or perhaps, as Rollie says, they raised each other. So she has been looking forward to seeing him tonight.

Instead of responding to her father's joke, however, Vic speaks to Rena. "I know you can't talk about it, Peter, but I want to anyway. I want to hear Dad's opinion."

"About what?"

"Oosay. That hearing yesterday, it was terrible. It started out like a show trial from Russia, and then we heard the pathetic whining by the Democrats. I was embarrassed. These people, members of Congress, they're supposed to be our leaders. They act like children."

He knows it will only make Vic angrier, but she is right: he cannot say anything.

Vic presses her case anyway. "How can the Republicans possibly believe anyone in the Nash administration wanted the Oosay tragedy to happen? That's absurd. And why do they think there's a cover-up? What's the evidence? It's self-destructive and cynical. Don't these people know they're tearing the country apart?"

If he could tell her what he thought, it would only make it worse. On the one hand he agrees with Vic that the hearings were embarrassing. But he also thinks that while some of Nash's critics are cynical and opportunistic, some are sincere, and he has little sympathy for most of the Democrats, who he thinks are blindly trying to help Nash.

At the same time, he thinks there *is* a cover-up involving Oosay. He just doesn't know what it is yet. And he cannot say anything about any of it.

Vic finishes her drink and waves the glass at the waitress for another.

"Rollie, don't you agree with me?" she asks, using the nickname she's used for her father since her mother died. During the battle over his nomination to the Supreme Court, Roland Madison often expressed dismay and bafflement at the cynicism of the capital city. Now, glancing at his daughter, Madison seems unperturbed by it, or at least unsurprised. "We're entering a presidential election season," he says simply, as if the rest were obvious. "So what do you expect?"

"I know that, Rollie. That's my point," Vic says.

In her expression—something between anger and sadness—her feelings are suddenly plain to see. She is worried that her father, a man who for so long has been a tower of intellectual honesty and candor in the law, is being changed by the jaded ethos of his new city.

Vic's next drink arrives. She looks at the two men, raises her glass in silence, and takes an unhealthy swig.

"The only point of investigating Oosay should be to make sure it doesn't happen again," she says, looking at Rena.

"That's what we're trying to do," he says.

"Are you, Peter? How would I know?"

Then she takes a breath and pushes her drink away.

"Look, this isn't about James Nash. We have taken a long time to get into this mess. But I blame the people who work in politics, who raise the money, who bring lawsuits, who work in campaigns, and the people they elect. I worry they're all getting so good at working the system they're destroying it. I just don't want it to corrupt you two."

"Vic," her father begins.

"No, Dad. Please. I feel like you're both wrapped up in the bullshit now so much you don't see it. Now that you're a justice, oh my, you can't talk about any issue that might appear before the Court. And, Peter, you can't talk about anything."

The silence is terrible.

Finally, Vic says, "I'm sorry. I shouldn't have begun this. Not here." But she isn't taking it back. She doesn't mean to.

And then they are rescued.

The hostess arrives, guiding Randi Brooks to the table. The rest of the evening is fine, thanks to Brooks's ebullience. The idea that Randi, with her candor and wit and high-wattage energy, has been changed by "the bullshit" seems impossible to consider.

As they drive back to Rena's row house, he and Vic say little. They do not make love that night and are polite but careful the next morning. Then, after an interminable hour trying to read in Rena's den, Vic breaks the silence between them.

"Why not come to California?" she says. "Why be part of this? You work for people you're not sure you trust, doing investigations you're not sure they want. You always feel that way. Don't you think it's cynical?"

Rena looks into Vic's smoke-gray eyes. Something about the way she has put it just now, as a question of cynicism, is clarifying. He has wondered about this himself, of course, about whether he should spend his life as a "fixer," an "apparatchik," ever since he wandered without meaning to from being a soldier into being an operative of the political city. Listening to Vic, the way she described it last night and the way she has asked him this morning, the answer that has nagged but eluded him for so long seems to come to him now with a sureness he hasn't felt before.

"Do I think what I do is cynical? I guess I think it would be more cynical not to be part of it. To stop trying. To give up and walk away."

Vic looks at him, considering what he has said. She nods but doesn't smile. She takes a long time to respond.

"That gives me something to think about."

They don't speak of it again, or the argument the night before. The day passes more normally, the pressure lessened if not gone, and late that afternoon Rena takes Vic to the airport for her flight home.

But they have touched some nerve, Rena knows, entered a new place in their relationship they had been unable to get to before. Vic had gotten them there, he recognizes, not him.

She has given *him* something to think about, too. And she deserves his honesty. She above all people. He doesn't know what his honest answer will be and whether this is the beginning of the end for them or the real beginning.

When he gets home from the airport there is a text from Brooks. "Check the *Tribune*."

## THIRTY-THREE

Two days after the drone story was published, Will Gordon had headed toward Jill Bishop's desk.

She saw him coming at fifty feet. With his shambling tall-man walk, head bowed, moving slow as if it were hard to stay balanced. It was her own damn fault, she thought. She should never have invited him into her thinking on the drone story. She now believed she had rushed that piece into publication. She should have held off on it until she'd made her source show her the video. Now she might never see it. That video had vanished. It had been two and a half weeks. Everyone in town wanted to get their hands on it, including Congress.

And when Congress announced it was moving the Oosay hearings up as a result of the story, she figured Gordon would want the paper to have something new to influence the conversation during the hearings.

Well, she sure as hell wasn't going to talk to him about it in the middle of the newsroom. She got up and met him halfway to his office. Out of the corner of her eye she could see one of her newsroom rivals, Gary Gold, watching them. Gold was a good reporter, but he was absolutely the kind of person who had gone into journalism for the pure, feral rush of it—if he wasn't involved in some big story, he felt a kind of death. He probably itched to get involved in the Oosay story.

"Your office," Bishop commanded when she reached Gordon.

The editor half grinned. "Yes, ma'am."

"And for chrissakes," she said, "don't call me ma'am."

They found space on the wreck of a sofa.

"I'm trying to get the drone video," she began, "but the problem—"

Gordon crossed his long legs and, before she could finish her sentence, said, "The problem is if someone gives you a copy of the video, it would have a digital signature and be traceable. The government would go to court to ask for it. We would have to fight that. Even though we would, your sources would be frightened, and that would make you even more dangerous to work with. If the government filed papers, your picture would be all over the Internet, which would only make your work harder."

"Right," Bishop said.

"And every other reporter in town is trying to get that video right now. So is the Oosay Committee. Which puts about ten times more pressure on anyone in the intelligence community who has it."

"That's right," said Bishop.

"And if everyone in town wants to know what's on that video, if anyone does find out, it will be easy to confirm the first story because all these sources have been asked about it already. Which means the video is a lot of work for a story that will remain exclusive for about an hour."

"That is also right."

"I think the thing to do is work a different story," Gordon had said. "Something no one else is working on."

Bishop had to agree that made sense.

It amused Gordon that reporters always seemed shocked when you could see things from a distance they missed up close.

"What's the biggest hole in the Oosay story?" he asked her. "What's the missing piece that makes other pieces suddenly fit?"

"The whole thing is a missing piece," she said.

"I often find it's what we stopped looking at that's important."

"Beg pardon. What the hell does that mean?"

"Well, there is usually something we wonder about a lot at the beginning of a story. And then we may lose sight of it when we get into the middle. For me, it was the question of who was the mastermind behind the Oosay attack."

"The man on the roof?" Bishop said, referring to a report in the early days that someone had seen a man on a roof near the Oosay compound looking through binoculars. That had never been confirmed.

"I know he might have just been a guy with binoculars up there by chance," Gordon said. "But the question of who was the mastermind is still actually more important than anything Congress seems focused on. Who did this, and how, and what does it portend about ISA in Africa? Not what the kindergarten on the Hill is looking at."

Gordon was becoming animated the more he thought about it. "Morat has slipped further into chaos since the attack," he said. "Who gained by doing this? What are the best theories? Where's the evidence point?"

Bishop had to smile. Gordon was not entirely useless, even if he was an editor.

"What questions mattered at the beginning that we've begun to forget about in the middle?"

Then Gordon stopped talking. It was better, he found, just to point his best reporters in a direction—not insult them with a lot of instruction about what to do after he'd pointed.

He stood up. "Just keep going, Jill."

Back at her desk, Bishop thought awhile.

Then she called Avery Holland.

## THIRTY-FOUR

Avery Holland had been just twenty-four years old when he began to perfect using artificial intelligence to track what everyone in the world said on the Web.

The idea had come to him when he was social media editor for the ABN-TV network, where he was given the lowly job of promoting the old TV channel's news stars and programs on a growing list of social media platforms like Y'all Post, Little Bird, and Me, Myself and You.

During the Arab Spring in 2010, Holland began to realize he could track the revolution online by monitoring the social media posts of influential activists and triangulating their conversations. He knew more, and knew it faster, than journalists working on the ground where the protests were occurring. He learned how to weight each voice he heard based on their influence—the number of followers they had—and their reliability—whether their past digital conversations turned out to be true, thus weeding out the fakes, the spoofers, and the blowhards.

He began to write computer code that could identify which accounts were "organic"—meaning real people—and which were bots—

meaning either machines posing as people or actual people being paid to run multiple fake identities. At twenty-six Holland coined the term "Little Bird Revolution" to describe the protests in Egypt— which six months later he repudiated when he discovered most of the "sparrow tweets" posted on Little Bird were either military spoofs designed to catch protesters or protesters putting out fake tweets on Little Bird to deceive the soldiers.

By then, however, his discredited term was misunderstood, and he had become one of the most recognized interpreters in the world of social speech on the Web—though ironically he was now becoming one of its skeptics.

Holland left ABN for a Ph.D. in computer science at the Massachusetts Institute of Technology, where he began to write more sophisticated code. He began creating maps of great depth and detail. He could take any topic in the world and know who was saying what about it, eliminate the fake traffic, and identify down to the person, either in the Dark Web or the open Web, what they said and who listened to them. Or he could map a city and everything that was said online inside that city. He knew better than most residents of those places what their neighbors thought, liked, and in secret kept from their family members. He began predicting elections and even crime. He could track the reputation of a corporation or a person and know everyone who liked them, everyone who hated them, and everyone who talked about them.

The CIA was the first to come calling, visiting Holland's graduate dorm at MIT to talk about his algorithms. He created a company, VoxMapia, that the CIA helped finance indirectly, and then they hired Holland and his company to track dangerous extremists online. In time, the CIA had learned enough from Holland that it began to try to emulate his work itself, though he still spent some time as an occasional advisor. But Holland was considered a little too idiosyncratic for the CIA. Gradually his company moved into more commercial areas, which were also more lucrative. Food conglomerates and consumer product giants hired him to track what was being said about their shampoos or deodorants, and how to shape that conversation. There was a lot of damaging corporate sabotage and espionage now. Candy turns up in a convenience store in Ames, Iowa, with a trace of arsenic. Twenty-four hours later, a campaign of hate could rise up online costing the candy manufacturer a billion in stock valuation overnight. Avery Holland could identify that it was a rival candy manufacturer behind the social upheaval. He never engaged in such behavior himself. But he could spot others doing it, and he was paid a good deal by brands to know about it, though they were not always able to stop it.

On the side, Holland still had an interest in news, and there were a few reporters in town who understood what he did and for whom he was willing to work. It was her intelligence source Talon who originally had told Jill Bishop about Avery Holland.

"This boy can zero in on what the head of ISA is saying, even if the man is using anonymous accounts in some part of the Web we didn't even know existed. He has figured out the real identities of these extremist voices online. He knows who the person is doing the sparrow tweeting, where they actually live, and their real name. It's pretty amazing."

If anything, Holland was a lot more cautious than most actual spooks, Bishop had discovered. He operated with cash, rarely used credit cards, and met Bishop face-to-face only on those rare occasions when she sought his help on a story.

This time she said only that she needed something. It wasn't until she arrived at his brownstone on Capitol Hill, where he ran his company and also lived, that she explained what she was after.

"I want to figure out who masterminded the Oosay attack," she said.

Holland stared at her a long moment. "I thought we did this already. We said there was a lot of social traffic that night in Oosay. The U.S. government should have seen it."

Holland had been her source for that aspect of the original Oosay exposé.

"This is different. A different story. This time we need to go deeper and find who was directing things. Who was behind the Oosay attack. If you get me that, I can pry loose what the intelligence community thinks."

Holland looked like an overgrown boy. He was pudgy, had a round face, a hipster's beard, and friendly, soft green eyes. Yet Bishop sensed a sadness in him, as if Holland knew he would spend his life looking at how anger and hate would spread, not the liberation he thought the Web would bring. At age thirty-three, he seemed to her a weary soul.

"It will take a day or two," Holland said. "And I will need five thousand dollars."

"Do it."

As far as Bishop was concerned, Will Gordon had given her a blank check.

"I need some clues to get us started," Holland said. "Some people to look at."

Bishop handed him the pieces she had collected, most of them written early, speculating on who had been behind the attack. There was a piece by Roland Garth in the *New York Times* that mentioned eyewitnesses recalling men who seemed to be observers supervising the attack from adjacent buildings, including the so-called man on the roof. The *Guardian* in England had surfaced some names, too. The *Guardian* also had reported that the Nash administration wasn't keen on trying to talk about who it thought was responsible for the attack, lest the man vanish. That had led the conservative online media to condemn the Nash administration for not having a clue about who it was. Bishop tapped her tablet and grabbed the pieces from her file and emailed them to Holland.

"What do your intelligence sources tell you?" Holland asked.

Bishop scrunched her nose in frustration. "They're pretty quiet about that," she said. "I wonder if the masterminds of Oosay actually are people who began to disappear online as the attack got closer."

Holland smiled. That was the kind of thing he would wonder. He would track Oosay months before the attack and then look for who began to get quiet.

Bishop came back two days later to check on Holland's progress.

As he began to show her what he found, Holland made a kind of humming noise.

"Is that a good noise or a bad noise?" Bishop asked.

Holland shrugged. "Got four or five suspects," he said.

He turned on his computer—which Bishop marveled was usually turned off when he wasn't using it—and opened a document with pictures and short bios, a little digital dossier he was building.

"If someone is trying to hide and isn't on social media or trying to be public, how do you know anything about them?" she asked.

"Everyone leaves breadcrumbs," Holland said. "Even when they think they don't."

A picture came up of a bearded man with a gun, from a blurry Internet photo.

"This one is an ISA commander who works mostly in Tunisia. Name of Abdul Hassan. But he wasn't in Morat that night. I know that for sure from tracking some of his aides, who you can locate. So if he was the mastermind, there was someone else on the ground in Morat doing his bidding who isn't usually one of his regular deputies."

"Who else?"

The next picture showed a man in front of a microphone giving a speech, another bearded man in a robe.

"This is a radical cleric named Ibrahim Ramzi. He held protests outside the compound. Exhorted people to resist the Americans. A lot of talk."

"So he's either hiding in plain sight or he's too obvious to be guilty?"

"I leave that analysis to you. I just provide the evidence," Holland said.

The next picture was of a younger man, maybe in his twenties.

"This is a local thug, a low-level Moratian gangster named Yousef Samir. He was coy in his comments after the Oosay attack. Powerful in the neighborhood of the compound. A suspect certainly. But I'm skeptical he has what it takes. He's on social media a lot. But he has no density."

"No what?"

"I've explained this to you before," Holland said. "Density is my measure of how many important people, or connections, follow a given person in various social realms and how much they respond to or pass on what that person posts. How much of a ripple someone makes if they throw a rock in the pond. This Samir tries to connect with powerful people. They don't usually connect with him. If he did this, it was a step up."

Click, and instead of a picture, a question mark appeared on the screen.

"And someone I know less about," Holland said.

"Who is he?"

"Well, he could be a couple of people. He could be a former carpenter or construction worker, who claims to be the head of a small militia group in Oosay. This man is not on social platforms himself. And he goes by several names. Mahmoud. Ghada. And Assam Baah. But I think, based on the location of a cell phone that might belong to him, he may have been around the compound a good deal for about a week before the attack. Staking it out, possibly."

"Was this the supposed man on the roof?"

"Perhaps."

"How do you know where he was? Especially if he is not on social."

"Cell phones ping off cell towers continually if they're on. You know location, even if people aren't doing anything online. The phone is communicating. That's how platform companies know where you are all the time. We know people who have phone numbers associated with this man. One of those numbers was around the compound a lot."

Bishop was reminded of the degree to which Holland, the master of tracking people digitally, rarely used a cell phone, or did much else online that wasn't from his secure computers.

"Or it could be another man named Amin Assani, who I think is this man's friend. Amin is the more visible presence."

"Why don't you think it's Amin then?"

"You know how in old war movies there is a radioman who moves with his commander? The commander is always telling the radioman, 'Tell headquarters this. Tell headquarters that.' But the officer himself is not on the radio?"

"You watch too many movies."

"You have no idea," Holland said.

## THIRTY-FIVE

## SUNDAY, FEBRUARY 2

The rest of Bishop's thread came from intelligence sources. She met with Talon and two others and ran the names by them. In a couple of days she had what she considered enough. At least enough for the kind of speculative story that would shake the tree a little more. The kind Gordon thought would help.

"While the Nash administration and law enforcement have not identified a suspect in the attack in Oosay that killed American army general Brian Roderick and three others, intelligence sources and evidence gathered independently by the *Tribune* have narrowed the search down to five men," her piece begins.

It walks through the different characters, naming Amin Assani as one, and his unnamed friend as another.

"The unnamed suspect is the leader of a small militia group in Oosay that has emerged in the last two years as claiming credit for different acts in the name of ISA."

The story runs big, leading the paper's evening briefing that Sunday night. It would run on page one in print the next morning and be the second story in the paper's morning lineup online.

**THE SECOND HEARING** on Oosay is scheduled for two days from now in closed session.

After dropping Vic at the airport, Rena reads the *Tribune* story and considers what Vic had said about Congress—how it was focused on the wrong things. Perhaps any public inquiry should focus on the larger war on terror and how to conduct it—not on the Oosay incident.

The story contained a subtle message to Washington, Rena thinks: stay on what matters. He wonders what hand Will Gordon might have played here. He is decoding the news the way Washington insiders often find themselves doing.

He plays *Go* by Dexter Gordon and mixes a Grey Goose and Dolin martini, but after the first sip he loses his taste for the alcohol.

He picks up his phone and begins to type a message for Vic, who is still in the air en route to California: "I miss you already." Then he hesitates. She would appreciate the sentiment, he thinks. But he wonders if she will think the message is manipulative, a form of pushing her away when she is here and pulling her back as soon as she leaves. And why does he think she would suspect that? Is that what he does? Vic is so honest, he thinks, she deserves better than that. She deserves the truth. What does he want? Certainly he wants Vic, but what does he want for himself, and what is he willing to give? He erases the message, and then, unsure of what to write in its place, he sends nothing.

## THIRTY-SIX

## MONDAY, FEBRUARY 3
## QUANTICO, VIRGINIA

The next morning, Rena calls Tommy Kee, the man who taught him how to be a military investigator.

Kee, now in his fifties and close to retirement, is still in uniform, a sergeant—high as he will go—and perhaps wondering if he has stayed too long. Tommy is investigating crimes by soldiers the age of his children.

He is stationed in Quantico, Virginia, nearly halfway to Richmond. Rena drives the Camaro, stuck in traffic on 95 both ways.

They go to a frozen yogurt stand on base and sit outside in the cold, the only customers.

"How you doin', Pietro?" Tommy says, using Rena's Italian name, the way Peter's father always had.

"We can't get what we need. We're being frozen out," Rena says.

Tommy nods. "Whatever they're hiding, they're keeping it deep. And maybe from the boss, too, and you're working for the boss." Kee means the president.

He is a small, hard man with leathery skin and small watchful eyes. Tommy looked old when Peter met him fifteen years ago and doesn't seem to have aged. He speaks in a hybrid English of his own, part his Korean parents, part East L.A. where he grew up, part military—a staccato syntax that Rena thinks a kind of poetry.

"It's always the same story," Kee is saying. "The president asks his generals, 'How do I win this war?' They tell him, 'Give us more men on the ground. Don't tie our hands.' Then he asks the foreign policy people and they say, 'Don't get trapped in a ground war. Only the people of the country can win it.' The president goes halfway, it doesn't work, and the generals say they must now fight the war their way but in secret. Eventually they begin to hide the worst from the president himself. Korea. Vietnam. Iraq One. Iraq Two. Afghanistan. It is always the same."

Kee is telling Rena he may never know what he is looking for.

"What do you know about Brian Roderick?"

"He's dead."

"I need to know what he was doing there," Rena says.

Kee tosses his frozen yogurt into the trash.

"I know him by reputation. He was one of those Technicolor generals. Everything bright, big—his heart, his brain, his stubbornness. Half visionary, half crazy. Saw the warrior thing as destiny." Tommy pauses to examine his friend. "Brave as a superhero and just as absurd. Did something like six tours in Iraq and Afghanistan."

"Seven," Rena says.

"He liked to get out of the Green Zone. Be with the people. Always in harm's way."

"I know his theories," Rena says, telling Kee he isn't helping enough. "But I don't know the man or what he was doing in Morat."

"What do you suspect he was doing?"

"Maybe trying to recruit spies, double agents, in country."

Tommy's expression is sour.

"Hard to do in that part of the world when you're the invader," Tommy says. "But we could use it. Practically the only good inside sources we have over there are from the Israelis. And that isn't good enough."

"You ever heard of the Office of Special Directives?"

Kee thinks, not answering for a moment. His memory, even now, is one of Kee's great, almost mystical tools.

"Sorry, Pietro. *Lo non só nulla*." I know nothing, in Italian.

Rena tosses away his own yogurt.

"How about Henry Arroyo? Colonel."

"Know that one," Kee says. "That guy is as hard as dried crocodile skin. Fucker was a Marine in military intelligence who believed in enhanced interrogation. Almost no one in uniform thought that CIA torture shit was a good idea. But Henry Arroyo did. Guy is right out there on the edge."

Rena hands Kee a piece of paper with the number of his secure encrypted phone. "If you want to reach me," Rena says, "use this line. We figure they're tapping everything else."

Kee is shaking his head now and a mischievous smile is forming.

"Peter, you always make the same mistake, and I warned you over and over: 'Never do a bad job well. They'll keep asking you to do it again.'"

Rena smiles a distant, worried smile.

"Yeah, I still need teaching."

Kee wonders if he has taken the teasing too far. He slaps Rena's knee.

"So come at them without them seeing you, Pietro. Without them seeing you coming."

## THIRTY-SEVEN

## TUESDAY, FEBRUARY 4, 9:11 A.M.
## WASHINGTON, D.C.

The second hearing of the joint committee on Oosay is being held in closed session.

They are meeting in the "secure" hearing room in the Capitol, a little-known chamber down a protected hallway, away from reporters and casual passersby. The star witness of the day will be one of two survivors of the Oosay attack, a wounded private contractor named Adam O'Dowd. The second witness will be the director of the CIA, Owen Webster. Tomorrow there will be another closed hearing, with another survivor, Sergeant Major Garrett Franks, and General Frederick Willey, director of the Defense Intelligence Agency.

For Curtis Gains, chairman of the Oosay Committee, the last few days since the first hearing have been difficult.

He has been the subject of extraordinary criticism, and even hate, from both the left and the right. More media leaks: the *Tribune*'s "mastermind" story inspired a storm of criticism that the committee was looking at the wrong problem. And after the criticism of the first Oosay hearing, there's been even less cooperation from some in government. The air force is refusing to provide the drone footage, or even to allow the drone pilot to testify. Almost no one is agreeing to testify in public, not the soldiers who survived the attack nor their superiors at the Pentagon, let alone the CIA.

Waiting for today's hearing to begin, Gains is sitting at a small conference table in the anteroom next door to where the committee will convene. The space—the Democrats have their own across the hall—is little more than an oversize foyer, barely big enough for the small conference table, a single bookshelf, a mini refrigerator, and a coffee machine.

When Senator Dick Bakke enters the anteroom, he thinks Gains looks miserable. Gains had told Bakke he expected to draw on his experience as a prosecutor in Florida to chair the Oosay Committee—as if this were going to be a kind of national prosecution of the Nash administration. Instead, Bakke thinks, the young congressman is getting a lesson on the meaning of federal separation of powers.

Gains was also not prepared, Bakke thinks, for the kind of public scrutiny a national story now received. He had no idea how intense, unrelenting, and sometimes deranged it could feel. Gaggles of reporters waiting for him every time he stepped out of an elevator; daily call lists from angry donors, lobbyists, reporters, so lengthy there weren't enough hours in a week to call them all back; the jabbering wannabes on cable; and the scalding hyperbole in social media. If you didn't have the right kind of personality—didn't find the TV lights a kind of energizing adrenaline rush—you could wake up every morning exhausted from it, as if you had been scrolling through Y'all Post in your head all night.

The Internet, he thinks, is bipolar: it is all fury or euphoria. It has no middle.

Bakke sits down next to Gains. He likes the young man, so he feels bad about what he is about to do, but he has no choice. They are in the arena. He has his own role to play, and if the committee continues to falter as it did on the first day, Bakke still has to get from it what he needs.

"Curt, may I have a word?"

"Of course, Senator."

"In light of the latest *Tribune* story, the resistance of administration officials to cooperate with the committee, and our inability to get our hands on the drone footage, I've written a letter to the White House," Bakke says. "I'd like to read part of it today before we question witnesses. I don't have to read the whole thing—it's ten pages—but I'd like to describe it."

Gains turns to look Bakke in the eye.

"It's a closed hearing today, Senator," Gains says. He sounds pained at the prospect of yet another difficulty to manage. "Why not just release the letter to the press? We can't talk about what's said in the hearing anyway."

"We can't leak what happens in the hearing," Bakke agrees. "But I can say that I read this letter. Then, when I release it, reporters will write about the letter because I mentioned it in closed session. It will have the air of something special, something leaked. They will ask Democrats about it. The Democrats will be infuriated."

Bakke leans closer: "You see, don't you, Curt? If I simply release the letter to the press, well, it's just a letter."

Gains inhales as if he can't get enough oxygen.

"Yes. I see. But after last week, I think we need to demonstrate to the American public that we're being fair."

A concerned smile forms on Bakke's face and then a sterner, more fatherly look.

"Curt, I just hope you understand which public to keep in mind," he says.

Some people might have mistaken this remark about "the right public" as a racist or ideological allusion to "real Americans," flag-waving whites rather than people of color or liberals. But Bakke's meaning is more subtle.

"I'm talking about your public," Bakke adds. "Back home. These days no matter who you are, y'all need to worry about your primary."

Your primary. It's as simple as that when you're in the House. And the math is clear. The people who matter for Gains to keep his job do not include the Speaker of the House or even the American public at large. They are the angriest Republican voters who might show up in his next primary back in Escambia County. And those people could turn on him in a heartbeat if they felt he was insufficiently aggressive now.

That's how fragile primaries can be, especially in a place like Pensacola.

In the off years—without a presidential campaign—only 7 percent of Republican voters even show up for House primaries. In Gains's district, as in many others, that's fewer than forty thousand people. Total. Get a few hundred angry, saying you didn't do enough while chairing the Oosay Committee, and you could lose your primary and your seat.

Gains won his first primary by three points. Nine hundred people. Bakke had looked it up.

"That's who you need to worry about, Curt."

Curtis Gains is the sixth-most conservative member of the House, according to vote ratings—sixth out of more than two hundred thirty Republicans. That doesn't mean someone couldn't convince a few hundred people in Escambia County it isn't enough.

"I understand, Senator," Gains says.

"Good man."

Behind Gains, Bakke notices Senator Wendy Upton coming to the table where they're sitting.

"Mr. Chairman?" she says, using Gains's honorific title as their temporary leader. "Morning, Dick," she says to Bakke.

"Hello, Senator," Gains says.

"Since it's a closed hearing today, Mr. Chairman, I propose we dispense with any opening statements," she says. "There are no cameras. No public record. No need to score rhetorical points. Especially after the pyrotechnics of last week. Don't you agree?"

She knows, Bakke thinks. She's gotten wind of the letter he wants to read. She is trying to stop him.

And mixed with his irritation, Bakke recalls his reaction to her opening statement last week, and he begins to think that perhaps he should view Wendy Upton in a new light. Everyone knows she agreed to join this committee reluctantly at the request of Majority Leader Susan Stroud—to be "Lil Susie's" eyes and ears—in no small part to keep an eye on him.

But he had tended to consider Upton overrated. The old moderate Republican establishment, he thought, was too taken with her good looks and good manners, and it yearned for someone young to emerge as its new champion, a new national figure, even a presidential contender, a rival to Bakke himself. Now he is wondering if he should reconsider his skepticism of her. If Upton's operation knew about his plans for the letter, he had to tip his cap. Add that to the statement last week that made her look like the only adult in either party and he will need to keep his eye on her, just as she was keeping her eye on him. Perhaps she is more interesting than—and not as nice as—she seems.

Bakke looks at Gains. He can see the poor congressman's misery. He can also see that Upton has won today. There will be no opening statements.

But he can see in Gains, too, a dawning look of recognition, a realization that in the end he will have to choose which public matters most to him. And Bakke can already see, whether Gains recognizes it yet or not, what choice the congressman will make.

Bakke has learned something else. It is Wendy Upton, not Curtis Gains or even Susan Stroud, he should be worrying about.

## THIRTY-EIGHT

A few minutes later Gains bangs his gavel and looks down at the military contractor Adam O'Dowd, arm in a sling, and thinks the young man looks not just wounded but damaged.

"Mr. O'Dowd, thank you for being here today," he begins. "The committee wants to commend you for your bravery, for your previous service in the U.S. Army and your continuing service to the nation as a private contractor. You are, young man, an American hero."

"Thank you, sir."

O'Dowd's voice sounds as brittle as a Wheat Thin. The lawyer next to him whispers in the young man's ear.

The committee's goal, Gains explains, is simply to get to the truth of what happened that terrible night. "So please, Mr. O'Dowd, tell us about it in your own words. I don't think we will burden you with many questions."

That is the compromise they'd made. "Let him make a statement followed by a few simple questions. But don't cross-examine him," O'Dowd's lawyers had insisted. "The man is coping with enough stress."

The optics ruled. The committee agreed.

His own words. O'Dowd looks down at a written statement in front of him and wonders whose words they are.

**HOURS LATER,** O'Dowd is standing at Garrett Franks's front door in Virginia.

Their lawyers had warned them to stay away from each other until after Franks testified tomorrow. But when O'Dowd called that afternoon sounding lost and upset, Franks invited him to dinner anyway. Standing in front of him now, O'Dowd looks even worse than he sounded. They go into the house. Franks introduces Charlotte and the kids and then suggests the two men take a walk.

It is cold out: a dry, gray, empty cold. A Virginia winter, Franks thinks, all the charm of a vacant apartment.

O'Dowd talks mindlessly, trying to keep the silence away as if it were a bad smell. When they reach the woods by the creek, O'Dowd stops.

"Jesus, Garrett, what have we got ourselves into? Congressional hearings? Lawyers? We should have said no, Garrett. We should have done our job."

Franks puts his hands on the smaller man's shoulders, squaring him up and looking him in the eye.

"You did your job, Adam. And more. You did what you were ordered. You are a righteous warrior."

"I lied today to Congress, Garrett."

"No, you didn't. Not if you read the statement you were supposed to. Did you say anything different when you answered questions? Is there anything I need to worry about?"

O'Dowd looks up and closes his eyes, taking a deep breath.

"No. Christ. No."

"Then stop berating yourself. They don't even want to know the truth, Adam. They're just playing their games. It has nothing to do with us. It has nothing to do with what happened."

* * *

That night, at home, Peter gets a call from Tommy Kee on the secure phone line he had given him.

"Got an address for you, Pietro. I found that office you were looking for. The one that doesn't exist."

Tommy Kee is still the better investigator of the two of them, Rena thinks.

"But the name on the office door isn't going to say Office of Special Directives."

"How did you get this?"

"Let's just say, now that you're an asshole in a suit, I have more friends than you do."

Rena writes down the address.

"And remember, Peter, don't let them see you coming."

## THIRTY-NINE

## WEDNESDAY, FEBRUARY 5, 9:20 A.M. CRYSTAL CITY, VIRGINIA

When Henry Arroyo was a boy in Puerto Rico, he was an undersize kid, poor and picked on. But he always knew he was smart. And by eight or nine he began to discover he was tough. He ached to get away from what he called "the old nets" of the island, the way its poverty had cracked and dried out his father's spirit and made his mother an old woman by thirty-five. In school Henry poured all his viscous, angry drive, his secret pain, and his endless capacity for work into wrestling. He won a scholarship to the University of Georgia and in college joined the ROTC. Of course he found the Marines—or maybe they found him. As he had with wrestling, Henry found something that satisfied him, that he understood, in the discipline of the Corps. He seemed to understand intuitively how the Marines worked. He knew how to get things done in its system when others couldn't.

In Afghanistan he met Brian Roderick, the best soldier he had ever seen, a true warrior, and an inspiring leader. Arroyo thought the two men shared something that was hard to define, a hungry heart, a kind of yearning for finding a better way when you were locked in patterns of failure. Roderick called it a seeking soul. In other ways, the two men could not have been more different. Rod was an idealist, always thinking about the big picture that others couldn't see. Arroyo was a pragmatist, someone who knew how to make things happen.

If someday we were ever in the right spot, Arroyo said, imagine what we could do.

They would need a sponsor, he told Roderick, a protector, someone to give them enough cover that they wouldn't be destroying their careers. If they had that, Arroyo could find the means, the capital, in the fine print of the DIA's black budgets that he had learned to master.

Then things began to happen.

Daniel Shane became secretary of defense, and Arroyo found his own protector in General Frederick Willey, Shane's new director at the DIA. Arroyo and Willey were old hard-ass, shit-kicking comrades. The day Willey was promoted he called Arroyo. "You can be a real son of a bitch, Henry. But you're gonna be my son of a bitch."

Arroyo rented space in an office near Crystal City, an innocuous place not far from the airport, not too far from the main DIA campus at Joint Base Anacostia-Bolling.

The Office of Special Directives needed to be off campus. Since it was off the books.

And it needed to be low-profile. So the sign on the door said GLOBAL ENTERPRISES. And they didn't have uninvited visitors.

**SO IT IS CONFUSING** that Wednesday morning when the security button at the front door buzzes and the security cam shows a man and woman standing outside.

Arroyo's assistant Colin has to get up from his office to open the door.

The two people identify themselves as Peter Rena and Hallie Jobe from the White House Counsel's Office. They are here to see "Colonel" Henry Arroyo.

Fuck me.

Arroyo tells Colin to sit them in the conference room while he punches keys on his computer. These were the assholes who had been hired to investigate Oosay for the president. He knew something about this man Rena. A West Pointer, once a rising star. The unofficial version was that he destroyed his own career on the cusp of making colonel when he had pushed a sexual harassment investigation too far. A fool for principle.

Rena ran some consulting firm now. The president had hired them before.

Click clack, hunting around. The woman, Jobe, was an ex-Marine and former federal agent who worked for Rena's firm, he learns from his quick search.

This is a shit sandwich.

He lets them stew a little longer while he thinks. He makes a call but doesn't get through. It never occurs to him to just leave. That would be a chicken-shit move. And it wouldn't solve a thing. He ponders a little longer. And finally heads down the hall to meet the two assholes in suits.

* * *

Arroyo bursts into the room.

"Apologies for your having to wait. I'm sorry. Terrible day. Henry Arroyo. My goodness, we don't get many visitors here. What on earth can do I for you?"

Rena responds to the manic bravado with a slow-motion look, setting his hands on the table and giving a long glance at Jobe. He is trying to absorb Arroyo's energy like water into a sponge. Two veteran interrogators vying for control of the room.

Then, in the most laconic manner he can muster, Rena introduces himself and Jobe. They are here from the White House Counsel's Office with personal instructions from the president, Arroyo's commander in chief, to talk about the Office of Special Directives and the death of General Brian Roderick.

Arroyo makes a confused face. But he sits down.

He is compact, maybe five nine, in a dark blue polo shirt, khakis, and tasseled loafers. No Marine-brown uniform and colonel's bars when you are running a classified operation in suburban Virginia under deep cover. He has sharp, darting eyes and a thin caterpillar mustache.

"I know you," Arroyo says, as if it were just coming to him now. "Ex-army, right?"

The manic bravado at least is gone.

"Colonel, if you couldn't figure out who we were in the last ten minutes, it's because you already knew who we were."

Arroyo's mustache flattens into a smile.

"I love it," he says. "No bullshit. Cards up." His eyes are sharp, intelligent, and mean. "Make your play."

"We want you to watch something, Colonel," Rena says, leaning down and taking a laptop out of his bag. "And we'd like you to explain to us what you see."

The computer wakes and Rena opens the file Marty Wallace had set up. It is a copy of the video, with the signatures of origin removed, a copy of a copy of a copy. It is cued to the point at which the first figure who is heading toward the Manor House, Lieutenant Joseph Ross, is hit.

Rena freezes the image.

Arroyo says: "That video is classified." Peppery voice.

"We've been cleared," says Rena.

"Not as far as I'm concerned."

"Call the White House Counsel's Office. They will confirm it."

Arroyo is good. Only the slightest quiver in the caterpillar mustache.

"I don't give a good goddamn what the White House counsel says."

"Colonel, have you seen this video?"

Arroyo doesn't answer.

"Why are these men running the wrong way?"

Arroyo's smile is back but it's as tight as a fist.

"There must be some enormous misunderstanding. Yes, I hold a colonel's rank. But I'm on loan to a civilian company trying to export food supplies to Africa. You can call *my* commanding officer."

"No, sir, you are running a black budget operation from this office," Rena says. "You were supervising the classified operations that night in Oosay. You were working with General Roderick the night he died."

Arroyo's stare has enough menace to fuel a Humvee.

"What the hell do you think you're doing storming in here like this?"

"Why was there no drone on the scene for ninety minutes?" Rena asks.

"I am not going to discuss this video with you."

"Why was General Roderick guarded by only one member of his security detail at the Manor House?"

Arroyo's smile is now gone for good.

"Same answer as before."

"Why were Ross, Halleck, Phelps, and O'Dowd not with Roderick guarding him?"

Arroyo says nothing.

"Why were they rushing toward him and arriving so late?"

Arroyo looks from Rena to Jobe and back. And recalibrates.

"Look," he says. "I don't want to insult you two. You're serious people, obviously. So understand this. I've worked in military intelligence for a long time. One thing I've learned: you can't gather intelligence and be transparent with the American public at the same time. We can't fight a war on terrorism and let everybody know what we're doing."

"I agree with you, sir," says Rena.

"Then you should understand this, too. The Chinese and the Russians are inside our systems. That is the next war after this one, and we are already losing it. So the more we share what we are doing inside our own government, the more they know. Every memo. Every secret. And they aren't above selling that to our enemies if it serves their purposes. Including the jihadists. The only way to fight is to keep information tighter, closer, more compartmentalized than ever before."

"You want sympathy?" Rena says. "You should still be leading a platoon, Colonel. You went too high in rank for sympathy."

The mustache bends in irritation.

"I'll tell you why we lost those guys in Oosay," Arroyo says. "Because we got on the ground. We didn't stay up in the air, looking down from eight thousand fucking miles away. We can't win the war on terror by killing people from the sky. It's not that kind of war."

"What kind of war is it?" Rena asks.

"It's a war of ideas."

"I agree with you about that, too," Rena says. "But it's beside the point."

"I'm not gonna answer your questions, Mr. Rena, Ms. Jobe. You wanna cream my ass? Have the president fire me? Be my guest."

And slowly the colonel rises from his chair. "We're done."

At the door, Arroyo stops and turns back to look at them. "If you see me again, I won't be so nice. This is me, nice."

"**WHAT DID WE JUST ACCOMPLISH IN THERE,** other than tipping our hand?" Jobe says in the parking lot.

Rena's eyes brighten. Behind his usual deep stillness, he is pumped.

"First off, we learned Arroyo's the guy. He had seen that video before."

"How'd we learn that?"

"Because he didn't look at it. He knew what was on it."

"And why did we tell him what we knew?"

He hadn't told Jobe much beforehand, only that he wanted her to come because she was ex-military.

"We put them on notice we're getting close. That we know they're lying. We know which off-the-books division Roderick was reporting through."

"How did that help us?"

"Look, Hallie, we were stymied. The only progress we've made in this whole thing is when we flushed them out—first Howell, then Webster. This is the guy we needed to flush most, the one who was hardest to find. So he is the one who is going to react the most."

"I can't wait to see what happens when that guy reacts," Jobe says.

Watching them drive away, Arroyo picks up the phone and dials a number direct.

When he reaches the person on the other end, he says, "I tried to call you before. You won't fucking believe who was just here."

\* \* \*

Randi Brooks is waiting for them at 1820.

"Tell me goddamn everything."

Her eyes dance as they walk through the ambush and Arroyo's reaction.

Then, one more time, they walk through what they know so they can anticipate what may come next.

They know there was some kind of cover-up over Oosay. The

president didn't know about it in advance, and when it went wrong he didn't trust his own people to level with him. Since coming in, they have learned that the survivors in Oosay are lying about where they were. They ran to Roderick too late. He was in the Manor House alone, protected only by one man, Garrett Franks. His security team tried to get to him and couldn't. And Roderick died in some kind of explosion. The CIA and the army and the DIA have also lied about what he was doing there. It was some kind of covert black operation run out of the classified Office of Special Directives under the command of Henry Arroyo. But they still don't know what the operation was. Only that the president had not been informed of it and now the men involved were trying to cover it up.

This was more than Congress knew. It was more than the *Tribune* knew, though the paper was not far behind. The Oosay Committee will recess this afternoon, after it completes two days of closed hearings, the second going on now. They have no idea what was learned—but so far there've been no leaks, which suggests nothing dramatic. If there had been, Brooks thinks, she would have heard something.

"So, for the moment, we wait," she says.

"Not long," Rena predicts.

*  *  *

That night, Samantha Reese knocks on the door of Rena's row house.

He answers it carrying a cat in his arms. Reese does a double take.

"I didn't take you for a cat person."

"Me either."

Rena and the cat step aside to make a path for Reese to come in.

"You want a drink? I'm having a martini. And I may have another one."

"You have whiskey?"

They sit in the kitchen, overlooking Rena's patio garden. The *Washington Tribune* sitting on the counter has pictures of Los Angeles ablaze from seven wildfires. Wildfires in winter in California. The world off-kilter.

"What's wrong, Sam?" Rena asks.

"You're being watched. I don't know why now, but there are eyes on you."

Rena nods just slightly.

"You don't seem surprised."

"Not really," he says, and then tells her about the ambush interview with Arroyo.

"I would have liked to have seen that," she says with a smile.

"Tommy Kee told me not to let them see us coming. They didn't see us coming today."

"You worried?" Reese asks.

"Should I be?"

Reese shrugs.

"I'm weird, Peter. I was raised to hunt. It's bad juju to worry. Your prey can sense your fear."

After a moment, Rena says, "Then I am not worried."

*FORTY*

## THURSDAY, FEBRUARY 6, 2:22 P.M. ASPEN, COLORADO

Senator David Traynor steps out of the midnight-blue Gulfstream G650 into the sting of Colorado winter. The pain feels good.

It is Thursday afternoon. The second of two listless hearings of the Oosay Committee ended yesterday. Traynor couldn't wait to get out of Washington. He'd thought he could use a seat on this committee to protect Jim Nash from a witch hunt, and, admittedly, enjoy some of the limelight. But the whole committee thing has proven more of a crap fest than even Traynor expected. Over the last two days, they'd listened to one frightened survivor of Oosay, a man named Adam O'Dowd, who was too damaged to say much of anything, and a second, Garrett Franks, who was too disciplined to say much more. They'd been stonewalled by the director of the CIA and gotten the runaround from the head of the DIA.

Honestly, Traynor could hardly blame them. These people hate talking to Congress in the best of times, and these, children, were not the best of times. Clearly something had gone hugely sideways in Morat. And the generals and spymasters were not going to confess their mistakes to Congress, the most broken, polarized part of government. Even the national security people who didn't much like Jim Nash weren't going to give knuckleheads on the Hill more opportunity to exercise control over them. The whole thing, Traynor thinks, feels false and ritualistic. He couldn't wait to get away.

Philippe Benoit, the former Paris cop who looks after the Aspen house, has the SUV waiting on the tarmac. Traynor and his bodyguard, Scott Souder, get in and Benoit makes the six-minute drive. Traynor designed the house in Aspen, a combination of bungalow style and cowboy chic, after Will Rogers's place in Los Angeles. It's his favorite getaway.

The housekeeper, Carmelita, is making *ropa vieja* for dinner, and Traynor can smell the rich aroma of seasoned beef. He has meetings with strategists and donors later this evening, but no one is expected for a couple hours. Souder goes to take a nap.

"He here?" Traynor asks.

Carmelita points the chef's knife in her hand toward the south yard.

Traynor pours two glasses of small-batch rye, grabs two cigars, and heads outside. In one of two Adirondack chairs pointed to capture the view of the Roaring Fork River basin sits an older man in blue jeans, a cowboy hat, and boots.

"Alligator?" Traynor says, looking down at the boots.

The cowboy hat makes a slow, deliberate turn, and the man underneath it looks up.

"Yep."

"Jesus, Jimmy, what are those, eight thousand dollars? Spend your money on something worthwhile."

"Five thousand. And it's mostly your money."

Traynor sits down and hands the man a tumbler of rye followed by a Cuban cigar and a box of small wooden matches.

"While we're on the subject of my money, how do I know you're not hacking into it to cover your boot addiction?"

A grin forms under the cowboy hat. "Number one, the security system would tell you instantly. I should know. I built it. Number two, I'm not stupid enough to try. My own people would catch me."

Traynor takes a sip of rye, which burns pleasingly on its way down.

"What are we doing here, David?" Jimmy asks.

"We're not having a conversation."

That gets a doubtful look from Jimmy.

"We're not having *this* conversation," Traynor clarifies.

Jimmy's cowboy hat nods up and down. "We've had a lot of those. What is this one *not* about?"

"Can your people get into the House of Representatives server? Is that system secure?"

Jimmy gets very still.

"Is it?" Traynor repeats.

"Those are two different questions. Is it secure? Hardly. If the Chinese can get into the fucking federal Office of Personnel Management, and the Russians can get into the Democratic National Committee, I can assure you they can get into the House server."

"And?"

"*Will* I hack it? It's just not worth it. Congress is the leakiest institution in the United States. Everything about it is public eventually."

"Well, since we're not having this conversation, let's say someone wanted to anyway."

Jimmy takes a deep breath and an exhale of steam rises into the air from under the hat.

"Look, business competitors used to hack us all the time, right?" Traynor says. "And if they did, we hacked them back, right?"

Jimmy doesn't answer.

"The point is to let them know you hacked them. It's the threat that matters. You're trying to make them feel vulnerable."

"Congress ain't some business competitor," Jimmy says.

"The hell it isn't."

Jimmy frowns and then makes a counteroffer.

"Do a few personal accounts, Senator. Some key people. But not their congressional email." He is warming to his own suggestion. "You'll probably get better shit that way, if you pick the right people."

Traynor is looking into the gorge. "So, you'll do it?"

"We're not having this conversation," Jimmy warns, as if he would ever answer that question directly.

Traynor takes another sip of rye.

"No fingerprints, Jimmy. Do it from Ukraine or someplace. A country that ends in 'stan.'"

The alligator boots cross and uncross nervously.

"And I need it fast. Next week."

"Goddamn you, David. You are one fucked-up dude."

"I promise you, only good will come of it. Only good."

The cowboy hat tilts backward and Jimmy puts a cigar to his mouth, strikes one of the little wooden matches, and sets about lighting the cigar in the cold.

## FORTY-ONE

## THURSDAY, FEBRUARY 6
## WASHINGTON, D.C.

At almost the same time Traynor sits overlooking the Roaring Fork River basin, Richard Bakke is sitting in the Senate cloakroom with his friend Senator Aggie Tucker. It is late in the day, and they are alone.

"You need to make something happen on the outside," Aggie has just said.

Bakke looks back uncertainly. "Something on the outside?"

Bakke feels almost the same about the last two days of Oosay hearings as David Traynor, though he doesn't know it. Not only had both hearings been closed, but Bakke is frustrated he's heard nothing that would be useful even indirectly.

He had found Tucker, the junior senator from Texas, in the cloakroom, and shared his feelings and asked his advice.

Though they were only a year apart in age, Tucker had always been Bakke's mentor in the ways of the Senate. Now it was Bakke who was becoming more prominent nationally. He yearned for bigger things. Only presidents changed history, he argued. The Senate bored him.

Tucker had no such savage impulses. He actually liked the intrigue of the Senate. And he didn't think the presidency was worth the price. Run and you're most likely gonna lose, and you may come away diminished. So he had reconciled himself to the fact that his friend was eclipsing him as the face of the hard right in the Senate. Strategist in chief suited him fine.

"Yeah, Dick, you gotta work the outside," Tucker says. "Inside a Senate committee you got all those rules and people and voting. The Democrats. And even on our side. Wendy Upton. And, hell, Lew Burke for God's sakes sticking his nose in, whispering in Susan's ear. Outside, you got no obstructions. Dick, we've talked about this before."

Yes, they had talked about it before, and Bakke knows Tucker is right. While he had pushed for congressional hearings, Bakke had few illusions about their real purpose. Congressional hearings are not really a form of inquiry at all—not in the twenty-first century. Members face too much pressure from donors to hew to the party line; witnesses are too well prepared to reveal much you don't already know. Congressional hearings are really just set pieces around which you can focus attention elsewhere—in the old media, in social, and in the new blazing-hot channels of conversation online. Being on the committee gave Bakke standing to shape all that. And he could get as much traction trolling the Web for accusations and then demanding they be investigated as anything he could do inside the committee room. That's all Tucker was reminding him.

"It's simple physics," Tucker explains. "Create an outside action that causes an equal but inevitable reaction."

"Simple physics," Bakke repeats.

The other problem inside the committee room, with all its rules and procedures, is that you have too many rivals.

One of them, David Traynor, the dot-com guy from pot-smoking Colorado, has a natural ability to phrase things in a way people find entertaining, and he has a kind of charisma that reminds Bakke of Paul Newman in *Butch Cassidy and the Sundance Kid,* a sort of infectious bluster where you know you're being conned and enjoy it anyway. Traynor is crazy like a fox. Bakke gets it. He understands the man.

Substantively, it is Wendy Upton he is beginning to worry about more. She is more subtle, and more of a puzzle. She is serious and elusive. People respect her—in both parties. Bakke cannot get a read on her.

The first presidential primaries are still a year off. But Wendy Upton, with her military background, her support for women in the military, her good-girl rectitude, could attract serious backing—especially from private equity types, and their money moved in bunches. He will need to watch her. If she did something dramatic, the Oosay hearings could become prologue to a dangerous rivalry he hadn't entirely seen coming.

"Right, do something to change the dynamics," Tucker says. "Then you'd be driving that committee. Not just sitting there watching David Traynor and Wendy Upton battin' eyes at each other."

## FORTY-TWO

## FRIDAY, FEBRUARY 7
## WASHINGTON, D.C.

He needed only a little reminding. If there is one thing Dick Bakke knows how to do, it's create an outside force. He was born an outside force.

Each day Bakke made sure one of his communications staff followed the voices of the far right in America—the Web videos posted on WeTV (almost all of them by men), a half dozen important podcasts, a list of highly followed conservative bloggers, two dozen key websites. An analytics firm he uses has identified the ten thousand top conservative "influencers" on the right in social media based on the size and value of their network of followers, and an algorithm using keywords summarizes what they discussed yesterday. A press aide has a summary of it to Bakke by email each morning by 7:30. He wants to know these people, hear their fear and anger, feel the pulse of their hearts. To Dick Bakke they are not the fringe. They are the leading edge.

As he skims the morning summary he finds something promising. A podcast, called *Deep State*—the anchor calls himself "Hackford Stone"—has woven a theory about the death of General Brian Roderick that is showing up in fragments on different websites around the world. Stone has connected the dots and ordered them into an organized narrative. "Was it possible General Brian Roderick was killed by friendly fire? Perhaps even assassinated by American interests? Was the tragedy in Oosay, in other words, a contract hit by the Nash administration?

"Seem far-fetched?" Stone had asked rhetorically. "Hear the facts for yourself. Then you decide.

"If you don't know, General Roderick was a controversial figure in military circles," Stone explained for his listeners. "He's hailed as a martyr now, a fallen hero. But in life, Roderick was a man bold enough—or some said impudent enough—to be an outspoken critic of Pentagon policy and the Nash administration. He was a decorated soldier, however, and too beloved to be fired. But it worried the brass that he was winning supporters among a silent majority of rank-and-file soldiers. And the more supporters he won, the more angry he made the administration."

Stone walked through "the evidence." The general had written a controversial essay in an influential foreign policy journal attacking U.S. policy, which he said was breeding more terrorists than it was killing through its reliance on drones. Roderick himself had nearly died in a bombing three years ago in Iraq, and there were "questions" then about the circumstances. A website in Austria last year published a story citing unnamed intelligence sources to the effect of "it has been said that there have been calls for the outspoken Roderick to be 'taken out.'"

"Ugly rumors," Stone said. "But they make it plausible to wonder if General Roderick's death might be different than we have been assuming.

"Who knew Roderick was in Oosay? With whom was he really meeting? Why didn't he leave that night? Who knew he had decided to spend an extra day in the compound? The answers all point to his superiors, many of them his critics. Only a theory, but something that needs to be investigated."

Some things you do yourself, Bakke believes. Aides came and went, and when they left they might begin to leak. He gets out one of his three personal phones and sends an instant message to a writer he knows, Marc Filippo, an editor at the popular conservative website True Flag.

"You should listen to this podcast," Bakke messages. "I think it might make a good piece for True Flag. Please message me if you decide to publish something."

Two hours later, a grateful Filippo posts a piece summarizing Stone's podcast. Filippo has adopted a tone of even greater skepticism. Thus at the blog's conclusion, when Filippo credits Stone's theories for having some merit, it has the added weight of apparent surprise.

True Flag has 40 million followers a month. And Filippo's team knows how to write headlines for the Web: *"Could General Brian Roderick have died from friendly fire—that wasn't entirely an accident?"*

**THAT AFTERNOON,** in a scrum with reporters by the members-only elevators, Senator Bakke is asked how he feels the committee is progressing.

"I think we should be looking at some new possibilities about what happened."

"What possibilities are those?" asks a reporter from NewsMix, a new conservative website, which has been tipped to pose this question.

"I keep getting sent messages from my constituents that we look into theories that General Roderick was killed by friendly fire, and possibly—that his death was no accident."

"What do you mean no accident?" a reporter from the *Wall Street Journal* asks in surprise.

Bakke is careful not to say the words himself: "It's just a theory, but it connects evidence from several sources. So it's worth looking at. We owe it to the American people to be thorough, all the more because we are a single committee representing both the House and Senate. Because of that, we need to make sure no theory has been overlooked—or covered up—especially by the administration's own so-called internal inquiry."

"Are you referring to the inquiry led by Peter Rena and Randi Brooks?" asks the *New York Times*.

"I am."

And with that, the stray claims of Hackford Stone's obscure podcast have made it into the mainstream press.

Bakke turns and heads into the elevator. A single aide rides with him, a young woman who is his body person that day, keeping his schedule and keeping him on time.

The aide is pretty and young, and she is tempted to ask, "You're not serious, are you, Senator?" But she manages only, "Senator, do you think that theory is even possible?"

"Oh, we need to investigate *everything*."


**ARVID LUPSA SPOTS THE ARTICLE** in Political Animal an hour later. It not only mentions Bakke's accusation but also describes the groundswell of talk in social media about friendly fire that has built up from the True Flag posting online.

Lupsa carries his laptop into Randi Brooks's office and the two of them wander down to Rena's.

"Flesh-eating zombie time," Brooks says, handing Rena a printout. "And remember, nothing in Zombieland ever dies." Rena scans the story. "Bakke is a man not to be underestimated," Brooks says. She looks at Rena a moment longer than usual. "Given where we are."

The comment does not need elaboration. Rena knows where

they are. They are convinced members of President Nash's national security team are involved in a cover-up. The two Oosay survivors who had lied to them had both testified this week in closed session. So had two other men they suspected might be involved in the cover-up, or were at least aware of it, CIA Director Owen Webster and DIA Director Frederick Willey. And two days ago Rena's team confronted the man who they thought might be at the center of it, Colonel Henry Arroyo of the DIA.

Now this—an accusation by Senator Bakke that Roderick's death was an assassination. Was it possible? Is that what was being covered up? Or was Bakke simply trying to shake things up, much as Rena had with Arroyo yesterday morning?

His cell rings: Matt Alabama calling.

"Turn on BNS. You have incoming."

*Incoming,* the old military word for artillery dropping on you, is Washington-speak for someone attacking you in the media.

Senator Bakke is a guest on Jack Anthem's afternoon news roundup *Focal Point.*

"I have proof that the outside investigators in the case, Peter Rena and Randi Brooks, have the drone footage and are withholding it from the committee. I worry, now, in light of new reports, that they might be suppressing it because it provides evidence that General Roderick may have been killed by friendly fire. Or worse."

"Are you suggesting, Senator, an assassination?" Anthem asks. He looks genuinely shocked.

"We're trying to arrange a special witness for the committee in a few days who will shed light on this."

Anthem tries to unpack what Bakke has just said. *Has he seen the video?* Anthem asks.

No, that's just the point.

*How does he know what it shows?*

That is exactly what the committee and the American public need to learn.

"You watching?" Alabama asks.

"The pace of chaos," Rena says.

"What?"

"Something I read," Rena says. "It's the idea that there is no such thing as chaos. The idea that something is chaotic is just the perception people have when things begin to move faster than they can process them. We get confused and perceive the normal random pattern of events as things spinning out of control. They were never in control in the first place. Chaos is a constant state. It's just our ability to perceive that changes."

"Well shit, Yoda," Alabama says. "If you really have that video, and you are obstructing Congress from getting it, you and Randi better get lawyers."

It is the new Washington: public service and private lawyers.

Brooks is yelling at the television. "That is so fucking outrageous!"

Rena is off the phone.

"You know what this is, Peter. It's classic diversion. People are criticizing his committee. So you pretend you're on to some conspiracy, something else, to distract from your own problems."

The term du jour for this sleight of hand in town is "what aboutism," as in "Hey, what about this?"

Rena's feelings about Bakke's claims are different than his partner's, however. Yes, the idea that they are part of the cover-up surely is a diversion. But is the theory that Roderick was assassinated by U.S. interests completely out of the realm of possibility?

Rena's phone is vibrating. He is getting multiple calls now. He recognizes some of the numbers as reporters. His office phone begins to light up as well.

"Can you handle the press for me?" he asks Brooks.

"Where are you going?" Her partner has a habit of sometimes vanishing without explaining himself. He always had a reason. But it is still annoying.

Rena begins to gather his bag.

"Me?" Rena says. "Gonna see a man about a murder conspiracy."

## FORTY-THREE

On almost any day Congress is in session, one will find senators having a drink or dinner at Bistro Bis. Often the people with them are more powerful than the senators they are trying to influence. The food is a mix of French and modern American, and the bar is large enough to provide privacy for those in the dining room.

Rena has not picked the place. Dick Bakke has.

He is waiting for Rena at the bar holding bourbon that has the word *Kentucky* in the name twice. *Kentucky Tavern Kentucky Straight Bourbon Whiskey.* Rena thinks you should never order anything that has to try that hard. He orders a Grey Goose martini.

"What are we doing here, Mr. Rena?"

"I want you to tell me what you have."

That wins a smile from Bakke, and Rena notices Samantha Reese enter Bistro Bis and take a seat near the front of the bar by the windows.

"You want me to tell you what I have?"

"Whatever it is, I promise we will pursue it. If Roderick was killed by friendly fire—on purpose or not—we want to get to the truth. That's all. No cover-up. I promise. You don't know me, but I have a problem with that sort of thing."

A long look from Bakke.

"Just hand it over?"

"You have my word."

Bakke's reaction is something between a snicker and a gasp. "You are a Boy Scout, aren't you?"

"An Eagle Scout, actually."

"You'll be seeing things in the next few days that will be very interesting," Bakke says. "It will start to come out."

Rena gives Bakke a stare that Randi Brooks calls "the read." It is something he has done his whole life, trying to understand people by watching them. He refined it in army interrogation rooms around the world, and now he was paid to use a variation of it on some of the most powerful people in the country.

Randi Brooks would call this whole meeting "a read," Rena's habit of wanting to confront antagonists in person, ask them questions, and observe their body language, speech, and mannerisms as they try to answer.

It has taken less time to read Bakke than Rena expected.

"You have nothing," he tells the senator. "You don't have the video. You don't know what's on it. You have no witnesses."

"What does that drone video show?" Bakke says. He has raised his voice.

"I'm not authorized to tell you that, Senator."

"If it disproves General Roderick was killed by Americans, or people working on their behalf, you *will* tell me, Mr. Rena."

Rena leans closer and, slowly, just above a whisper, says, "The video is classified. If I were to reveal anything about it to you, that would constitute a federal crime."

Bakke smiles a strange, chilling smile back, the kind you recall in the middle of the night. "You are a traitor to your party, Mr. Rena."

"You can only be a traitor to your country, Senator."

"You know where this country is headed?" Bakke asks.

"I find it's hard enough to understand where it's been."

The Bakke smile is back. "Those who don't understand the past are doomed to repeat it? You really should have come armed, Mr. Rena, with more than clichés."

"You know the one about ends never justifying means?" Rena says. "That one's true, too. It's why conducting yourself with honor is so important. Because in politics there is no end, is there? The battles just go on and on."

Bakke doesn't like being lectured to, which is why Rena is doing it. He wants to see the senator angry, to see what he has.

Bakke frowns and leans in toward Rena. His voice has become more liquid. "My party conducted itself with honor and good manners for decades. We compromised on everything until the government became so bloated it was an addiction. And now the Democrats are out of ideas. And the country is failing. I'm fighting to change that, and if I need to scorch the earth a little, so be it."

"And after you have scorched the earth and made the truth into a joke," Rena says, "how do you govern?"

Bakke's unsettling smile has been replaced by something angrier and more sincere. "The truth? Don't underestimate me, Mr. Rena. I'm not the cynic you think I am. But I understand that the truth is bigger than a few grubby facts. It's a mistake to be too literal. Knowing that is why my side is winning."

"Good night, Senator," Rena says, rising.

He has learned what he came for.

"I'm going to take you down," Bakke says.

Rena stops. He doesn't like bullies. They're usually cowards, and the threats they make are usually empty. But that doesn't mean the people who make them aren't dangerous. He looks hard at Bakke, a man who is balding, overweight, physically awkward, cunning, and relentless. Rena studies him a moment longer. Then he turns and leaves.

**ON THE SIDEWALK,** he has to pause to calm his breathing. He's learned two things.

One, Bakke is bluffing about having evidence Roderick died of friendly fire—let alone some kind of assassination.

Two, the man is more dangerous than Rena thought.

He pulls out his phone. There are two text messages.

One from Vic: "Heard the accusations from Bakke. Hope you are ok."

She'd called earlier, and he had not called her back.

The other message is from Brooks. The Oosay Committee would be resuming hearings next week. There are rumors of a surprise witness.

About ninety hours away.

How much more could happen, Rena wonders, in ninety hours?

# PART FOUR

# WELCOME TO THE JUNGLE

## FEBRUARY 8 TO FEBRUARY 13

## FORTY-FOUR

## SATURDAY, FEBRUARY 8
## OOSAY, MORAT

From the fall of 1908 until early 1910, American novelist Thomas Strong Adams lived in Oosay, Morat, in rented rooms near the waterfront neighborhood called "Nuit," or the "Night." It was a poor area full of coffeehouses, bars, and dance halls, but it was a favorite at the time of a small knot of young American and European expatriate artists and writers. It was in these rooms that Adams wrote his second novel, *The Forgotten Heart,* which would propel him from a promising curiosity to a contemporary of Ford Madox Ford and E. M. Forster, and would even draw comparisons to Henry James. Adams would write two more novels of loss, love, and manners set on the African continent. Together, the "African trilogy" became the core of his literary legacy. Well into the 1960s, Adams remained a source of pride to the educated elite of North Africa. Even during the regime of Ali Nori, the Adams home was still a prominent attraction in guidebooks. The house, open for tours, and nearby spots featured as key scenes in his stories were highlights of "literary Africa" day trip excursions. In the evening, tourists liked to visit the Nuit cafes Adams had frequented.

In the latter part of the twentieth century, Adams's work started to become a source of angry reconsideration, particularly among

Islamic intellectuals. They described the writing, and especially his innocent white young female heroines, as subtly anti-African and anti-Muslim.

At just after 11:30 P.M. local time in Oosay on Saturday, February 8, a series of remote-controlled bombs were detonated around the foundation of the Adams house. The explosions and subsequent fires destroyed the house and several other buildings in the Nuit.

According to the cursory police inquiry, residents of the adjacent buildings had been warned to be out of their homes at the time of the explosions, which reduced the loss of human life. International investigators would subsequently note this fact—a desire to limit civilian casualties—as a new feature in the tactical handbook of the Islamic State Army, after ISA contacted the media to take credit for the attack.

From his watch point near the old Catholic church on Owl Hill above the city Assam Muzaar Baah watched the explosion and the fires for only a few minutes. Then he instructed his friend Amin to deliver the message to Agence France-Presse and Moratian state radio. The message was five sentences long:

> The people of Morat are shedding themselves of the oppressive history of the West. Tonight Moratian patriots have destroyed the building where the infidel American Thomas Adams lived and wrote his shameless, obscene and oppressive novel. Today Morat is taking back its history. We venerate its own poets. We are eliminating the memory of yours.

## FORTY-FIVE

## SUNDAY, FEBRUARY 9
## WASHINGTON, D.C.

The bombing of the Adams house fills only about twenty seconds on the three old-style broadcast nightly news programs Sunday evening in the United States. In the simple algebra of news, the limited number of dead makes the story less important.

The incident receives more attention on the various U.S. cable news channels. The one most critical of the Nash administration, TNC, devotes the largest portion of its Sunday programming to the incident, including a prime-time special from 9 to 11 P.M. focused largely on the question of whether the Nash administration has done more to destroy the legacy of Western civilization on the African continent than any other administration in history. The question is essentially rhetorical. No one is invited to question the underlying premise. The only discussion is about how much damage Nash has done.

On the BNS cable network, anchor Jack Anthem interviews a Carleton College historian with a more measured view of the incident's impact. While certainly the house had literary significance, Thomas Adams lived in many homes during his lifetime, many of which have been torn down now. "A writer ultimately lives on his pages," the historian says. The bombing, he concludes, has a symbolism that matters more to Moratians.

Of the wire stories that circulate, the BBC account is the most complete. It is also the one Ellen Wiley spots sometime late Sunday morning and sends electronically to Rena, Brooks, and the staff.

One fact in the story strikes Peter Rena above the others. Although no link is made directly, a Moratian security source is quoted as saying the "bomb signature" on the explosive device could be similar to that used to destroy the gates on the American compound in Oosay in December, which killed General Roderick and three others.

Most bomb makers, Rena knows, build their devices employing certain techniques that they repeat, even unconsciously, so-called bomb signatures that identify the makers almost like fingerprints.

That same detail catches the eye of computer network analyst Avery Holland. Late on Monday morning, he calls Jill Bishop of the *Washington Tribune*.

"After this bombing thing, I did a little digging. A couple of things were starting to bug me," Holland says.

"What things?"

Holland thought in maps and numbers, and Bishop sometimes had trouble following his words.

"Senator Bakke's friendly-fire theory, for one."

"Seriously, Avery?"

"Look, even bullshit has an origin story, Jill. These things usually connect to something. Even if it's a movie or a novel or whatever."

"Unless you have some evidence, put me in the bullshit category. Was there a second thing?"

"It's complicated. But related."

Although Avery's mind is often a mystery to Bishop, when she does finally break its code, it's usually worth it.

"You gonna tell me?"

"It's something we should discuss in person."

They meet at Brixton, a new British-style pub in an old plumbing warehouse in the Shaw neighborhood of D.C., a formerly poor area now popular among white millennials and dotted with million-dollar rehabbed row houses. Brixton's food is pub fare, and the place features what Bishop considers a fetishistically large number of beers.

After they order two of the beers and some food, Bishop can control herself no longer. "I'm gonna blow my brains out, Avery, if you don't tell me what the other *thing* about the bombing was that was bothering you."

"The bomb signature," he says.

"What's a bomb signature?"

"Every bomber is unique. The way they build their bombs, the way they utilize fragmentation, wire, timers. These signatures identify bomb makers in the same way handwriting can identify an author. The bomb signatures here suggest the guys who blew up the author's house were the same guys who killed Roderick."

"So what?"

"I wanted to see if I could maybe test that. See if there were any digital markers from anyone near this bombing that resembled markers the last time. Remember when we tried to pinpoint who masterminded the first attack?"

"Yeah, I remember. I put it on page one. So what?"

"'So what' is there's a digital imprint from this site that appears to have been in contact with a device associated with the U.S. government."

"Sorry, Avery. Can you try that again in English?"

"Someone was near this bombing who was also at the first Oosay attack, the one that killed Roderick."

"Of course they were," Bishop says. "You just told me it was likely the same bombers."

"Yes, but that device, that person, had been in digital contact with someone in the U.S. government. In fact right before the incident that killed Roderick. That night. And more than once."

"You telling me that someone involved in the death of Roderick was in contact with the U.S. government?"

"No. I can't go that far. What I know is that a digital phone near the bombing two nights ago was also at the scene of the first Oosay attack two months ago. And that phone has been in contact with a phone associated with the U.S. government. For all I know this is some CIA guy who's hanging around watching. Or maybe it's something else. Maybe it's an American who killed Roderick, like Bakke's nut-job network says. But why would that person then also blow up a historic landmark? I don't have any idea. I don't know what this is. But it's there. The digital connection is there. And you should look into it. I can't take it any further. But you can."

Bishop tries to process what Holland is saying.

She runs it by him a couple more times. Then she plays out in her mind how she could track down those facts—that someone at both bombings had some connection to the U.S. government, or the U.S. military.

Jesus.

It would be hard. Talon won't help her. This involves trying to understand "sources and methods," the hallowed ground of how American intelligence people gather what they know. For all she and Talon trusted each other—no, it was more than that—for all they were friends, Talon never went near sources and methods. She had never discussed with Bishop the techniques and technology used. That was sacrosanct. That got people killed in the field and fired back home. Talon would leak to stop operations she considered stupid. She would expose lies and hypocrisy. But she would never reveal sources and methods, never endanger colleagues in the field. No matter where it led. Never. Bishop would have to find other ways to track this down.

She leans back in her chair and ponders.

When lunch is over, she begins making phone calls, using one of the burner phones she employs for phone work, since the damn

*Tribune* lines are so easily tracked. She works all afternoon. She gets a couple of people who say they will try to help. When she doesn't hear back, she presses. And begins to sense she is touching a nerve.

**CHANGING INTO CLOTHES** for a night run a few hours later, Peter Rena receives the text from an unknown number.

"You have a visitor. Look at the vehicle in front of your house."

A black SUV so enormous only a political figure or a drug dealer could be inside is idling out on the street. Rena's sense of alarm jumps to level ten. He has a gun, rarely used, locked in a gun safe in his bedroom. He wonders for a moment where Samantha Reese, his mystery bodyguard and her team, might be. Then, unable to see any other choice, he walks outside.

The back passenger-side window starts to slide down. For a moment Rena considers diving into a bush that separates his row house yard from his neighbor's.

"Hello, Peter." The voice comes from half a face, the other half still in shadow. The face leans forward. It is Anthony Rousseau, the old CIA man.

Rena can feel the wet of an adrenaline sweat release over his spine. He relaxes slightly and walks toward the Escalade.

"What are you doing in D.C., Tony?"

"I've been in town awhile."

Rousseau pushes open the door.

"Come inside the car, Peter. So we can talk."

Rena slides in. The car has the smell of being recently detailed, a clean antiseptic odor.

"You piqued my interest, Peter, with your visit at Christmas. I've been trying to help you since. I assume you knew that."

What men like Rousseau consider help, Rena can only imagine. This whole mess was caused by people of influence imagining how they could help.

"Why are you here, Tony?"

"I need to alert you to something. That reporter, Jill Bishop, is beginning to ask questions about something dangerous. I don't know what she's got, honestly. But my sources say she's getting close to something critical—something she herself doesn't understand. And it will damage the United States in a significant way if she keeps going. She is bumping into something that must remain a secret. In other words, you and Randi are running out of time. You need to move now. You need to wrap this up now. Put an end to this."

For an instant, the words echo in Rena's ear and then begin to swirl together with all the advice, all the commands of the last few weeks—then from years back, converging into a stream of admonitions, a river of instruction and obedience. They must stay ahead of Congress. He must pick a political side. They must do this on their own. They must put an end to this now.

"An end to what?"

"Bishop's story," Rousseau says. "You need to make it go away. To do that, you need to once and for all find out what happened in Oosay. But you better do it now. I mean tomorrow or the next day. Even tonight. Whatever cards you have left, play them."

Rousseau is serious.

"Do you understand? The Oosay Committee resumes Wednesday midmorning, less than two days from now. And Bishop's story could break before that."

All Rena can feel is his exhaustion, but he summons himself. "If we're going to wrap this up, I need a favor from you. We need to see Shane. As soon as possible."

Shane, the secretary of defense, the iconoclast, like Roderick, who was trying to change the war on terror. Shane, who has eluded them longer than any other of Nash's people.

Rousseau gives Rena a hound dog stare. "I'll call you," he says.

Rena steps out of the Escalade and watches it pull away.

Back in his house, Rena thinks about calling Vic, to hear her voice and talk through things they have been avoiding. But he can't now.

He needs to make another call instead. They had sent Walt Smolonsky back to Europe last week to find the missing communications analysts who had been in the Barracks that night. It is one of their last cards to play, and they are already playing it. He needs to call Smolonsky.

## FORTY-SIX

## MONDAY, FEBRUARY 10
## WASHINGTON, D.C.

In Washington, David Traynor lives in a brownstone on P Street near Dupont Circle. His wife, Mariette, had restored the outside to its auburn brick Victorian glory. Inside she'd created a stunning example of architect Mies van der Rohe's twentieth-century modernist Bauhaus vision.

The cybersecurity consultant Jimmy Collins is sitting in Traynor's minimalist living room. Collins is not wearing a cowboy hat, but he does have on a pair of black Lucchese boots, the better ones made in El Paso, not the ones done now in Mexico. He is playing with the fireplace remote, which has a series of buttons, one that says fireplace on/off and another that indicates temperature.

"This thing for the heat or the fireplace?" Jimmy asks.

"Both," Traynor says.

"The fireplace heats the room?"

Traynor sighs. "One button controls the fireplace. The second controls the heat, so if the fireplace heats the room, it won't get too hot."

"Screw it," Jimmy says, handing Traynor the remote. "Too many buttons."

"You build computer security systems, and you think the remote on my fireplace has too many buttons?"

"Yeah. And you have too much money."

Traynor changes the subject: "So this was ridiculously easy, after all," he says. "Only took the weekend. What ya got?" Down to business.

"We got juice from tracking two personal emails. Dick Bakke and Curtis Gains's chief of staff, a guy named Tom Beyers, who is also operating as chief of staff for the Oosay Committee. You really wanna know this?"

Traynor sits down and gives a look that says yes, I really want to know. Jimmy takes a breath.

"Dick Bakke is one relentless guy. Hundreds of emails a day. Like nine hundred—and that's just his personal account. I didn't touch the Senate stuff. No need."

"And?" Traynor says.

"Bakke loves his wife fine," Collins says. "Gains's guy, Beyers, is having an affair. They both think they're running the free world."

"Did you happen to find anything useful?"

"You gonna give this to WeLeaks?" Jimmy asks.

"Jimmy, as bad as the other side is, my side seems to be losing at the moment because of a right-wing conspiracy that James Nash murdered a U.S. general in the field in some kind of cover-up. I'd like something that could blunt that insane theory and connect us back to reality. If possible. You on my side?"

Jimmy sighs and makes a show of it. Then he takes a manila envelope out of his briefcase. Inside are printouts of the contents of personal emails for the last month of Senator Dick Bakke and Oosay Committee chief of staff Tom Beyers.

Jimmy hands the envelope to Traynor. "Let's just say there is a lot of bragging in private about how they're gonna use the hearings to screw the administration and win the next election."

Traynor smiles.

"You shouldn't be doing this," Jimmy says. "I shouldn't be doing this."

"You should be helping Dick Bakke win the next election? That your point?"

Jimmy says: "Is that what we're doing? Fixing elections?"

"It's what we're stopping," Traynor says.

Jimmy lets go of the envelope. The computer expert knows Traynor is thinking of running for president himself. The senator has even asked Rena and Brooks, the Oosay investigators, to conduct opposition research on him so he can anticipate what would come at him. In other words, Jimmy thinks, in theory stopping Dick Bakke from being president could help David Traynor get the job instead.

Traynor opens the envelope.

"I have to worry about you, Senator?" Jimmy says.

"Now you sound like my mother. She's always asking me what I'm going to do with all this money. Like it was a mistake to get rich."

Jimmy raises his eyebrows to suggest it is always good to listen to your mother.

"You got any rye?"

"Other room," Traynor says as he reads. "Next to the bookshelf."

Jimmy has highlighted some of the best emails in yellow marker. Senator Dick Bakke speculated on the best ways to pin blame on the administration and hurt Daniel Shane, the secretary of defense who was also considering a run for president. There were a lot of emails soliciting questions from different interest groups that he could ask in the hearings to damage both Nash and Shane and also Traynor himself. That was a way of currying favor with those interest groups—to carry their water for them on TV.

As for Tom Beyers, the Oosay Committee chief of staff, he is mostly a braggart. In a lot of the highlighted emails he is telling people he thinks the Oosay investigation would be a career maker, a path to the White House for the GOP—and for Tom Beyers.

The young, Traynor thinks, are so dumb.

"What you gonna do with these?" Collins asks as he returns with his drink.

"Not me. You," Traynor says. "Use one of your anonymous hacker friends to send this to those assholes at WeLeaks."

"Your mother is right," says Collins.

"Hey, dude," Traynor shoots back, "as Guns N' Roses said, 'Welcome to the jungle.'"

## FORTY-SEVEN

## WEDNESDAY, FEBRUARY 12, 9:50 A.M.
## WASHINGTON, D.C.

The email story breaks twenty-four hours later, Tuesday evening.

Senate Majority Leader Susan Stroud quickly postpones the Oosay Committee hearing scheduled the next morning.

Instead, she summons a small group to her private Capitol office.

Three are there to be taken to the woodshed—Senator Richard Bakke, Congressman Curtis Gains, and Gains's aide Tom Beyers.

Four are there to judge them: Stroud, the Speaker of the House, Senator Wendy Upton, and Senator Llewellyn Burke, the Republican from Michigan.

"I asked Lew to join us as chairman of the Armed Services Committee," Stroud says. "And for his good sense."

Every media outlet in the stratosphere has run with the emails, which were sent by an anonymous hacker group in Europe to the website WeLeaks. *"Emails Reveal Oosay Committee Insiders See Probe as Largely Political,"* reads the headline in the *New York Times*. A few mainstream outlets mused about the ethics of publishing stolen emails. But the emails were real, the editors concluded, and in the twenty-first century, the public, not the press, will be the arbiter of their propriety.

Stroud herself never loved this committee, everyone knew, but she had assented to it to accommodate the rising powers on the right in her party, powers that she knew in time would engulf and destroy her. But not, she thinks, today.

Bakke sits on a sofa across from Stroud. Next to him, looking as if they have been called to the principal's office, is Gains, and beside him his chief of staff, Beyers.

On a facing sofa sits the Speaker of the House, hands cupped on his stomach, and next to him Burke. Stroud has taken an armchair.

Wendy Upton is standing at the window overlooking the National Mall, too agitated to sit. In a single glance, she can see the Smithsonian museums, the Washington Monument, the memorials to Vietnam, Korea, and World War II, the reflecting pool, and the Lincoln Memorial. Halfway down the mall on the right, in what were marshy flats at the time, Thomas Jefferson and his architect Pierre L'Enfant placed the White House, so the people's legislatures would always look down on the country's chief executive.

Bakke has already started talking.

"Before we go too far, let's remember this leak was a criminal act. Private emails were stolen." He glances at Stroud, the only person here with even nominal authority over him. "And in private there's nothing wrong with speculating on the political impact of hearings. Indeed, I said nothing in those emails I have not said on the record."

Chairman Gains has his eyes in his lap.

Stroud raises her hand, palm out, a signal she uses to get people to stop talking, particularly men. Bakke stops, and Stroud turns to Senator Burke.

"Lew, I asked you here *because* you're not part of this committee. I wanted an outside read on the damage and what we might do."

Burke shifts his body toward Bakke in a way that conveys respect. It is one of Burke's gifts that he can make everyone in the room feel listened to.

"I sympathize, Dick," he begins. "We can't govern the country in a fishbowl, without some zone of privacy. Any more than we can govern it on cable TV." The last remark is a gentle reminder how often Bakke is in front of cameras.

"But we need to recognize a political reality. Our party controls both legislatures, so the responsibility here is entirely on us as Republicans. We need to show skeptics we can be serious and fair, and show our faithful we can be thorough. To do that, we have to be above reproach."

Burke wrinkles his brow in concern. "Your emails, Dick, have brought reproach on us."

He turns to the staffer, Beyers. "And Mr. Beyers's emails, which put his personal ambition above his responsibility, do worse than that."

"Respectfully," Bakke answers, before anyone can agree with Burke, "we're ignoring the elephant in the room, which isn't my emails. The problem is this committee has gotten nowhere."

Bakke glances at Gains. Stroud uses the slight hesitation to interrupt.

"Mr. Speaker," she says, "what do you think?"

She looks at the frumpy man on the sofa, third in the constitutional line of succession, two heartbeats from the presidency. The Speaker shifts his girth. He knows what the people in this room tend to think of him. It's fine. He has learned the advantages of being underrated.

"The elephant in the room, if I may, isn't the committee's progress. It's the presidential election. Young Senator Bakke here is almost certain to be a candidate. And there are some in our party who would also like to see Senator Upton here run as well. And on the other side, Senator Traynor looks like he might run. And possibly Senator Kaplan, a former comedian, God help us."

No one laughs.

"My fear is if we let this committee become a campaign event, we all suffer. I say let's contain the committee, focus it, and not let it turn into a fishing expedition trolling for anything bad we can find about the Nash administration."

The Speaker is talking in code, but everyone in the room has the decryption key: he hates Dick Bakke and the new right in his party— even more than Stroud does. Every House member has to run in the next election, and if Bakke is head of the ticket, the Speaker thinks they all may suffer. So make Bakke pay for the email leak. Never let the opportunity of a good disaster go to waste.

Bakke is reading the code, too, and the code in this room, he thinks, is awful. Stroud has set him up. The only other genuine conservative here is Gains, and the congressman is terrified. The only way out of here alive, Bakke thinks—the only way the conservative movement has flowered in the first place—is to blast his way out.

"Mr. Speaker, I'm sorry. Not only can this committee's findings be whatever we discover. They must be. If we find the Nash administration is hiding something we weren't looking for, we have a responsibility to get to the bottom of it. If we find out they murdered someone in the White House, would we tell the American people we didn't care because that isn't what we were asked to look at?"

"Do you have evidence someone was murdered in the White House, Senator?" Burke says with a flash of more genuine anger than he usually reveals.

"Do you have evidence someone wasn't?" Bakke answers.

"Is that the standard now?" Burke says. "We imagine a crime and ask the president to prove his innocence?"

Bakke smiles like a hungry crocodile. "We're not a court. We're a congressional committee. So let's not fool ourselves: this is about politics. And frankly it feels to me as if you're embarrassed by that. Even afraid of it. Don't be. When we look back at this committee, no one will care what liberal newspaper columnists wrote. What they will wonder is one thing: Did we win the next election? Or did we lose it?"

The room is silent. For a moment, Bakke thinks perhaps he has prevailed.

"Enough."

Every head turns.

The voice belongs to Wendy Upton, and it contains an authority many of them have not heard before.

"The problem, Senator," she says, "is not any lack of passion by the people in this room, or some fear of politics. The problem is we used the discovery of political emails by a Democratic aide at the State Department to trigger this committee. Now, your own private emails suggest the motive behind the committee was always just to harm the president and gain ground in the next election, perhaps for your own candidacy. That makes everyone in this room, and in our party, a hypocrite. Whether the emails were private or not, whether their being stolen is illegal or not, whether anyone agrees with you or not. That is the politics of this."

Bakke's heart begins to sink. He has never heard the polite and careful Upton sound so venomous.

Upton moves from the window to the center of the room and the rest of the group.

"Our job now," she continues, "is to limit the damage those emails have done."

She looks at the Speaker.

"Sir, I know you prefer to handle these things in private, before they get out of hand. Perhaps you could do that today by asking Mr. Beyers here, whose emails have embarrassed the House, to tender his resignation this afternoon, and ask Oosay chairman Gains here to accept that resignation. That would be your acknowledgment that this committee is fair-minded and more than a political proposition."

The Speaker is kneading his hands together in his lap as if he were feeling the idea in his fingers. "Yes," he says. "I believe that is a good idea."

Upton turns to Bakke. "I can't tell you what do, Senator," she says, "but when Mr. Beyers's departure is announced, reporters will most assuredly call you for comment. I suspect the majority leader would appreciate your promise not to embarrass her, or yourself."

It is a subtle twist of the knife, getting him to pledge to make Stroud happy.

Bakke's own hard life had taught him something about defeat, and when he arrived in the Senate Aggie Tucker had given him an axiom that put it into words: never forget and never forgive and always nurse your resentments longer than your enemies do. He will remember this moment.

## FORTY-EIGHT

## WEDNESDAY, FEBRUARY 12, 12:30 P.M.
## WASHINGTON, D.C.

What could happen in ninety hours, Rena had wondered.

A U.S. senator had tried to implicate them in an alleged assassination plot of an American general in the field. The senator's private email, and that of a congressional aide, had been hacked and leaked to the press. The former CIA director of operations had come to Rena's house and told him the *Washington Tribune* was about to break a story that could do irreparable harm to the U.S. war on terrorism. And the only thing they knew for sure about what had happened in Morat was that the president and his own national security team no longer trusted each other.

The country feels at war with itself, as if the foundations under the stone and marble federal buildings that lined the city, which were built to express the nation's pride in the idea that people could self-govern, were decaying from some long-neglected rot and were about to collapse in on themselves.

Dick Bakke's voice still rang in Rena's ears from five nights before, mocking the word *truth*. Maybe knowing the truth about what happened that night in Africa *was* a fool's errand. Maybe thinking that knowing the literal facts about anything would get you closer to the truth *was* as simplistic as Bakke suggested, a worn-out trope, or a naïve antiquated notion from another time, like a gentleman's honor.

They have one more chance, a Hail Mary. Then their time will be up. The Oosay Committee will reconvene, delayed a day or two. Or the *Tribune*'s mystery story will run. And they will have failed.

He and Brooks have almost reached the entrance to the Four Seasons hotel in Georgetown, where they've been summoned by Anthony Rousseau.

Brooks's phone rings. She looks at the number—the *Washington Tribune*.

"It's Jill Bishop," she says. "If I answer this, even to tell her I can't talk, she could say she's reached me. That might be enough for her to run her story, saying we offered no comment."

"Let it go to voice mail," Rena suggests. "Then she hasn't reached you."

He has no idea whether that gambit will work at the moment, but eventually it would not: "The investigating firm Rena, Brooks & Toppin did not respond to repeated efforts to reach them for comment."

Brooks lets the call go.

"I wonder if we're at the end of the road."

Brooks only murmurs the words, as much to herself as to Rena.

Sometimes his partner's wonderfully strategic mind works against her, Rena thinks. She can see all the possible moves on the chess board. And the effort of trying to assess which one to make can paralyze her.

"We're only at the end of the road if we stop," he says out loud.

At the entrance to the Four Seasons, Anthony Rousseau is waiting. He has not told them why they should come, and he says nothing as they follow him through the revolving doors and down the hotel's long, wide hallway. Rousseau leads them to the darkened entrance of the restaurant called Bourbon Steak at the rear of the hotel, where you can order an ounce of forty-year-old single-malt scotch for $230. Rousseau whispers something to the maître d' and they're led to a private room. Security agents with earpieces stand outside the door.

They enter, and the secretary of defense, Daniel Xavier Shane, turns from the window overlooking the Potomac.

"Mr. Secretary," Rousseau says, "I'm afraid I can't join you for lunch after all. I have to go back to Seattle suddenly. But my friends Randi Brooks and Peter Rena can keep our date for me. I know how much the president would appreciate it. And I know how much you have been trying to see them. I'm so glad this worked out. Please excuse me."

And before Shane musters a response Rousseau is gone.

The secretary regards the two fixers he has been avoiding for weeks with something between fury and surrender.

"I should throw you two out on your ear."

But he holds out a hand, inviting Brooks to sit at the small table set for four, and pushes her chair in for her as she sits.

Rena has no idea what to expect. But now they can ask their questions, which in the end amount to only one: What went wrong in Morat you are covering up? They are convinced now Shane is the only one likely to tell them. Shane moves to a chair and sits.

He is tall and athletic, even at sixty-two, still a quarterback's frame inside his navy-blue suit. Big hands, dimpled chin, Irish handsome. It is a face etched by a large and successful life.

"You two have a helluva job," says Shane.

"Finding the truth?" says Brooks.

"Yes, tough town for it," Shane says.

His voice has the familiar timbre of so many soldiers Rena has known. The words start low in his gut and sound as if they were filtered through gravel.

"I looked up your record," he says to Rena. "You remind me of me. Order of the Arrow." It's a reference to an honor society of Eagle Scouts to which Rena and Shane both belonged. "And foolishly

bullheaded," he adds. "A right and wrong complex." That's a reference to the end of Rena's military career.

Shane had spent his life rubbing against the grain, too. He was the
kind of boy adults admired but most kids thought too straight—an
Eagle Scout, high school quarterback, president of the Young Republicans and the Catholic Youth group. In the rebel 1970s at William &
Mary, Shane had grown more religious and dutiful. He joined ROTC
when others were protesting its presence on campus and wrote college editorials calling for universal mandatory government service
while Nixon was ending the draft. There was a quote in Wiley's file
of Shane saying that in college he felt a growing call to public service
but anguished over whether to become a priest or enter politics.

He chose public life, becoming an intelligence officer in the air
force, attending law school, joining the staff of the Senate Armed
Services Committee. He ran for Congress and four years later won a
seat in the Senate from Pennsylvania after 9/11.

In the most deliberative body in the world, Shane became
even more independent. He compared the war in Iraq to Vietnam
and drew fire from his own party for a speech in which he declared
that "questioning the government does not embolden the enemy, it
makes our government stronger."

*Going viral* was a new phrase then. Shane was among the first
politicians to whom it was attached.

James Nash's relationship with his military was getting worse.
On the eve of his reelection campaign twenty-eight months ago, he
asked Shane to join his administration. Frustrated by the Senate,
and about to change parties, Shane agreed.

Critics saw an opportunist. Supporters saw a man of intellectual honesty and old-fashioned independence.

"He's a fount of contradictions," Wiley's file had concluded. "A
devoutly religious spy, a soldier skeptical of war, an ambitious politician who goes to mass every morning. He's like a chemical compound that's inherently unstable."

The expression on Shane's face in front of them now is playful and intrigued, not fearful. It reminds Rena of the first time he met President Nash. His joy in the arena seemed to grow as the events became more intense. If Wiley's speculations about Shane are correct, there is some roiling going on underneath the secretary's smile.

"For a public man, you're hard to find," Brooks says.

"There is a congressional investigation ongoing. I was advised that speaking to you two was unwise." A pause. "Since this meeting isn't on my schedule, I have to ask if this conversation is official."

"We didn't know we were meeting you any more than you knew you were meeting us," Brooks says.

"So, how can I help, unofficially?"

"We've seen the drone footage. And we have some questions," Rena says. "And there is an urgent deadline. We've been told that if we cannot resolve this quickly, the *Tribune* is close to breaking a story that will be far more damaging than you talking to us."

Shane looks surprised. They know something he does not.

"So ask," he says.

There is no interview strategy, no careful winding path. They are improvising.

"What was Brian Roderick really doing in Oosay?" Brooks asks. Shane hesitates. "It was more than meeting with moderates."

Shane is trying to guess what they know.

"No, I think you could say that was the reason. But not all the meetings were public. And not all took place in the compound."

He is still being coy with them.

"Where did they take place? And with whom?" Brooks tries.

"Rod was more than a warrior," Shane says. "He believed there was a way to win the war by helping these countries find their own way out of oblivion. That was how he believed we could defeat the enemy."

The secretary is recalling his friend, Rena thinks, but not answering their questions. Time to mix the chemical compounds.

"There is no more time for this dance," Rena says, his voice so soft Shane has to lean toward him to hear. "Let's assume you didn't have your friend assassinated like Senator Bakke says. What went wrong that night? What are you hiding? A failure by his security people? Their cowardice?"

Shane's expression hardens.

"There was no cowardice that night. Just the opposite."

The memory of his lost friend seems to surface in Shane's face.

"Brian Roderick was the bravest man I've ever known. The most extraordinary soldier. The best man . . ."

He doesn't finish. Shane's professional mask has slipped, just for an instant, the stress of the last months unexpectedly washing over him.

It catches Rena off guard. And he begins to feel sympathy for his prey, for the responsibility Shane has taken on. People like Shane bear the paradox of being responsible for problems they didn't create and no one can solve, and then being blamed for them. We salute the soldiers, ritually, but condemn those trying to keep them safe.

"We're not the enemy. Why won't you tell us what happened?" Brooks asks.

Shane, grave and pained, tells her, "You two have no idea what you are doing."

Now Brooks is out of patience, too. "You're our last stop on the bullshit train, Mr. Secretary," she says. "The Oosay Committee is going to come even harder at you now because they're embarrassed. They will retaliate. And the *Washington Tribune* is coming for you, too. You are about to become known as the man at the center of a cover-up. A man whose career ended protecting a lie."

"I'm sorry," he says. "Tell the president, he should ask me himself."

Shane rises from the table.

"And tell Tony Rousseau, it was a nice try. A nice trick." Then he is gone.

## FORTY-NINE

## WEDNESDAY, FEBRUARY 12, 5:03 P.M.
## NORTHEAST OHIO

The white Sierra hurtles south on Route 57, heat on, windows down. The late January cold burns against Adam O'Dowd's cheek. The pain comforts him.

He sticks to state roads, through farm country, two-lane black-top and broken white lines. The land rushes by outside, frozen and gray. Rolling land, tossed and uneven, like an unmade bed. The V-8 growls.

He isn't like Garrett Franks. He can't bury it so deep. He doesn't have kids to command him, "pick me up, Daddy," and help him forget. Or a wife to slide next to him at night, move her hands down, and dig her nails in. He isn't like Franks. He never was. His Kevlar wasn't that thick. And now, sweated through and exposed to too much sun, it's begun to wear out.

The week has been terrible. Nights especially. He bolts awake after an hour or so feeling ghosts in the room with him. Sometimes he sees the dying. Often he doesn't know if he's slept at all. What is dreaming and what is awake? Every night, it starts all over again. He cannot seem to get his wounded mind to rest.

And, over the weekend, a new bombing in Oosay.

The land rushes past. Small white houses, pickups with rust

stains from highway salt, old cars on blocks people are trying to get back to running—so a sister or a daughter can stop taking the bus.

O'Dowd feels like he knows all the stories from inside these houses. Soldiers spend years telling each other what their lives were like in those places. They couldn't wait to leave. Then once they were over there, they couldn't wait to get home again—to stop being afraid. And then when they're back home, it isn't the same. They're not the same. They don't know where to be. Something has eaten up some of their insides, like rust on the pickups in the driveways.

It was bad for everyone. And it was worse if you were African American.

He loves America. God bless America. Fuck you, America.

Even his name, O'Dowd—a name a slave owner gave them. Even his name.

Last night he dreamed about Oosay. He could see Franks, firing over him, firing at the Ali Baba coming toward him, firing, firing, and shouting at him, saving him, and ruining him, and he saw the Manor House explode, the roof bolting up into the sky, as if all the air in the world had been sucked into the stars and then came down like concrete rain.

He has no plan. Just drive. Stay in motion. Keep the outside rushing by. Till maybe he can lie down and maybe, if he is tired enough, sleep.

"Dude," he says into the phone.

On the other end of the line, Garrett Franks says, "Adam?"

"Hey, dude, you good?"

"Adam, where are you? I've been trying to call you."

"You see the news?"

"What news?"

"Another attack in Oosay. They got us and they're still at it."

"Adam," Franks says.

There is no answer.

"Adam?"

"It's the same guys," O'Dowd says.

"Adam, you don't understand. It's okay."

"Same guys."

Franks wonders if he can tell him, but O'Dowd isn't stable. Isn't safe.

"Adam, where are you?"

O'Dowd has put the phone down, though he hasn't turned it off, and Franks can hear the sound of the wind rushing and the low rumble of O'Dowd's engine. The sound reminds Franks of when he was a child, sitting in the backseat of his parents' car at night driving through a tunnel near where they lived. Tourists sometimes died in that tunnel, his father said, because they failed to turn on their headlights. Franks would hold his breath whenever they drove through that dark place, frightened by the picture in his mind of a car crashing and a family dying. He hasn't thought of that tunnel in years, but he thinks of it now, for just a second, when O'Dowd puts down the phone. He waits, and then he hangs up because he knows Adam doesn't want to talk.

For years afterward, Franks will wonder—if he hadn't gotten lost in the memory of that sound of wind in the car—if anything would have been different.

## FIFTY

## WEDNESDAY, FEBRUARY 12, 8:17 P.M.
## WASHINGTON, D.C.

When Rena and Brooks left the Four Seasons hotel five hours ago, there was a message to call Hallie Jobe.

Walt Smolonsky, she said, had just called from the Netherlands. That's where he had finally found one of the five men who had been working communications in the Barracks the night of the Oosay attack.

It had been a long journey finding him. Smolo had been trying for nearly two months. The men working the Barracks were military contractors, and the night of the Oosay attack they had been shipped off to Germany, kept under wraps, and finally left to scatter and told to disappear. Smolo had worked every old friend and loose contact he could think of to get their names. Finally, it had been Samantha Reese who had done it. She'd had a friend, a military contractor himself, who knew two men who worked the Oosay compound from time to time. No one had heard from them since early December. She gave the names to Smolonsky. He discovered one of the two men had effectively vanished, not returning to his home in Virginia. But the other man, a former navy communications officer named Emanuel Nariño, was now living in Amsterdam.

Smolo had gone off to Europe a week ago to find him. He had

tracked Manny Nariño's movements for days, identifying the club in the red-light district where Manny spent a lot of evenings. By then Smolo knew as much about Manny Nariño as he did about most of his own family. At the club, Smolo managed to buy a drink just as Nariño was ordering another round for himself. Hey, an American. An exchange of introductions. Your name's Nariño? Whoa, Smolo lied, he knew a Sally Nariño in Modesto. No way, Nariño said. That's my cousin. They toasted the coincidence, ordered another round, and began a club crawl that lasted till dawn. It was around 4:30 A.M. when Smolo had gotten out of Manny Nariño what he needed.

"Peter, now we know why Ross, Halleck, Phelps, and O'Dowd were in the wrong place," Jobe said to Rena outside the hotel.

"We've waited long enough, Hallie. Why?"

"They were in the Barracks, all of them, even Roderick," she said. "That's what this guy told Smolo. Then, Roderick went *back* out there, back to the Manor House. After the attack had begun. Just him and Franks."

Rena had halfway guessed something like this from talking to Shane.

"Hallie, tell Ellen, Arvid, and Maureen to print out everything we have about the Manor House. Everything. Bring it all to my place. Bring everyone with you. This might take all night."

Now, five hours later, the papers are strewn across Rena's den, on the tops of furniture, chairs, and the seat of his chocolate-brown Stickley leather sofa. On the floor, too, with little paths between the papers to walk through.

Nelson the cat wanders among the documents, getting in the way, rubbing his head against the investigators.

They'd gathered most of these documents weeks earlier when they first got the assignment. On his first trip to Oosay, Smolonsky had even paid a local fixer in country to go to the city's hall of records, or what remained of it, and bribe someone to make copies of everything about the building. Sales history. Zoning documents.

Maureen Conner had dug up whatever there was at State. The U.S. government would have meticulously documented everything it had done to the Manor House since acquiring the property four years earlier.

But they had not looked at any of it before.

Rena feels like they have wasted time, been too methodical, stuck too long to their plan, to the Grid, to the idea of working from the bottom up. And they'd put too much faith in what Rena and Brooks had come to realize was a mistake: they'd believed that if they said they represented the president, people on his national security team who knew what had happened would help them.

But then they got the video. And now, thanks to Smolonsky, they knew part of what it showed.

Roderick had gone *back* to the Manor House. There was something there he needed. Something worth going back for *after* the fighting began—with only one man to protect him.

"What are we looking for?" Lupsa had asked when they had begun spreading the papers out across Rena's town house hours earlier.

"We don't know," Rena had said.

"Anything odd. Or that you don't understand," Wiley had guessed.

"Exactly."

It is a quarter past eight now.

Lupsa is poring over the documents from State. The old house was deteriorating when the United States bought it four years ago. The U.S. government had installed a new kitchen. Done structural work.

"What's a Seef?"

"A what?" says Rena.

"A Seef."

Lupsa spells it out. "S-C-I-F?"

"It's pronounced skiff," Rena says. "Like the small boat."

"What does it mean, a small boat inside a room?" asks Lupsa.

Of course, a SCIF, Rena thinks. He glances at Brooks, who is thinking the same thing.

"A SCIF is a room, a place where you can have classified conversations, keep classified documents, and only certain people are allowed in," Brooks explains to Lupsa.

"And it means I think I know what Roderick was doing in the Manor House, and why he was there alone. And maybe why he died," Rena says.

He looks at Hallie Jobe. "Are you feeling charming tonight?"

"What plan are you cooking up for me now, Peter?"

"You know the man you disliked most in this whole mess? I want you to sweet-talk him."

* * *

When Jobe arrives, Garrett Franks is sitting in the hanging swing on his front porch. He had needed some privacy, some time to think. He is worried about Adam O'Dowd. He has called O'Dowd back but now Adam's phone is off.

Franks puts his weight onto the balls of his feet and pushes, then lifts his feet and lets the momentum swing him back and forth. The lightness makes him feel better, like he is floating, and he sees how many swings he can get each time until the floating stops, his feet touch, and he has to push again.

She comes up the walk slowly.

"You lost?"

"We need your help."

"Then you have a problem."

Jobe thinks Franks looked faded, like something that has been left outside in bad weather.

"Help us put this right, Garrett."

## FIFTY-ONE

## WEDNESDAY, FEBRUARY 12, 9:30 P.M.
## MCLEAN, VIRGINIA

They meet outside the front gate of the big house.

Hallie Jobe had brought Garret Franks.

Rena and Brooks had come in Peter's Camaro.

"Thank you," Rena says to Franks.

Rena introduces the sergeant major to the tall woman next to him as his partner, Randi Brooks.

"You sure he's home?" Jobe asks Rena.

"We'll find out."

As Rena pulls out his phone, another car pulls up, a rented blue Ford Fusion, and Samantha Reese gets out with two men.

"My surveillance team notified me you were here. I thought I might make an appearance," Reese says. "In case there was security here that tried to push you around. But once again you seem to be living a charmed life."

Rena gives her a look. Then he dials Daniel Shane's number and announces they are out front with Sergeant Major Garrett Franks.

Rena has used this method before. In interrogations he has brought family members into rooms or let subjects see a child in the hallway. In the case that ended his military career, Rena had confronted a general who had sexually harassed women by bringing the general's own adult daughter to the meeting. People had told Rena he was crazy to do these things. Some said he was shaming people. "It doesn't shame them," Rena always answered. "It reminds them of who they want to be. That, in the end, is what interrogation is."

The secretary of defense answers the door in an old sweater and frayed khakis. He is divorced, his children grown, and he lives alone in the big house.

An expression of surprise gives way to one of resignation. He would not be one to make a scene. "I thought we were done," he says.

"Is there a place we can spread out some documents?"

Shane leads them to a den in the rear of the house. Out the window, they can see a forest sloping down a hill. It is an old house, stone and wood, and the den has been tastefully added. In this part of Virginia, a town called McLean, colonial and Civil War plaques dot the roads, and one can find two-hundred-year-old houses once surrounded by wooded acres. Over the last fifty years, the land has been carved up and filled in with gaudy mansions. Shane's house has been here more than a century.

On a library table they lay out the plans of the Oosay Manor House. Brooks, Shane, Jobe, Franks, and Rena stand around the table.

This is a gamble, but a plausible one, Rena and Brooks have reasoned. They need to press some theory on Shane, even if it's the wrong one.

"Please look at this," Rena says, pointing to a spot on the architectural plans.

Shane squints. "I don't know what I am looking at."

"It's a SCIF," says Rena.

The word—or acronym—has special meaning in national security. SCIF is shorthand for one of those soulless phrases only governments seem capable of inventing:

"Sensitive Compartmented Information Facility."

In layman's terms, a SCIF is a safe place where you can keep secret things, classified things, and have classified conversations. But it is also a physical reality, a secure room built according to strict national security standards. There are rules about soundproofing, special wiring, protection against fire and electronic eavesdropping. Until those standards are met, no classified material can be placed in a SCIF. No classified conversations can take place. Once the SCIF is certified, only accredited people can enter it. No documents can be removed. SCIFs are difficult and costly to build.

And they are dangerous to have in overseas outposts.

If you are under attack, there are specific instructions and protocols on how to destroy the contents of a SCIF, or, if necessary, how to destroy the SCIF itself and the contents inside.

Shane's eyes are fixed on Rena.

"Roderick was safe in the Barracks," Rena says. "We've confirmed that."

A crease of tension forms around Shane's eyes.

"Roderick went back to the Manor House. In the middle of the firefight. He ran back across those hundred yards. Because of that SCIF. Didn't he? Something there had to be destroyed. And only Roderick was cleared to go in."

When Shane doesn't answer, Rena looks at Franks but the sergeant major's face is a mask, his feelings buried soldier deep.

"Mr. Secretary, I think General Roderick killed himself that night. I think he did it to destroy the SCIF, to protect whatever secrets it contained. That's why he went back alone, why he ordered everyone in his security detail other than Sergeant Major Franks to stay in the Barracks, and why the sergeant stayed outside on the terrace."

The graceful set of Shane's expression has been replaced by something else. Grief and exhaustion.

"I think the rest of the detail died rushing back to protect Roderick in defiance of his orders. I think everyone there died a hero protecting a secret you are still trying to protect. You need to tell us what that secret is."

Shane is staring at the building plans, at the word SCIF.

After a long breath, Shane says, barely audibly, "All right."

## FIFTY-TWO

Shane cannot tell it simply.

He wants to explain it.

"You need to understand Roderick," he says. "He was fearless. A true visionary. And I don't use that word lightly."

They already know much of what he is telling them, but Shane feels he has to tell it anyway—his way. He talks about Roderick's unconventional approach to leadership, his seven deployments, his time with everyday people in country, his preference for enlisted soldiers, his theories on how to fight the war on terror.

"Rod was brilliant, part genius, part warrior, part diplomat, part priest, part . . ." Shane looks like he is going to say "madman." He says "visionary" again.

"But he was not a Pentagon politician. So I sent him back, to redeploy. 'Put your plan in action. A free hand. Somewhere no one is watching, Africa, and make it happen. Prove your case.'"

Shane looks at Rena and Brooks. "This afternoon you asked me what Rod was doing in Oosay. That is what he was doing."

"What was the secret in that SCIF that Roderick considered worth dying for?" Brooks asks.

Shane looks at Franks, not Brooks.

"No, sir," Franks says. The sergeant would keep this secret buried still.

Shane, too weary to stand, finds an empty chair and sits.

"The SCIF contained documents that would identify an ISA leader who is actually working for the United States. It was Roderick's operation. He cultivated this man for almost a decade. And that night, this whole thing, was the culmination of that recruitment."

"What thing?" Rena asks.

Shane glances at Franks again.

"This whole attack. In Oosay. The attack on the Manor House. It was our operation. Our man's. His way of finally elevating himself into the high echelon inside the Islamic State Army in Morat. He would arrange an attack on the U.S. facility while a brigadier general was on the property."

"Jesus," Brooks says.

"To kill Roderick?" Jobe asks.

"No," says Shane. "No!" He tries to compose himself.

"You two were pretty close to guessing today at lunch," he says. "Rod was supposed to be in the Barracks. The Barracks was never vulnerable. That's why the whole operation made sense. The Manor House was basically expendable. The plan was to allow ISA to breach the compound and do whatever they wanted to the old house. They would score a symbolic victory. In reality it would do us no real harm. We would take the embarrassment of the attack in exchange for having someone at the top of a leading jihadist group. Something we've never had. Something we've always needed."

Rena guesses what comes next.

"But Rod discovered there were classified documents left in the Manor. In the SCIF. And he feared it would blow the whole operation."

Shane closes his eyes and nods in agreement. "It was just a goddamn mistake. A simple screwup. No one in Oosay knew about the planned attack, of course. That was basic operational security. On the scene, only Roderick and Franks knew. Everything classified on the property was supposed to have been moved to a new SCIF in the Barracks. As the attack began, Roderick asked to see it, the secure room in the new building. He was told it hadn't been certified yet, and thus all classified documents on the property remained in the old building. He realized the risk of what was taking place. Everything could have been undone if the attackers had penetrated what had been left behind in the Manor House. Including the identity of our man and others. Rod made the decision to go back, to go out there, to destroy the old SCIF, to protect his man inside ISA. By the time he got there, he had no choice but to trigger the tempest."

*Tempest* is the term of art for the operation of destroying a SCIF.

"So Roderick blew the Manor House up," Rena says. "It wasn't the attackers. They were firing assault rifles. They didn't have the ordnance to blow that old building that high."

Shane nods again. "That's right."

"That's the secret you're lying to protect. Your mole inside ISA," Rena says. "And the fact that a simple oversight, a delay in certification of a room, nearly exposed it and led to the explosion of the Manor and the death of General Roderick."

Shane looks at Rena and Brooks and Jobe and says, "And now you have to protect that secret, too. That asset is your asset."

## FIFTY-THREE

It takes a minute to absorb, and Brooks seems strangely agitated.

"Did the president know?" she asks.

Shane, exhausted, says, "No. Months earlier the president was briefed that we were trying to elevate someone inside ISA, a plan nearly two years in the making. That was all. Not the details. Not even that it involved Roderick or Morat. Not the attack. Nor would he be. This was advance action."

Shane pauses. "I know you may think it's strange to keep things from the president. But you know why we created advance action? Because the government has started leaking as never before. Sometimes people at the top leak without even realizing it. And some people leak to kill plans they don't like. Diane Howell and Secretary of State Arthur Manion had seen a plan like this more than a year ago, allowing someone to rise in ISA by condoning a terror attack. They had been vehement in their opposition. We couldn't risk their being in the loop. We couldn't risk their leaking it to kill it.

"When it became clear our man could get very close to the top if he masterminded a major attack, we looked for a target opportunity for that to happen soon," Shane says. "The plan for Oosay came up quickly, in a matter of a week or so—that Roderick would be there, that the Barracks would be complete. Frankly it was sufficiently risky that we were not going to ask permission."

"Does the president know now?" Brooks asks.

"You mean has your task been a sham?" Shane says. "No, the president doesn't know."

Brooks looks like she is trying to decide whether she believes him. "Why didn't you tell him?"

Shane straightens in his chair.

"Ms. Brooks, you have to understand something. General Roderick died. But the operation succeeded. Our man is there. In fact, Rod's death made the operation more successful. It elevated our man higher inside ISA."

Rena can see Roderick as he ponders killing himself to protect his man thinking along similar lines. Protect the operation; protect his man; Roderick's death makes the covert operation a bigger success.

"Rod's death was terrible, but our asset is still in the field. Our best chance was to keep operational security at the same level we always intended. That hasn't changed."

"So you told no one?" Brooks asks.

"I almost did. I called Spencer Carr that first night," Shane says, referring to the president's chief of staff. "I told him the Oosay incident involved an advance action operation and the president had not been fully briefed—but that the operation was still active and that our best chance to protect it was to maintain operational knowledge at the same level. He agreed and told me not to tell him anything more. The next day George Rawls called you in. I knew what Carr was doing. He was protecting our operation. And he was protecting the president at the same time."

"Christ," Brooks says.

"You two were public proof the president didn't know the details."

It sounds like Carr, Rena thinks. And Rawls.

Protect the president. It is the ultimate law of Washington.

"When the *Tribune* story broke, establishing that some of your cover story didn't add up, you didn't tell the president at that point?" Brooks demands.

"You were already investigating by then. We decided to see what you would learn. We figured you would always get closer than Congress would."

Brooks glances at her partner. "And Diane Howell?" she asks.

Shane pauses.

"Diane puzzled some of it out. After the *Tribune* story broke, she came to me and Webster and confronted us. We told her this was an advance action, that Carr had told us not to tell the president or him. We asked her to abide by that instruction, to continue to protect him and keep operational security—not to go to the president with her suspicions. By then everything was in lockdown and everyone was wondering who had leaked to the *Tribune*. Diane kept her head down. She kept out of it."

On one level, Rena thinks, their investigation provided Nash cover. And those involved waited to see how far he and Randi could get. Shane, Webster, Arroyo, and even Howell would judge what to tell the president, what to say to Congress, and how to protect their new asset inside ISA, based on what Rena and Brooks could learn.

"Who did know about the operation?" Rena asks.

"In general terms. Roderick. Me. Henry Arroyo. Willey at DIA. Eventually Owen Webster. We needed his cooperation. And then afterward Howell guessed some of it. I assume at some point Rod told his sergeant major," Shane says with a glance at Franks.

"I don't know who else on Webster's staff. Or Arroyo's. I would guess fewer than a half dozen people know the whole story."

"And that night?"

"The plan came together very quickly. Days. General Willey at

DIA and Arroyo came to me with it. I signed off. It was my responsibility. Not Rod's. Not Henry's. Not General Willey's. Not the president's."

The tortured public servant. The Boy Scout. The devout soldier.

* * *

No one sleeps well with the secret they have uncovered, waiting for morning. In the middle of the night, Hallie Jobe receives a call. At first she doesn't recognize the man's voice.

"I'm sorry. I'm sorry I couldn't tell you the truth."

Then it comes to her. It is Adam O'Dowd.

"I didn't tell you the truth. But I didn't lie. I didn't abandon my team. I followed orders."

The words are slurred, and they remind Hallie of the last time she saw her father in the hospital before he died. They frighten her.

"Adam? I know. Where are you?"

"You know what's it like out there."

"Where are you, Adam?"

"I wish you knew better, Hallie."

Then the line goes dead. And when she calls back O'Dowd has turned his phone off.

## FIFTY-FOUR

## THURSDAY, FEBRUARY 13, 4:38 A.M. SOUTHEASTERN OHIO

He parks the Sierra up the ridge at the end of the road and hikes the rest of the way down to the water's edge. He knew the lake as a boy, fished here and hunted, near Bannock, where his grandfather had owned land.

He would sit and dream, his eyes open, imagining himself grown. He felt something special was headed for him.

Now he wonders if he is in the wrong spot. The aspens are leafless in winter. The lake looks smaller.

Play by the rules and you still lose. Like that bank that opened accounts and stole people's money and ruined their credit, all because the more accounts the bank opened the higher the stock price went.

Is that what we were fighting for over there? American values?

Once, when it was just the six of them, they had talked with the general about why the jihadists could recruit Americans. He asked Roderick if he thought America had become a less moral, less righteous country. You could talk that way with Roderick.

"I don't think any of the six of us here is immoral. Do you?"

Maybe Roderick was wrong about people. About America.

He doesn't know what to think.

He looks at the lake through the steam of his own breath. In battle, you learn that if you don't breathe, you lock up, your muscles tighten, and you begin to panic. People who don't know how to breathe get killed.

\* \* \*

Around midmorning, an Ohio state trooper spots the white Sierra parked at the ridgeline. When they contact O'Dowd's home in Elyria, his mother says she hasn't seen him for three days.

It is late afternoon, just before dark, when they find O'Dowd's body below the surface of the lake, weighted down with rocks stuffed in the pockets of his jacket. The case is listed as a suspicious death, a likely suicide, awaiting results of an autopsy.

The autopsy is authorized with priority status, given that O'Dowd is a public figure, someone, in a certain way and for the moment, famous. Or at least a person whose death, the sheriff's communications office anticipated, will get media attention.

"Soldiers commit suicide all the time," the assistant coroner says as they begin the examination of the body.

"This one was a hero, though," the county's chief medical examiner says.

"So what?"

The autopsy, however, is inconclusive. O'Dowd was alive when he went into the water and apparently struggled afterward, but the depth of the lake, the cold, and the fact that his jacket was zipped closed meant he had little time or chance to escape or get to shore.

"A guy committing suicide who began to have second thoughts?" the medical examiner asks his assistant.

"Probably. Who would want to kill a hero?"

Peter Rena will wonder the same thing, though Hallie Jobe said the man she had met certainly might have taken his own life.

Brooks asks only one thing: that Rena not head off to Ohio to solve whatever lingering mystery there was behind O'Dowd's drowning until after they are finished with Morat.

## FIFTY-FIVE

## THURSDAY, FEBRUARY 13, 10:15 A.M.
## SENATE MAJORITY LEADER'S OFFICE

Word of Adam O'Dowd's death ricochets through Washington all morning.

And once again, Susan Stroud orders a meeting in her office, this time just herself, the Speaker, Chairman Gains, and Wendy Upton.

"We cannot look as though we hounded this man, a hero in Oosay, to his death," Stroud says. "Have you put out a statement yet?"

The question is directed to Gains, but it is Upton who answers. "Members of the committee are doing that separately. You both should, too," she tells the Speaker and majority leader. "People can be more personal, and there is more of a drumbeat of sympathy that way."

"The committee is putting out a formal statement of condolences as well," Gains adds.

"What the hell did O'Dowd tell you in that hearing?" Stroud asks.

"He read a statement. We praised him. But he refused, for the most part, to answer questions," Gains says. "I knew he was hiding something. But we didn't want to drag a hero through the wringer."

Stroud's look at Gains is withering.

"PTSD," the Speaker says to no one in particular.

Then the majority leader's secretary walks in with a note.

Stroud looks up after reading it.

"Spencer Carr, the president's chief of staff, is asking myself, the Speaker, and Chairman Gains to come down to the White House, along with the minority leaders of the House and Senate. He would like us there immediately."

* * *

They are brought through the East Wing, where they could move unseen by reporters. They are taken not to Spencer Carr's office but the Map Room, a larger space that has chairs arranged for a formal meeting. Gains vaguely remembers Roosevelt and Churchill took meetings together in this room.

Chief of Staff Carr, White House Counsel George Rawls, National Security Advisor Diane Howell, Secretary of Defense Daniel Shane, and Director of Central Intelligence Owen Webster are there when they arrive. So are the outsiders, Peter Rena and Randi Brooks. Spencer Carr asks the newest visitors to sit.

Gains has never met Rena, but he dislikes him instinctively. A political fixer, an apparatchik who works both sides of the party fence. In Gains's prosecutorial mind, he is the equivalent of a dirty cop.

Six of them from the Hill have come—Gains and the ranking Oosay Democrat, Fred Blaylish, plus the Speaker and the majority leader and the two top Democrats, the minority leaders of both houses.

A door opens and President Nash enters the Map Room. They all rise, and observe the ritual of sitting again only after the president has thanked them for coming and asked them to sit. Nash cups his hands in front of his chest and looks gravely around at each of them.

"We have a mutual problem, and I think we need to help each other arrive at a mutual solution."

Gains tenses. He doesn't trust this man, though he has to admit, every time he sees him up close he is struck that the president is even more graceful and charismatic in person than on television.

"What you are about to learn, I learned only this morning. It will be obvious to you that this knowledge can never leave this room. What you are about to hear is the story of an honorable lie that we must now all protect. A good lie.

"Peter and Randi, would you describe what you learned last night?" the president asks.

The request catches Rena off guard. He is still unsure about some of what they heard from Shane. He expected the president to ask the secretary of defense to explain it.

They had called Rawls last night from Shane's home and came to Rawls's office first thing this morning. Rawls had quickly said it was time finally to brief the president. Nash, in turn, had decided instantly how to react. They had to brief the Speaker and majority leader and the two party leaders of the Oosay Committee in person. How soon could they get here?

The president had met in private with his chief of staff, national security advisor, Shane, and Rawls. Rena and Brooks waited outside.

Now the president is asking Rena and Brooks, who know the least, to begin. Their doing so would reinforce the point that the president himself did not know until now, that Rena and Brooks, acting independently, had tracked down what happened and are now telling how they discovered it. Perhaps the awkward and uncertain explanation will be the most authentic.

Brooks looks at Rena. You, her eyes say, it should come from you.

He describes it plainly. This was a covert plan and there is an agent still in place. He describes how they arrived at the discovery: their suspicions after talking to Franks and O'Dowd, the drone video, their deduction from that of something valuable in the Manor House, the discovery of the SCIF, their confrontation with Shane, their realization that Roderick took his own life to destroy the SCIF and protect their agent now rising in ISA.

In Rena's telling, Roderick is the hero, the president the innocent, and there is no villain. The only evil is revealing the secret.

"You see our problem," the president says. His eyes move to the different congressional leaders. "Your committee cannot get to the truth of all this. At the same time, I don't want your efforts derided. Or for you to be blamed for Adam O'Dowd's death."

Nash is offering them a deal. Find some honorable conclusion to your committee investigation—one that protects this "good lie"—and the White House and Democrats will not condemn the committee's work.

In the ashes of Oosay, the president is seeking the rarest of Washington artifacts: a compromise. Common ground in a shared secret.

"We cannot go back empty-handed," Stroud says. "My conference will not accept that."

"I agree," Nash says. He looks at his national security advisor. "Diane?"

This is what they have been working out for the last hour while they waited for the congressional leaders to arrive, Rena thinks. While he and Brooks waited outside.

"The State Department failed to adequately protect the facility," Howell says. "Reforms are required in the program to upgrade security at foreign installations. That may also require additional funding from Congress, something limited, a few million dollars."

In other words, Arthur Manion, who is not present, will be the first to take blame.

"That is not enough," the Speaker says.

"I agree," Stroud says. She has to back the man. Many of her future senators will come from the most extreme members of the House GOP conference.

Nash glances at his chief of staff, Carr. *It always comes down to the Speaker's conference,* his eyes seem to say, the rising anger in the House.

"We're not done," says Nash. He looks at Howell.

"Our efforts at intelligence coordination in real time are still inadequate. Same problem as on 9/11," she says. "We still need to do better. So the CIA, DIA, NSA, and NSC will work with the heads of the intelligence committees in Congress to arrive at a better plan."

This is mumbo jumbo. The intelligence traffic in Morat that night was deliberately ignored to protect the operation. But this reform will give Congress a role, however symbolic, in developing new rules. They've never been satisfied with the Directorate of National Intelligence, set up under George W. Bush. The intelligence community will hate what it sees as more meddling by congressional amateurs, but by the time it is resolved, Rena knows, Nash will be gone. The problem will belong to his successor.

"Congress will also set up new rules for security details to protect visiting high-ranking officials," Howell says.

More symbolism, but it's an issue that the Common Sense wing in Congress has cared about—that Roderick had too few people guarding him.

The Senate majority leader is shaking her head. "I need a resignation. Things went wrong. Someone has to pay. We can't go back up the Hill without that. I apologize if I'm being blunt."

Stroud stares at Daniel Shane, the moderate, the turncoat who had left the party, then gone to work for a Democrat and who is now thinking of running for president. He stares back at her, his former Senate colleague, with a look that reminds Rena of scorned lovers.

Diane Howell says, "You will have my resignation."

This catches everyone by surprise.

But obviously it was the other part of what they worked out behind closed doors for the last hour, Rena and Brooks recognize. The Oosay plan hadn't been Howell's idea. It was Shane, Roderick, and Arroyo's. But she was responsible for two fateful mistakes that had animated Nash's critics. First she had gone on television mischaracterizing the events of the attack the first day. And it was her man, the aide she had sent to help Manion at State with communications, who had written the clumsy memo about how to attack anyone criticizing the administration over Oosay. Those two mistakes, in turn, triggered the congressional investigation.

Then, after guessing most of what happened in Oosay, she had sided with Shane, Webster, and others—the boys—not to tell the president but instead to wait to see how much Rena and Brooks could figure out. Now, in her final act of loyalty, she was agreeing to take the fall for Oosay, both to protect the real secret and the rest of Nash's team. It might even bring Nash and the rest of his national security team closer in their final months.

Susan Stroud stares at Howell, and Rena catches a glimpse at Brooks. Howell's resignation will give Nash's critics someone close to him, but not someone who would ever reveal the secret of Oosay. She is too loyal for that. And she had a life beyond politics, which had proven a rougher game than perhaps she had anticipated.

## FIFTY-SIX

**THURSDAY, FEBRUARY 13, 1:45 P.M.**
***WASHINGTON TRIBUNE* OFFICE**

Will Gordon is squinting over his reading glasses, and Jill Bishop wonders how bad the editor's eyes must be.

"You think the man who killed General Roderick was working for the Americans?" he asks.

She is briefing him on the story, looking at a memo she has written, trying to decide whether they have enough.

"Well, whoever he was, he was in contact with Americans," she says.

Her voice is toneless. She is cold-eyed when working like this, sorting facts as if they are jigsaw puzzle pieces, assessing the corners and the shapes and seeing which fits into which. She is not rooting for her story. She is trying to find its weak points.

Gordon bends his awkward body over the printout of the memo on his desk. A strange vague smile appears on his face, like a cat's.

"Connect the dots for me again," he says. "Explain it to me as if I were a reader, as if I were coming to this fresh."

Bishop goes through it one more time: Someone with "a particular digital footprint" was in contact with Americans before the Oosay incident. That digital footprint may even have been in contact with General Brian Roderick in the days before he died. Then that same person in Morat, the same digital footprint, was in contact with Americans again before the bombing of the author's house in Oosay two months later.

"The man who had the same bombing signature as the bomber in the Roderick incident," Bishop says. "So, yes, there appears to be some contact between Americans and someone who is near the bombings in Oosay."

"If you're right, Jill, Dick Bakke's theory that Americans might have assassinated General Roderick could be true," Gordon says.

"Maybe," Bishop answers. She doesn't want to leap that far yet.

"You think that might have something to do with the death of this private security contractor? O'Dowd? You think maybe he was involved? Or even killed to keep him quiet?"

Jack Hamilton, the national editor, shifts uncomfortably in his chair. "Let's not get ahead of ourselves, Will. You know how many veterans kill themselves every day? The latest estimate is twenty—each day. That's one every seventy-two minutes."

Will Gordon likes arguing over stories. He thinks arguments make stories stronger. But he has little patience for what he considers the often-spurious use of data. "And every one of those suicides is unique, even if they form a larger pattern," he tells Hamilton. "Our problem is *this* suicide. If it was a suicide."

Bishop watches Gordon narrow his eyes again in concentration and then speak to Hamilton.

"If we report that on the day O'Dowd died, the Oosay bombers were talking to Americans, readers are going to leap to the conclusion those facts are connected. They're going to think O'Dowd killed himself—or worse, that someone killed him—so he would not get caught for killing Roderick. True or not, that inference will exist."

"Are you saying hold the story because people might jump to the wrong conclusion?" Bishop asks.

"No, if there are gaps, we need to point those out to the reader, too."

"Maybe we should wait? Get more," says Hamilton.

"We don't have that luxury," says Gordon. "Not today. Not with O'Dowd's death. We need to share with people what we know. And what we don't."

Hamilton nods.

"Jill, do you think Roderick was assassinated by American interests? Do you think Dick Bakke could be right?"

Bishop has no interest in speculating.

She is pleased when Gordon's desk phone rings, but he ignores it and waits for her answer.

"I have no idea," she says.

Gordon's secretary is now standing at his door.

"It's the president."

"President of what?" Gordon barks.

"The United States."

In the end, most cases in which government officials persuade journalists to hold stories don't last. They just buy time. But sometimes years, and that is enough.

The CIA in 1975 convinced some of the biggest news organizations in America, and some of the best reporters, to hold stories about a secret spy ship that had sunk to the bottom of the ocean near Hawaii with nuclear warheads on board. The spy ship was being salvaged by a company owned by reclusive billionaire Howard Hughes. The whole thing sounded like fiction. The *New York Times, Los Angeles Times, Washington Post,* and others all agreed, after separate and candid meetings with the CIA, to hold the story.

It bought the Agency roughly a decade. When the full tale of the failed spy ship with secret nuclear weapons at the bottom of the sea—"Project Azorian"—finally came out in a book, it was history but no longer news.

In 1961, President Kennedy personally convinced the *New York Times* not to expose plans to invade Cuba at the Bay of Pigs. After the invasion to overthrow Fidel Castro failed, Kennedy said he wished he'd been less persuasive.

There are dozens of smaller cases—and hundreds more when

the Agency failed to persuade journalists to hold back. In every case
in which journalists chose to publish, they did so arguing that the
public good outweighed any proven harm. And in virtually every
case, people in intelligence said the harm was profound—but classified so they couldn't talk about how much damage the reckless
and self-serving press had done to the nation. They just seethed in
secret over whether the United States had a free press or a treasonous one.

Yet most of the cases of stories being held, modified, or negoti-
ated came from another time, an era when there were fewer news
outlets, and the people working in them mostly operated by a common code. Now anyone with a gripe or a rumor or a fantasy could
publish. There is less of a code, and what little there is isn't held in
common.

Rena doesn't know whether any journalist in the twenty-first
century would decline to publish a secret in the name of national
security and public good. In the last ten years, more damaging secrets had leaked—especially through offshore hackers and groups
tied to the Russians—than Rena ever thought conceivable, leaks so
vast it was impossible to comprehend their damage. Henry Arroyo
had been right about that.

But one thing that hadn't changed much was human spying.
You blow the identity of a human spy and you get that person killed.
The Russian government killed with an impunity these days beyond
anything from the Cold War: political opponents, journalists, sus-
pected double agents, even former colleagues who knew too much.
The Chinese had recently killed a slew of agents thanks to a mole
it had placed in the CIA. It was hard to tell whether much of the
American public noticed.

Rena had known Will Gordon briefly long ago. He liked him. So
what? As far as Rena could tell, Gordon never protected his friends
or anyone else from what he published. That was his ethic, at least as
he saw it: truth above all. Chips fall where they may.

Rena considered that simplistic and convenient. But he conceded that at least Gordon had an ethic. And he held to it.

They also had to figure out how to meet with journalists in a way no other journalists would know about. That is a problem—in the presidential mansion in a free country.

The last meeting, with congressional leaders in the Map Room, was on the White House schedule as a meeting with Chief of Staff Spencer Carr. The president had simply "dropped in" unannounced. It wasn't necessarily going to attract the attention of curious reporters. Meetings with congressional leaders in the White House happen all the time.

But a gathering of people from the *Washington Tribune* was different, even if it were scheduled with Spencer Carr. It would still attract the attention of other journalists who'd want to know what they were missing.

They needed to meet the *Tribune* team somewhere else, somewhere off-site. And even then, the president would be accompanied by a press pool, a handful of reporters who expected to be briefed on the president's activities and who would write a summary about them to be shared with the press corps and posted publicly online.

Secret meetings with the president are harder to manage than most people imagine.

"I have a way we can do this," Brooks says. "My apartment backs up onto the Myriad Hotel. The president could do a meeting with someone there. You would set up a holding room, right, where the president can wait and prepare with his people in private before the meeting?"

"Of course. There's always a holding room," Carr says.

Holding rooms are common for staging these kinds of unseen and unrecorded meetings. There is no list made of who might spontaneously stop by a holding room. Have people join the president in a holding room in private. Then neglect to tell the press about the visit.

"If there can be a way in and out of a holding room that is un-seen," Brooks says, "put the holding room in the back of the hotel on the first floor. My patio backs onto an alley behind the hotel. You can walk from the hotel through the alley to my back gate."

They would bring most of the same team that had met with congressional leaders—Chief of Staff Carr; White House Counsel Rawls; Defense Secretary Shane; CIA chief Webster; Howell from the NSC; and Rena and Brooks. But the president needed to be there in person, too. On that they all agreed. James Nash needed to look Will Gordon in the eye and do the talking.

"Don't try to bullshit Gordon," Rena says, catching a look from Carr for giving the president orders. "He will react instinctively if he feels he's been lied to or manipulated and will say no."

"I've met the man," says Nash.

**WILL GORDON BRINGS FOUR WITH HIM:** two top editors, a lawyer, and Bishop.

Brooks meets them at the door of her apartment and escorts them to the living room, the only space in her home large enough for the group. She's brought her dining room chairs into the room, arranged alongside a sofa and armchair. It looks like her book group is coming.

The president rises and shakes hands with the people from the newspaper, then everyone sits.

The president stares at the tall, rumpled editor. Then he turns to Bishop, the reporter whose face never gives anything away except the feeling you wouldn't want to play cards with her.

"I'm going to ask you to do something you won't want to do," the president begins. "I'm going to ask you *not* to publish a story."

Nash pauses—a familiar, even famous moment of hesitation, a timing trigger he uses to signal: *the next sentence I utter will be especially important.*

"I am going to be honest with you as to why I am asking you to do this. But I cannot tell you everything. In fact, I'm going to try to tell you as little as I can. But I am going to tell you the truth."

It's a good start, Rena thinks from the other side of the room. In encounters such as these, the government often offers journalists a story that is only partly true—to create confusion. It is a time-tested intelligence technique. Make journalists doubt the true story they have by telling them it was wrong and giving them another one, which contains just enough fact mixed with fiction to be plausible. Then, unsure what is true, the journalists will have to run around and re-report. The idea is they will never fully be sure what is true and what is not and will give up. Nash has said he won't do that.

Rena glances at his partner. She is watching Bishop, not Gordon, knowing it is usually the reporter, the hunter, who is harder to persuade.

"Do you agree that what I am about to tell you is off the record? You cannot use it?"

"It's a standing rule at the *Tribune*," Gordon says, "that the president of the United States can never be off the record."

"If you like, then, I can ask someone else in this room to say what I am about to tell you—since apparently they can be off the record and I cannot. But that seems ludicrous to me, simply because you insist on what you call a standing rule."

Gordon is not the type to make decisions democratically. He stares at the president. Then, only half-angrily, he mumbles, "You have manipulated me into having no choice, sir. You are now off the record." But something in his eyes suggests the gruff editor is a little impressed, even amused, by his president.

"What I'm about to tell you is classified as advance action," Nash says. "That means knowledge of it is held by only a handful of people in the world. It did not have explicit approval from the president. Advance action is designed to move more swiftly and minimize chances of leaking. I had authorized the secretary of defense to use advance action if he deemed it necessary for the goal we had in mind. Whether you believe this or not, I was unaware of the details we are about to share with you until this morning. This insulation is why we had an outside investigation of the Oosay matter in the first place."

Gordon has that squinting look of concentration. The *Tribune* lawyer, someone named Goffin, crosses his legs in a way that suggests he finds this fascinating. Bishop's expression could be described, charitably, as suspicious.

Then Nash tells them almost everything. The Oosay bombing was sanctioned and approved by the U.S. government, he explains, as a means of placing an American-sponsored agent into the top ranks of the Islamic State Army. A mistake was made during the operation. Classified materials that could have revealed the existence and identity of this agent and compromised years of intelligence gathering, as well as other secrets, were left in a secure location in the old Manor House, a so-called SCIF. It was such a simple mistake no one had imagined it possible. General Roderick was the only person on scene that night who knew these materials might be contained in the SCIF and was authorized to enter that room. He made the decision in an instant to follow prescribed procedures when such materials are at risk. He destroyed the SCIF and its contents. That decision also meant that the general sacrificed his own life. He did so willingly. He made the decision to do so himself.

"If the *Tribune* or anyone publishes this story, it would almost certainly result in the death of the most highly placed agent we have ever had in the jihad movement. I cannot imagine what public good would come from this consequence. If you can describe any public good from publication of this information, I will listen. But I can tell you, without any doubt in my mind, that publishing this will result in the loss of innumerable lives that we will save from having this source in place."

Gordon shifts uncomfortably. Governments regularly ask journalists not to publish information on the grounds that it would "destroy intelligence efforts" and "damage national security." Journalists believe most of the requests are made to avoid political embarrassment.

Nash adds that he has never made such a request personally to any journalist before. As president. Or at any other time in his public life.

The walk-through takes ten minutes.

When it is over the president simply stops.

Gordon says, "Do you expect us to give you an answer now? Here?"

"I do," Nash says.

They eye one another a moment. No one else in the room matters.

"With all due respect, Mr. President, you've ambushed us. This is unfair."

"Hardly," Nash says. "I've trusted you. With one of the most important and fragile secrets I have. I have made myself, and this country, vulnerable to you. I've taken you at your word about having a confidential conversation."

Gordon turns and looks at his colleagues. Bishop says nothing: Anything she might say, Rena thinks, could hint at a source.

"At least allow us to talk by ourselves," Gordon says.

"Of course," says Nash.

And for the next half hour, in what both Rena and Brooks would long remember as one of the oddest times of their many years together, the president of the United States and his aides stand around in Randi Brooks's small kitchen waiting for the people from the *Tribune* in the other room to decide whether they will agree to protect a secret that had been so strangely shared with them, that four men had died to protect, and that the country had now spent two months anguishing over.

* * *

Rena and Brooks never do learn the identity of the man who was now rising inside the ranks of the Islamic State Army. They know he masterminded the attack on the American compound in Oosay and the bombing of the Thomas Adams house. They know he provided intelligence of varied quality over a period of years. In various intelligence reports, they will learn, his identity was masked, as if he were a source reporting on himself—as if there were two of him. They learn only one pertinent fact about his identity, which they never share. The man for whom all this was done, for whom General Roderick gave his life, for whom Congress would shut down its investigation, and for whom the president would appeal in person to the *Tribune* to protect, bore the code name RIMSHOT.

# MARCH
# CRYSTAL CITY, VIRGINIA

In late March, the mysterious export company Global Enterprises moves to a larger space in the same office complex to accommodate its growing staff. The day before the move, Henry Arroyo receives a memorandum that is not merely classified "Top Secret." It also carries the additional and more exclusive designation of "SCI LEVEL Majestic." This is the highest possible "Sensitive Compartmented Information" category, indicating the most limited possible distribution list. It did not extend outside four offices in the DIA. It did not go to the White House.

The memo, which is sourced to RIMSHOT, the official code name for double agent Assam Baah, now officially Colonel Baah of the Islamic State Army, describes an unusual gathering of ISA leadership. The gathering is now referred to in this exclusive U.S. intelligence group as the Tunisia Summit. Such in-person gatherings of the ISA high command are rare, the classified memorandum says. ISA leaders are loathe to assemble many of their highest-echelon members physically in one place. But the meeting was considered critical. The summit was held to develop plans for ISA for the next five years. The reason, according to RIMSHOT, was ISA believed it was on the cusp of becoming the preeminent Islamist group in northern and eastern Africa. The supreme commander of ISA, Sheikh Ahmed Kamil, a man so secretive the American government did not possess a reliable photo of him, was in attendance. With him were the twenty-five top figures in the ISA command. Among them was Colonel Assam Baah.

The meeting was distinguished, according to the memorandum, by a growing rift inside the Islamic State Army. On one side were those who believed the organization needed to use discipline and physical intimidation to ensure the African population followed sharia law. These tactics, which mirrored what ISIS had used in Iraq and elsewhere, were designed to separate the devout and obedient from the suspect and unholy. Only by practicing and enforcing strict sharia law about women, technology, and other influences of the infidel could ISA be pure.

On the other side were those who believed that discipline over civilians could come later. This group argued that it was more important to win the confidence of the population by establishing security and ensuring prosperity. On the African continent itself, ISA should demonstrate its strength by acts of terror that had symbolic meaning but limited casualties of Africans, particularly Muslims. Repetitious acts of violence began to lose meaning, created fear, and ultimately suggested ISA was a chaotic force, not a source of strength. Such acts should be left for European and North American soil.

Though the memorandum didn't say so explicitly, Colonel Baah was clearly an advocate for the newer go-slow strategy.

Arroyo ponders the memo. RIMSHOT—this man Assam Baah—for whom they had arranged and then sacrificed so much, was dangerous. He was too reckless, too headstrong, for his own good. It would be safer if he were willing to blend in, to avoid being part of some argument inside ISA that could win him enemies. Arroyo wishes he would keep a lower profile.

But he trusts the intelligence. It is Baah's recklessness that makes Arroyo believe him. It is also what makes Arroyo worry.

Ultimately, Baah will be hard to control. The man clearly has his own agenda.

Then again, Arroyo thinks, it's true of everyone, isn't it?

## WASHINGTON, D.C.

Seven weeks after the meeting in Randi Brooks's apartment, she and Rena are invited to the annual banquet for Roberta Alton, a *Wall Street Journal* reporter killed in Iraq while saving a child. The annual fund-raiser in her name isn't famous, but it has become a popular evening among people in politics and media, largely because it still captures some sense of the professional comity that was once the aspiration of the White House correspondents' dinner.

Heading to his table, Rena notices Will Gordon, editor of the *Tribune,* who motions him to the side of the room.

"May I abandon you for a minute?" Rena asks Vic Madison and her father, who are accompanying him tonight.

"Go," Vic says with a smile. "And I'll see if Dad can identify anyone famous here."

"I hope not," Rollie Madison says.

Rena and Gordon lean against the side wall of the ballroom. It's the first time they've seen each other since the meeting at Brooks's apartment.

"If another organization ever gets this story, our bargain is off," Gordon says.

The editor, Rena thinks, is having regrets. Rena likes this man, but he doesn't like this moment.

"I know that won't happen because you or anyone else in that room gave someone a tip," he says to Gordon, in what sounds like a warning. "That includes Jill Bishop. You are vouching for her, too."

The two men stare at each other, something rising up between them where once there was goodwill.

"I'm trying to level with you," Gordon says.

Rena takes a long breath and says, "Will, you didn't make this choice because you were tricked into it. You did it because you understand. You were over there when this war began."

"I remember," Gordon says.

"Then you know it wasn't a bargain. You're not doing the president some favor. This is the right thing. Don't second-guess it. It's not just some news story."

"Nothing we publish is just some news story," Gordon says.

The man is a true believer. Rena will grant him that. Rena doesn't move his dark eyes from the editor's, and Gordon doesn't lazily half close his eyes, a habit Rena notices he uses for many purposes, including to change the subject.

Then Rena can feel whatever has risen up between them begin to shrink again.

"Matt Alabama says I can trust you."

"Does he?" says Gordon.

"You wouldn't make him a liar?"

A smile forms at the corners of Gordon's mouth.

"Matt is many things, but not that."

Rena holds out a hand, and Gordon takes it.

And after another moment, the two men look away from each other and into the room. There are clusters of friends and acquaintances talking, and in the center two scrums of people are spontaneously organizing themselves, almost like human whirlpools. One surrounds Senator Dick Bakke, who three weeks ago announced his candidacy for president, despite the controversies about his emails during the Oosay investigation. That seems a forgotten moment now. The emails will resurface during the campaign, Rena knows, and when they do, the question will be not what they reveal about Bakke's character, but how well he can deflect them. The ultimate test in any campaign now is not what you have done but how well you survive it.

The other cluster surrounds David Traynor, who is expected to announce his own candidacy for president next week. Rena had finally told Brooks he didn't like the man enough to take his money. They had turned Traynor down. Someone else would scrub his life for him.

Oddsmakers have the race in both parties a dead heat. No fewer than eight people are considered possible nominees, the most open and unpredictable race in years. Everyone knows polls eighteen months before election day are meaningless. Nonetheless, the *Tribune* published another today.

Rena has little doubt the race a year and a half from now will still be a dead heat. The country is split down the middle. And his political mentors and friends who try to occupy the center, for whom Rena and Brooks sometimes do work, are now often shot at by both sides.

Secretary of Defense Daniel Shane is talking to the chairman of the Joint Chiefs. Shane has announced he will be leaving the Nash administration in June and is still mulling a run for president himself as a moderate Democrat. No one gives him much of a chance.

Now Rena sees another circle forming around someone who has just entered the room. At the center of it he can see Wendy Upton, the senator from Arizona who behind the scenes did as much to control the chaotic Oosay Committee as anyone. Next to her, catching Rena's eye a moment and nodding, is Senator Llewellyn Burke.

Rena hears Gordon clear his throat, and he turns.

"Goodbye, Peter."

Rena nods and watches Gordon make his way toward the scrum of people around Bakke.

Rena would bet on Bakke, too, if he had to. People are tired of Nash, and rarely did the same party keep the White House more than eight years in a row. Bakke represents something new in Rena's party, much of which Rena disagrees with. But he fears Bakke also represents the future. Rena's job is not to fight history. A whole industry exists in Washington for that—raising funds, making promises, and vilifying the other side. Rena's job is to understand what will happen and why, and perhaps, in his own way, ensure that great deceptions aren't perpetrated along the way.

He had failed to do that here. Not only was the truth about Oosay a secret—one Diane Howell had resigned to protect; she was now headed to Harvard—but Rena could never look into Adam O'Dowd's death either, for doing so would raise questions he and Randi had just helped bury.

He wanders back to Vic and her father. She looks tan and natural in a cream blouse and yellow skirt, which are more casual than the semiformal gowns most women are wearing tonight. She looks fabulous without trying.

Rena had called her to apologize and ask for another chance the night after they had gathered in Brooks's apartment—the night they had hidden the secret of Oosay.

He remembered her answer, which had not come until after what seemed to Rena an excruciatingly long silence. "Aside from the fact that you never say anything, you live in the wrong part of the country, and you cannot tell me anything about what you do, I'll give you another chance," she'd said. "But you're on the clock, boy."

"I would be a moron not to take that chance," he'd answered.

"Well, you're not a moron. But you do have some bad moments."

Rena had imagined her expression on the other end of the phone, those smoke-gray eyes looking hurt and affectionate, a grudging smile forming beneath her freckled nose.

He smiled and Nelson, the cat she'd given him, nuzzled his face and purred.

Through the phone, Rena could hear Vic laugh.

## ACKNOWLEDGMENTS

Many people were generous in helping *The Good Lie* come to life. My friend Jim Risen was generous, educating me and wandering the haunts where he works his magic. The befuddlement of Jill Bishop in Tyson's Corner parking garages belonged to Jim and me both. Many investigative reporters I have known helped shape Ms. Bishop and her colleagues. The intelligence and military people I have met over the years, including in classes where I have had the honor to give talks, provided inspiration for many characters. To the gang who helped inform and reality check my imagined Washington—Jon, Mike, Drew, John, Tamara, David, and many others. Mike McCurry, among other things, helped me learn how the White House can bury the announcements and arrange meetings without being seen by the press. Drew Littman helped make my Senate scenes more real. Marty Kaiser, Marty Baron, and countless other gifted editors not named Marty helped shape Will Gordon. To my team at API, who are more present in this novel than they may know—Jeff, Amy, Jane, Liz, Kevin, Katie, Mel, Katherine, Laurie Beth, and Gwen. I am your student.

My debt to my editor, teacher, and friend Zachary Wagman just gets deeper and deeper. I am lucky to have found you, Z. The same is true for everyone at Ecco who has believed in me and my imaginary friends, Peter and Randi. I am honored to be with you—the wonderful Miriam Parker, Sonya Cheuse, Meghan Deans, James Faccinto, Emma Janaskie, Allison Saltzman, and the great Daniel Halpern.

To David Black, my friend and blunt, steadfast, funny critic, and backer, and to his team at the David Black Literary Agency.

Of course, to John Gomperts, my tireless buddy and reader: What could I possibly say that would be enough? And to Katherine Klein, my great, dear friend, who only keeps getting better: Doc, by far John's better half, you have made Rena better by at least half.

To my mother, Joyce Rosenstiel, my first editor, still my teacher, and the voice in the back of my head. Thanks to Craig Buck, my brother in fiction and in real life.

And last, but most important, ever to Rima, Leah, and Kira, "My Team."